FATE
DEALS THE
CARDS

A Stella Kirk Mystery #6

L. P. Suzanne Atkinson

lpsabooks
http://lpsabooks.wix.com/lpsabooks#

Cover Design by Majeau Designs
Editing by Tim Covell

ISBN
978-1-7776005-7-0 (Paperback)
978-1-7776005-8-7 (eBook)

1. *Fiction, Mystery/Detective-Cozy/General*
2. *Fiction, Mystery/Detective-Amateur Sleuth*
3. *Fiction, Mystery/Detective-Female Sleuths*

Distributed to the trade by the Ingram Book Company

Table of Contents

Inspirational Quotes..v

Recurring Characters Stella Kirk Mystery #6 1

Chapter 1..3

    Monday, March 15, 1982, 12:45 PM 3

    The Victim 3

Chapter 2:...5

    Wednesday, March 10, 1982 5

    The Players..5

    Earlene 5

    Deena 8

    Velvet 10

    Tess...12

Chapter 3..15

    Thursday, March 11 15

    Are You In?..15

Chapter 4..23

    Monday, March 15, 1982...23

    The Players..23

    Earlene 12:30PM 23

    Velvet 12:35PM 25

    Deena 12:40PM 27

    Tess 12:55PM 28

    Stella 1:30PM 31

Chapter 5..35

    Ample Opportunity...35

Chapter 6..45

    The Convenient Master Key 45

Chapter 7..55

    We are None the Wiser 55

Chapter 8..65

    Long Time Ago..65

Chapter 9 75
    Vagueness is Best 75
Chapter 10 85
    On My Guard 85
Chapter 11 93
    Dead Ends at Every Turn 93
Chapter 12 103
    Routine Inquiries 103
Chapter 13 113
    Suspicious Circumstances 113
Chapter 14 123
    Forensics Botched the Job 123
Chapter 15 133
    No Power is Often a Gift 133
Chapter 16 143
    Wednesday, March 31, 1982 143
    The Players 143
    Earlene 143
    Velvet 146
    Tess 148
    Mary Jo 150
Chapter 17 153
    The Beginning is Good 153
Chapter 18 163
    I Wouldn't Know Her 163
Chapter 19 173
    She Wanted to Hide 173
Chapter 20 183
    Uncontrollable Variables Are the Enemy 183
Chapter 21 193
    An Undefined Nervousness 193
Chapter 22 201
    Significant Miscalculation 201
Chapter 23 211
    Complications Happen 211
Chapter 24 221
    We Held the Higher Cards 221
    Saturday AM, May 8.
    Thirteen days until Shale Cliffs RV Park Opens 226

Life consists not in holding good cards,
but in playing those you hold well.
—Josh Billings

You can't have self-pity. At some point, you have to say.
"These are the cards I've been dealt, and I'm going to play them."
—Bret Michaels

Other works by L. P. Suzanne Atkinson

~Creative Non-Fiction~
Emily's Will Be Done

~Fiction~
Ties That Bind
Station Secrets: Regarding Hayworth Book I
Hexagon Dilemma: Regarding Hayworth Book II
Segue House Connection: Regarding Hayworth Book III
Diner Revelations: Regarding Hayworth Book IV

No Visible Means: A Stella Kirk Mystery #1
Didn't Stand a Chance: A Stella Kirk Mystery #2
Sand In My Suitcase: A Stella Kirk Mystery #3
Fictional Truth: A Stella Kirk Mystery #4
Mallory Gorman Won't Be Buried Today: A Stella Kirk Mystery #5

~E-Book Bundles~
No Visible Means / Didn't Stand A Chance: Books 1 & 2
Sand In My Suitcase / Fictional Truth: Books 3 & 4
Station Secrets / Hexagon Dilemma: Books I & II
Segue House Connection / Diner Revelations: Books III & IV

For David, always
Thank you to Marguerite, Harriet, and Beverley for your feedback, and a special thanks to my editor Tim Covell for his patience and support.

Finally, much appreciation to Patricia Brooks, who won a Cozy Mystery Party contest, and permitted her name to be assigned to a character in this book.

Recurring Characters Stella Kirk Mystery # 6

Stella Kirk ....Partner in Shale Cliffs RV Park; amateur sleuth

Aiden North ....RCMP Detective

Sergeant Moyer .... RCMP Sergeant

Rosemary North.....................Aiden's wife (Mary Jo and Toni are her sisters)

Nick Cochran .... Partner in Shale Cliffs RV Park; Stella's love interest

Paul Morgan..Park Employee

Eve Trembly .... Park Employee (Del. Trembly's granddaughter)

Merrilee Wild...................................... Park Employee replaces Alice Morgan

Duke (John) Powell ....Park Security (Cloris Kincaid – love interest)

Kiki .... Duke's Pomeranian adopted by Nick and Stella

Trixie Kirk ....Stella's younger sister (Val Reguly – love interest)

Brigitte & Mia Kirk.............................. Trixie's daughter and granddaughter
(Carter Stephens – love interest)

Norbert Kirk .... Stella & Trixie's father

RV Park Residents .... Mildred Fox, Buddy McGarvey,
Curtis Walsh & Elroy Brown,
Sally & Rob Black, Ted Metcalfe

Jewel & Ken Winslow ....Caretakers at Painter Farm

Cavelle Painter............................Real Estate Agent; friend to Trixie & Stella

Hester Painter..Friend to Stella

Angus Raspberry.. owns Raspberry Farm

Jacob Painter..Brother to Cavelle & Hester

Chapter 1

Monday, March 15, 1982, 12:45 PM

The Victim

The first blow numbs and blinds. The second doesn't matter.

****

Earlier in the afternoon, after one more spectacular steaming-hiss of the iron, she completed a perfect seam in her already pressed trousers. Her right shoulder and back ached, but perfection was her goal each time she met in the group lounge with the three other residents of the four-unit apartment building known by most as the G-plex. Her appearance wasn't a priority in the past, but Earlene and her tenants, besides their bridge-playing prowess, were vultures. The least hair out of place, and she would become the subject of their gossip until one of the others, probably Velvet, took her seat.

She was assigned the role of hostess for today's game—a circumstance causing both panting and chest tightening. Earlier, she'd prepared the card table with a clean cotton cover which, praise God, fit without wrinkles. She placed the cards—pictures of roses on the back of one deck and foxgloves on the other—at opposite corners; tallies and sharpened pencils poised at each place. She planned to offer homemade lemon squares for their lunch. One of them likes coffee but the others prefer tea. She glanced toward the kitchen. Her mouth was dry. She couldn't swallow. She mustn't forget to turn off the television. They complain when she leaves it on too loud. Croissants from the café might have been a better choice.

A small click distracted her while she zipped her pants. Did she leave the front door unlocked after she ran for the mail? Maybe she left the inside door to the common lounge open after she organized the table for their game.

"Hello," she shouted, making her way from the bedroom. At first, she didn't see the person standing in the living room beside her recliner. She assumed she forgot to lock her outside door. At least no one will be mad about the inside door. She understands why unlocked inside doors are a constant issue, but not for her. She attempted sternness and lifted her chin in defiance. "What do you want?" Her voice squeaked. "Leave now."

The intruder walked toward her with bold steps. Vaguely familiar indigo eyes snapped their rage. Without a word, sound crackled as her face endured the sting of a forceful and unexpected slap. Stars floated, and she staggered. Blinking, her vision remained black around the edges like she was peering down a pipe. She avoided the indignity of a fall and grasped the door casing to regain her balance.

When both of her arms were grabbed, she yelped in pain and toppled against the ironing board, which fell with a crash. The iron landed near her foot. A wave of pure hatred washed over her. She wanted to snatch her iron off the floor and bash her assailant, but she couldn't wriggle out of terrifyingly strong clutches. The result of an expert lunge meant the appliance now swung in the hand of her attacker.

She squirmed away and stepped back, freezing to the spot. Her vision cleared and questions niggled. "Why hurt me?" She attempted conversation, aware of her inability to outrun even a toddler.

"You don't know." Each word travelled on a droplet of spit toward her.

"I'm trying to understand," she panted.

"Think about me." The command flew from a flushed face with bulging eyes.

In a rush, she assembled the puzzle pieces. "Give me the iron and we'll talk." She slowed her breathing. "How can I help? Let me explain."

She believed, for a fateful moment, her words made an impact. As has often been the case in her life, she was mistaken.

CHAPTER 2

Wednesday, March 10, 1982
The Players

Earlene

Earlene Marigold surveys her domain. The best decision she made when she designed the fourplex, which her tenants now fondly describe as the G-plex, was the creation of this spacious room. Each apartment enjoys back door access into the room. Garden doors to a patio, and two generous skylights punctuate the lounge. The communal area has become the perfect place for a game of bridge, an intimate dinner party, or a movie night on the big television, complete with a VCR, purchased for the back wall. A kitchenette rounds out the amenities. If the thefts, and worse, the police reports, stopped, her stress might normalize. She hates to think of her investment, or herself for that matter, being the subject of attention from the authorities.

Tess prepared for today with adequate competence, she notes. The selected table cover shows the odd wrinkle, though. Earlene smooths an edge with a manicured hand. One must never engage in a bridge game before first enduring special attention to one's nails. She turns her water bottle around. Her name faces the players. She pats her black jumpsuit across her flat abdomen and clasps her hands in her lap while she waits, impatient for the others to arrive.

Velvet shuffles in and flops on the chair opposite. "Shall we be partners today, Earlene?"

She's mercifully tied her waist-length and static-inspired hair into a bun. Partnering with Velvet will prove unavoidable today, since they haven't played together for many sessions. Earlene nods. Velvet is a skittish participant. Even when she's dealt good cards, Velvet's often too nervous to play with the skill necessary to make the contract.

In response to her nod, Velvet presses her hand to her heart. Tess and Deena's apartment doors open simultaneously. "Hello, you two." Earlene glances at her watch. "Almost on time." Three minutes after one. She spreads her arms and points, so Tess takes the seat on her left and Deena on her right. "I'll deal, but first—a few items for discussion." She offers Tess a deck. "You make for me, Tess, while Velvet shuffles."

They do as they're told, which pleases her. Sometimes, her tenants are contrary. Today isn't one of those days. Cards snap and flutter as she begins. "The last police call happened on February 19. I must be blunt. I want no more incidents. Lock your inside doors, ladies. I can't make myself any clearer. There's a thief among us."

"You own the master." Deena's soft voice sounds insistent.

A blush creeps along Earlene's neck. She acknowledges the warm spot with a feathery touch. "I have never used my key for entry into any of your units. The purpose is for use in the event of an emergency or when a tenant vacates and I—me, the owner—clean and ready the space for someone new."

Deena sniffs.

"I resent your insinuation. I'm not the culprit. Keep your doors locked— an uncomplicated request. If I must, I'll install doorbells, meaning no excuse because you can't hear a knock. You leave the inside door open, right Tess?"

Her blond curls wobble when she nods. "Doorbells are a good idea, Earlene. I hate to concede, but my hearing has deteriorated."

She graces Tess with an abrupt nod. "And last, we won't play on Friday this week, because both Tess and I made other plans and I expect the weekend will be busy. Our next scheduled game is now Monday, March 15, at one o'clock, okay?"

Everyone nods in unison.

"Our friend Tess set up the room for us today. Thank you, Tess. Check the task roster on our little bulletin board for who is assigned as hostess next time. Don't forget."

Tess places the shuffled deck on her right. Earlene, the first dealer, slides the pack across in front of her for Deena's cut before she deals.

Seeing herself in no position for an opening bid because she has eleven points with face cards in every suit but Hearts, she passes.

She listens to Tess pass. Her point count is no doubt low because she adopts her glum expression whenever she opens a poor hand.

Velvet wiggles into her chair and pats her hair. "One Heart," she belts out, as if the other three were seated on the deck and not across from her.

Deena passes.

Since Velvet opened and Earlene has eleven points but no Hearts except for two losers, she answers with, "Two Hearts," describing her weak support.

Everyone passes. Velvet holds a Two-Heart contract. Play will take a while because Velvet can be slow. Earlene prepares her dummy hand as Tess leads the Ace of Clubs. Earlene presents her cards.

"Nice support hand, Earlene."

She nods, sure Deena's won her only Club trick, but wonders what else the woman will reveal. Deena plays well and follows quickly by offering a low Diamond. She's counting on Tess for the King, which Tess plays. Deena bounces up and down.

"Aha!" she exclaims. "You had the King, Tess. Good one."

After shutting her eyes for a moment, Tess leads a Club. She can't renege. She returns her partner's original lead in the hope Deena is void. Earlene murmurs her contentment when the King of Clubs on the board takes the trick. Next, Velvet follows the rules and runs her Hearts until the Trumps are gone, at which point she focuses on the Spades. In the end, she claims ten tricks, a score of Four Hearts, despite her hesitant bid of Two. "Well played, Velvet—a successful hand to start the afternoon." Earlene reaches for her score pad.

"A No Trump bid response after my heart opening might have made game," says Velvet, although Earlene senses no animosity in her voice.

"I worried because my Hearts were the Eight and the Five. If I had been dealt thirteen points, or even twelve, I could have responded with No Trump."

Tess presents the fresh deck for the cut while Deena shuffles the used cards. Sometimes the responsibility of ownership overwhelms Earlene. The thief among them must be caught, although she's unsure what her next steps will be. At least the talk regarding her husband's abrupt death has subsided. He was fit and healthy. No one expected him to drop dead on the doorstep. His story isn't hers to tell.

****

Deena

Well, that hand was a waste of time. She dislikes Earlene, Velvet, and Tess. Her mind wanders while Tess fusses with the deck. Deena Finch, shoulders back, posture erect, shuffles. First, she divides the cards in half. She forces each one to feather together in a perfect riffle, punctuated by the swish of the cards as they reassemble. She adjusts her new floral silk shawl. Not one of the women has complimented her. The purchase was expensive, and she knows she should have kept her money in her wallet. She fingers the fabric—irresistible—before she resumes.

Deena likes where she lives now. She fancies herself safe. Her unit is compact—nine hundred square feet. Two bedrooms—one no bigger than a closet—and one bath. The apartment is in the back, away from the street and prying eyes. She feels protected. Deena prefers her privacy. The rent is above the average, but Earlene covers utilities except for her phone. The long-term-disability people provide a paltry pension, which they will cut off when she turns sixty-five. Deena knows she should watch her pennies and caresses the shawl again.

She ponders each of her bridge mates.

Earlene is a rigid and irksome bitch. She owns the place, but there's no rule requiring her to play queen of the realm every minute. She's not chair of the board. Her husband dropped dead, and everyone thought she was involved, but in the end, a heart attack was the cause. They were well off. Earlene remains well off since she benefits from ample insurance. Deena admits her envy in silence.

Velvet is a lost sheep. She scares easily and proves ripe for manipulation at a moment's notice. Deena has no patience with Velvet. She's mentally ill, which explains most of her behaviour—especially her childish qualities and her anxiety. Harmless Velvet.

Tess, though, has the potential to be a problem. Tess can't abide her any more than she can tolerate Tess. The woman fancies herself to be a writer. Deena hisses and hopes she used her inside voice. No one noticed. Where's the discussion gone now? Connie, Tess' sister, wants Tess to author a book and tell her story of ALS? No way. She places the thoroughly shuffled deck to her right. "Are you writing a book?"

Three faces turn toward her. She loves to occupy their attention. She repeats herself. "Are you writing a book? I missed what you said."

"My sister, Connie, pressures me to pen her memoir, but I don't think I'm capable. It's hard enough to watch her deteriorate." Tess continues dealing, albeit with a slowness that makes Deena want to grab the cards from her hands. "Do you know, the nurses now tie a red sash around her forehead and the back of her headrest? The fabric keeps her from keeling over into her own lap." She inspects Deena. "The fabric resembles your shawl."

"Mine is raw silk with hand-sewn appliqués. The colour reminds you of my shawl," she corrects, while she caresses the garment again. "An investment purchase."

Earlene mutters, "You should be more attentive to your bank account, Deena, and pay your rent on time."

She gulps her embarrassment as her landlady mentions her delinquency in front of the others. "Earlene, I apologized for the oversight," she huffs. "I'll be more careful. Our business is a confidential matter."

"We're friends, Deena." Velvet gathers her cards before Tess completes the deal. Tess stops and stares at her. "I paid late once, didn't I?"

Earlene leans across the table toward her partner. "You did Velvet, but you forgot. Such forgetfulness happens with your condition, and the minute I reminded you of your error, you wrote a cheque." She straightens in her chair. "Deena, you spend your money on frivolous items and force me to wait for your mid-month disability payment's arrival to cover your rent."

Deena winces but decides avoidance of a further argument in front of everyone else is for the best. She has been caught twice accessing Tess' apartment. Convincing Tess she'd left her lounge door unlocked, and couldn't hear Deena's call, proved difficult. She miscalculated and is now positive Tess has suggested to Earlene that she, Deena, might be the G-plex thief.

"Will you write Connie's story, Tess?" Velvet casts a nervous glance in Earlene's direction as she talks across the board again.

Tess frowns. "Probably not, Velvet. How do I find a publisher? Who wants to hear my sister's tale of woe?" She squints at the cards which remain in her hand. "Now where am I? Let me finish."

Sucking in a deep breath unnoticed, Deena feels she dodged another bullet. She knows she should temper her remarks and keep her mouth shut, but the foibles of menopausal chemistry have rendered her in a permanent bad mood where shopping is the other cure—shopping she can't afford. Each woman has described her as irritable and difficult. They even made similar comments when the police were here—more than once. She admits she has no desire to make enemies of the other residents at the G-plex and silently vows to work harder to avoid their line of fire. Her other option is to move into a new community. She's sure someone is following her. Time for her to disappear again?

When Tess finally finishes the deal, Deena examines her hand. As she sorts, she deftly groups cards of similar suits in descending order. She hopes she has enough support and can reply if Tess makes an opening bid. Alas, eight points, again.

****

Velvet

"I know a publisher, Tess." Velvet Carmichael exudes confidence after the success of her firsthand. She wishes Earlene had mentioned her Spades, but no matter. She made her Two Hearts and the tension in her shoulders has released.

"What?" Tess drags her focus away from an analysis of her cards.

"Victoria Barlow, at Sailboat Publishing in Halifax, is a school chum of mine. I bet she'd be interested in a memoir focused on sisters where one develops ALS. Your story should include both of you."

Tess' eyes bulge.

"How did you get smart?" Deena sneers from her left.

"Stop, Deena. Don't be snide. She might have a point, Tess. Talk publishers later, not across the bridge table."

"Sorry, Earlene. Just a comment." Velvet snags a strand of her waist-length hair out of the chignon she worked hard at contriving before the game, holds on for dear life, and slips back into her hole of self-protection.

"A joint memoir might contain the hook you need, Tess. I expect you'd perform a random sexual act for poor old Theodore Gorman to persuade him to print books for you." Deena flutters her fingers.

Tess and Earlene huff in unison.

Staring at her cards, Velvet thinks she should have kept her mouth shut. She tried hard to pull herself together before the game today. She pressed her slacks and tied her hair back because she knows they complain how strands slough off everywhere she walks. Velvet hasn't cut her pride and joy in twenty years and won't entertain the idea. She'll move first.

She wishes Mary Jo lived here instead of Deena. Mary Jo Frost spares, when one of them can't play. Velvet met Mary Jo and Toni when they visited their sister in the hospital. Rosemary North—now she's a wingnut. Rosemary remained on the psych. ward long after Velvet found herself better managed. Velvet still slips into depression and prefers her own company, but the doctor said the various medications over the years affected her emotions. Her current beliefs lean more toward control and awareness. Doctors think they understand your soul, as well as your brain.

Velvet lives in the unit they call the spine of the G. Since the fourplex sits on a corner lot, her apartment faces the other road, perpendicular to Earlene. She enjoys seeing the street and has her favourite chair positioned where she can watch out the window, hidden from passers-by. Her unit covers the same square footage as Deena's and has two bedrooms and one bath. With no company and no immediate family, her guest room stores empty boxes, hoarded for whenever she moves again.

The stealing wears on her nerves. Earlene has a master key, but she doesn't need to steal a hair clip. She has hair, but not enough to support an accessory as heavy as the silver piece stolen from Velvet. She always locks both her inside and her front door. You don't spend your entire adult life treated for paranoia and not lock your doors.

"Bid, for God's sake." Tess' voice has an edge of impatience.

Velvet jumps. She startles, often for no reason. She glances at her hand before she passes. Her mind drifts back to Deena's smug remark, suggesting she's smart. She doesn't discuss her past, but Velvet trained as a teacher. Because of her mood swings and paranoia, she chose avoidance of the classroom and secured a librarian position instead. She toiled behind the scenes and spent minimal time with the public. Silent pride warms her heart because she earned an education degree despite her seemingly insurmountable challenges. She retired two years ago, at sixty, and now collects a partial pension and her Canada Pension. Once she reaches sixty-five, she expects a big raise when she qualifies for Old Age Pension, although her teacher's cheque will be reduced by fifteen per cent.

Everyone is tossing their cards into the centre. Each player passed and Tess must re-deal the hand. She promises herself she'll pay more attention next time around.

"Okay, people, let's improve our bidding." Earlene sits straighter in her chair. "Take a chance. Don't be shy."

"I had nine points, Earlene." Velvet accepts the criticism as personal, even though she understands, in the other part of her brain, that Earlene spoke to them as a collective.

"Well, we dealt someone points."

"If I have decent cards, I bid," Deena mutters.

"Okay. I'll do better. I had a sixteen count, but no suit."

Earlene winces. "For God's sake, Tess. Deal. Sixteen points," she hisses.

Tess pouts. Velvet notices the twinkle in Deena's eyes. She can't assess Deena's expressions. If she has a good hand, she plays. Deena's a show-off. She enjoys Earlene's annoyance with Tess. Under normal circumstances, Tess and Earlene are close. Velvet's loneliness surfaces when the two make plans for lunch or enjoy events with their friends here in the common room. She sits alone in her unit and fantasizes about the day when they include her.

Velvet straightens in her chair. She will not allow herself to drift toward her familiar abyss of self-doubt. Since there's no game on Friday, she vows to call Mary Jo and suggest they go to Port Ephron for lunch—the Purple Tulip would be nice. Tomorrow, she'll take a long walk and visit Yellow House, and see if sweet Brigitte Kirk can order her a book on playing bridge. She felt good when she made her bid earlier and she wants that experience again. Confidence is what she needs most—confidence.

****

Tess

Tess Boone clenches her teeth while she deals; her second stab at this godforsaken hand. She admits she's scared to open; afraid she'll earn the contract. The first is the worst. She annoyed Earlene. Velvet grabs her cards before Tess finishes. She knows better, having been admonished for rude behaviour at the bridge table before.

Despite her tiresome personality, Velvet made a valid point. She could write a memoir focused on herself and Connie. Connie Gee lives at Harbour Manor. She's a wonderful, capable woman who has struggled with her disease for years. Specialists took forever to confirm a diagnosis. At first, they expected slow progression, but in a matter of weeks, she couldn't go to the toilet without help, and decisions were necessary. Full credit to Connie.

She did her research, but when she needed to move, nursing home became her one option. She acts happy enough, spending her life, or what remains, with a red sash tying her head to the back of her chair. Jasper Nunn returned, and Tess experienced an overwhelming gratitude, knowing Connie has her dear friend by her side again. Thanks to Stella Kirk, Connie can experience love during her last months on earth. Tess' heart twists. She refuses to be jealous of her sister.

As she sorts her hand, she decides a visit with Frances might be in order. If Velvet's idea has merit, Frances will know. And Deena's wrong. If she authors a book and wants a few copies for distribution among friends, Gorman Printing happily provides the service. She likes him—more than she should. He buried his wife in the middle of December and has no interest in her. Besides, men are not her forté.

Although her apartment is small by any comparison, Tess enjoys contentment in her five hundred and fifty square foot space. Classified as a bachelor, her twin bed occupies one corner, which leaves adequate room for her table and chairs, a petite china cabinet, and a new sofa she saved for months to buy. She admits she must pinch her pennies, but people often think her lack of book sales causes a financial challenge. In reality, she received a settlement after the incident. Her tastes are simple. She hasn't worked since she was forty, but her frugality has paid off. If she plans well, she can take a pleasant trip each year. She's never made a dollar from her writing.

Tess gazes around the table at the three women with whom she shares the G-plex. Earlene's husband died. Everyone eventually said he suffered a heart attack. He had pots of money and excellent insurance. Lucky, although losing your spouse in such a blunt and unplanned way must be unpleasant. Tess likes Earlene. She can't imagine her as their thief, but she keeps the master key.

Deena lives on a disability pension. Tess doesn't believe she's disabled. Deena is mean. Tess expects she bullied Patricia Brooks at the Groceteria into filing a workplace accident report. Her imagination creates the scenario where Deena is their thief, but how can she slip into everyone's apartment if they lock their doors? And she claims items were stolen from her, too.

She watches Velvet twist her hair and hold a strand in her mouth for a second before her eyes dart around the table to see if anybody noticed. Tess knows Velvet has mental health issues and tries her best to be patient, although she avoids lengthy amounts of time with her. Tess believes her strands of horrible hair would turn up in her apartment if Velvet were the culprit. She never admits the woman inside her unit, except the hallway near the interior door.

Tess fans her cards and completes a quick count. Ten points. She can't bid. If Deena bids, she'll answer with two of whatever, and avoid the need to play. She didn't move into the G-plex because of the bridge, but Earlene accepted her as a tenant since she knows the game.

"Pass."

"One Club," Velvet mutters.

"Are you playing the low Club convention, Earlene?"

"For heaven's sake, Tess. I bid a Club, I mean a Club," Velvet mutters.

"Earlene provides the answer, not you, Velvet. Let Earlene tell me." Tess curbs her patience.

"No Low Club convention today, I gather." Earlene grinds her teeth in response.

In the end, the hand plays out where Earlene finds a match with Three Diamonds. She completes the play and gathers her nine tricks while Tess leans back in her chair. Velvet slides the fresh deck across for her to cut and begins the deal.

Tess makes her plan. She'll call Frances tonight and visit Connie tomorrow, if Frances thinks the idea of a joint memoir presents promise. She also wants to stop by the stationery store in Port Ephron and purchase typewriter paper in a variety of colours, which will help better organize her outline.

"What?" Deena made a remark, and she wasn't listening.

"I said Frances Ellis' publisher might take you on with your book, as a favour to Frances and Edward. They're successful and you know them both, right?"

Deena read her mind. "Frances and I have been acquaintances for years. I will talk with her and ask her opinion. I'm hesitant to tread on our friendship with such a request." She adopts a lighter tone. No need to reveal her innermost thoughts. "Now, if Frances offered…," she titters. "And I must discuss the concept with Connie before I consider a move forward." She turns toward Velvet and places her hand on the woman's wrist. "You gave me a sound idea, my dear. I'll thank you in the acknowledgements."

〰

CHAPTER 3

Thursday, March 11

Are You In?

Morning light wanders into their bedroom at six-thirty, washing across the pale walls and pine floors. Spring lurks in the corners of the property, poised to burst on the scene with crocuses, the smell of damp earth, and preparations for a change in season. Stella remains still and listens to Nick breathe. The alarm will bleat in a half hour. She curls deeper into the luxury of their down comforter. Kiki's sputtered snores continue. The weight of his arm rests on her breasts. His thigh presses against her own.

She expects a busy day. Duke and Cloris have returned home from the south. Duke maintains a trailer in the park in exchange for the provision of summer security services. He often helps Nick with projects—any reason to sit at her kitchen table. He said he'd work with Nick to paint the living room. Over the past month, Nick has, with a precision Stella admires, cleaned and restored the traditional Victorian brick fireplace. The revival will shock her father the next time they bring him to the old house for a visit. She stops mid-thought and closes her eyes. He might not even notice. He barely recognizes Trixie's daughter, Brigitte. Trixie faces the same situation as Stella has since her return to Shale Harbour. Norbert Kirk has forgotten both his children. Trixie seems untroubled by the loss. In contrast, the process has broken Stella's heart.

Her hand rests on the man beside her, nine years her junior and, as of December 31, 1981, a fifty percent partner in Shale Cliffs RV Park because Trixie sold her shares. Now, Stella and Nick will face the 1982 summer season together, as equals.

Today, they want to formalize their arrangement with Kiki, Duke's dog. Cloris, his most recent and most serious lady friend, doesn't like dogs. Nick and Stella took Kiki in while Cloris and Duke enjoyed Florida. Nick yearns to keep the dog, and she expects Duke will agree. If he wants Cloris on his arm, the pooch must be somewhere else.

With the sound of the alarm, Nick curls closer and tiny paws touch the side of the bed as Kiki barks for a morning love, too. Stella adores these early hours when the park remains closed and the down comforter puffs around them.

****

Downstairs, Nick lights the fire. Stella drags on her boots and tramples outside with the dog. Much of the snow has melted. She plans to work in her office today.

Back inside, they sit at the kitchen table, drink coffee, and eat homemade brown bread lathered in strawberry jam courtesy of her friend Hester Painter. Hester and Cavelle Painter live with their brother, Jacob, on a farm along the point. Over the last two years, Hester has been helpful as Aiden and Stella solved murders in the area. Hester, often socially inappropriate, but well-versed on a variety of topics, is an asset. She has improved considerably since her older sister, Opal, went to jail.

Stella admires Nick's angular good looks as he pours more coffee. Last summer's tan has receded, in time for 1982's version, which will invariably deepen his skin from cream to amber. Nick Cochran tans better than most. "Duke's coming over, right?"

"Yeah. He said he'd help me move the furniture and paint. I expect to discuss Kiki, too. We can keep her, agreed?"

"With pleasure. I hope whomever I hire to run the front office, likes dogs. Alice adored Kiki, who loved her." She knows her voice sounds as though a person dear to her heart has died.

"Alice is off on a new adventure." He looks toward the living room. "Here comes Duke, now. I unlocked the veranda door."

Duke Powell, whose real name is John, swaggers into the kitchen. Kiki wiggles her way to meet him. "Hi, you two. Great bein' back. Cloris thought she might come out later and check on her trailer."

"The rig is fine, but she's welcome to visit. Sit. I'll pour you a coffee. Did you enjoy your trip? We haven't visited since you came home."

"Busy, busy. Cloris and Aiden North were tryin' to put together a plan for Rosemary once she's discharged from the hospital, but her job prospects ain't lookin' good. You talked with him?"

"Nope. Not after we closed the Willy Saunders case. He took leave, I guess. You missed all the excitement."

His eyes widen.

"The circumstances were tragic. People are safe now, but aging alone without money and options isn't for the faint of heart." She notices Nick's frown and changes the subject. "About Kiki."

"Sure. She behaved for you? She's happy here?"

Nick sits straighter in his chair. "Kiki has been great, and we think life might be easier for you if she stays here."

He holds his coffee cup near his face. His pupils dilate. No one but Stella could interpret the meaning in his eyes. He's nervous.

"I hoped you guys would want her. I've moved in with Cloris in Port Ephron. Stopped rentin' my place at the hotel before we left, and never went back." He rests his fingers on Kiki's fluffy ruff. "Kiki isn't happy around Cloris, and Cloris will be upset with me if I take her back."

"You'll see her every day in the summer." Nick bounces on his chair. "She can ride with you when you do your rounds and visit you in your trailer when Cloris isn't there."

Duke's voice sounds lighthearted. "Great. We'll play in my rig because Cloris says my unit should be on the scrap heap, and that the carpet smells musty." He studies the dog before he resumes. "I don't want to sell in case me and Cloris don't work out. You understand, right?"

Adopting a more serious tone, Nick fortifies their decision. "Listen, Duke, if you and Cloris don't work out, Kiki still stays with us. Deal?"

The man who often channels John Wayne to cover his insecurities extends his hand. "Deal." He sniffs while his chin develops a tremble. "What colour paint has the Lady of the Manor chosen for the living room? Another shade besides eyesore dusty rose, I hope."

Stella and Nick exchange a glance. "Biscuit, Duke. I chose biscuit—to lighten the space," she explains. "Sorry if my mother's favourite shade has offended your sensibilities," she mutters, only half teasing.

****

In her office, next door to reception on the main floor of the old house, Stella composes offer letters to staff she expects will return to work for the season. Alice won't be back, and she senses tears welling. Sweet Alice Morgan, her right-hand person since she took over the park, has almost finished university and expects to set off along her own career path. Stella hoped for one last summer, but no such luck. She blinks her sadness away. Alice called from Halifax two weeks ago and told Stella she had found a fabulous new job which starts in June. Happy for the young woman, Stella can't imagine her summer without the redhead's perky good humour, consistent reliability, and superb assessments of the human condition.

She addresses her first letter to Alice's younger brother. Paul could live at the park year-round if given the opportunity. Nick teaches him more machinery maintenance skills each season. Since the septic system approaches operational status, she's sure Paul's excited to learn as much as possible. He's in university now, but she has a few more years before she needs to worry over his imminent departure. Nick depends on him.

After she slides paper into her typewriter, she begins. She checks her calendar. If the plan remains stable, their open dates are May 21 through May 24—the Victoria Day long weekend. She advises Paul he can begin the week of May 10 or May 17. The date depends on when his exams finish. Nick organizes the task schedule once he confirms. They complete mountains of spring work to ready the park. The sooner he comes on site, the better.

Once finished with Paul's letter, she dashes off a formal document for Duke. Although no money changes hands, she prefers documentation where his compensation for security tasks translates into a seasonal site on the property.

Her last letter is for Eve Trembly, Del Trembly's granddaughter. She has become an essential employee since she started with the park. Eve maintains the public washrooms, loves the flower gardens, and has never met a mower or weed trimmer she couldn't control. On top of her landscaping skills, Eve's studies focus on accountancy. She is capable and showed her ability to manage registration and the front office in Alice's stead. She can't work both positions. Stella writes to Eve, saying that her old job is hers, but Alice won't be back. If she prefers inside, she'll assign her Alice's position, but call the park as soon as possible because Stella will need to advertise for whatever job Eve doesn't want.

Almost coffee time. She heard Nick and Duke go into the kitchen for a break. A moment later, Duke pops his head in the door and tells her he'll take Kiki for a quick pee. "I'll help with her, you know, even if she don't live with me anymore." He nuzzles the dog.

"Lady of the Manor need a cup of Cochran's best?" Nick winks when he places a fresh mug of coffee at her elbow and sits in the chair in front of her desk.

"I've written the offer letters. We need staff to take Alice's place in registration, or Eve's place on the mower."

"I hate to lose Eve on the grounds, Stella. She has better skills than Paul with small machinery, and she works magic in the flower beds. I'll do the work in the fall but will miss her outside."

"You're right. I could change her letter and offer her registration back-up. We can search for an office worker." She reaches for Eve's envelope, which sits on her desk with the others.

Nick straightens in his chair. "Changing the subject, I want to present a proposition." As the veranda door bangs when Duke returns with Kiki, he shouts, "I'll be there in a minute, Duke! Grab a coffee and a treat for Kiki."

Tingling because Nick's propositions never disappoint, she wets her lips and asks, "And what might you have in mind?" Her blush betrays her.

"A romantic weekend in Halifax for your birthday."

"My birthday's in June." She leans back in her chair.

"Correct, and we never manage a proper celebration because the house is open, and we're swamped with park duties. I planned for this Saturday. We'll drive into Halifax in the afternoon and enjoy a surprise evening."

"And Kiki? Duke can't keep her."

"Talked with Trixie yesterday. She's thrilled to babysit. I expect she's shopping for a new and glamorous doggie wardrobe by now." He chuckles. "Are you in?"

She makes her way around the desk and holds the face of the man she loves in both hands. "I think I will come along with enthusiasm, my dear. No clues where we'll go or stay?"

"None."

****

Stella meanders into the kitchen after tidying her office. While Nick and Duke waited for the first coat to dry, they took Kiki for a walk around the property and checked on the septic. She assumes their inspection involved holding tank covers, seepage, and ground settlement.

While waiting, she assembles egg salad sandwiches, and a plate of carrot sticks, radishes, and celery. She made pumpkin cookies last week and fishes for half a dozen from the freezer in the pantry. By the time the two men return, she's placed lunch on the table.

"Here's your offer letter, Duke—more a formality, but I want proper documentation to verify the lot as yours."

He scans the paper while Kiki fusses at Stella's feet. "I see I got a raise." His guffaw rattles the windows and scares the dog.

Her relief becomes a muffled gulp. The park would suffer if Duke gave up his free site and didn't secure the gate and check on the guests two or three times a day. He has his challenges but has tempered any misogynistic behaviour since Lorraine Young died. She likes Duke Powell and would miss him.

Duke drops his round rump on to one of the oak chairs after he washes his hands at the kitchen sink and dries them on her clean tea towel. "Did I hear you say Alice ain't comin' back and you need help in the office?"

"Yup. Alice has a big-girl job now. I'll advertise, I guess. I hope you don't expect me to hire you." She snickers at the slur.

He ignores her tease. "Give the job to Cloris."

"Cloris? She won't want to work when she stays out here. She'll visit her trailer to relax, not to toil away in reception."

"Give her the same offer as me, and I bet you're wrong. Can I ask her?"

"She still has prospects as Rosemary North's caregiver. Aiden wanted to employ her." Stella frowns. If she hires Cloris, Aiden will be stuck with no help after Rosemary's discharge from the hospital, when and if a discharge ever happens. She won't undermine her friend.

"Aiden told her how his sister-in-law, Toni, wants the job again. I imagine the other one, Mary Jo, will pitch in. I guess they've both reconsidered."

Nick, with his back toward Duke, raises his brows and widens his eyes.

His expression seems cautious. "What do you think, partner?"

"Asking won't do any harm, eh, Duke? Didn't she plan to pop out, anyway?"

Stella struggles to hide her surprise and motions Nick out of the kitchen and into her office. Duke, with a mouth full of sandwich, doesn't notice.

"Listen, Stella." He touches her forearm and lowers his voice before she sputters her response. "Our donation of a seasonal lot for services might turn into a good deal. If she works out, I think we'll be ahead by a few dollars. The one with a problem is Kiki. She loved Alice."

"I imagine the dog will spend most of her time in the truck's cab with you and Duke. Let's go before our sandwiches disappear. I'm starved."

After they help clean away the dishes, both men return to painting. Stella, at loose ends because of the living room furniture piled in the middle of the floor, and uncomfortable about Cloris as an employee, grabs the dog. "I'll take Kiki for a walk around the property." Before anyone can object, she adds, "The paint has given me a headache and I need the fresh air. We'll be back for tea."

This day is one of those when the wind blows from the south. The warm gusts, grazing her cheeks, plant the idea spring might lurk nearby. Kiki runs ahead, well-aware of her route. Cloris Kincaid, Duke's latest flame, dragged her trailer from Port Ephron RV to Shale Cliffs last fall. She fell out with her sister, Duke's previous girlfriend. Her rig sits snuggled behind the house for now. She'll move it to her permanent site and hook into services in May.

Stella wanders along the main road. She notes Mildred Fox's old Cardinal standing strong against the wind, reminding her how Mildred stands strong against life. Aiden and Rosemary's unit sits near the cliffs, on the far right—a beautiful 1976 Holiday Rambler which belonged to Lorraine Young before her murder at the hands of her boss in the summer of 1980. This was Stella's first collaboration with Aiden. He had recently moved back to the area. They have a history from high school.

Duke's girlfriend is nice enough, Stella guesses, but she remains unsure how the woman will manage. She could be the type of person who controls instead of helps. Alice pitched in, made lunches, grocery lists, bank deposits, and even cleaned the downstairs with Eve on a rainy day when the office was quiet. Stella's eyes narrow. But Alice never exceeded her authority.

Stella believes Cloris doesn't need to work. She has a place in Florida, her trailer, and her three-bedroom bungalow in Port Ephron. She assumes Cloris started private caregiver services as an escape from the house and imagines she still hopes Aiden will want her help.

After turning left at one intersection where she passes Ted Metcalfe's unit, she pulls her cap lower over her brow, and thinks she must call him and report the rig is fine. "Don't run too far away from me, Kiki," she shouts between the gusts, always nervous when the little dog is off leash. Nick insists she not worry.

The rumble of a motor distracts her from her musings. The Jeep appears over the rise. She trots ahead, fetches Kiki, and scoops the canine into her arms before the vehicle approaches.

"Hi," Nick bellows above the wind. "Duke called Cloris, who's now on her way out for a visit. I told her we were painting, but she wasn't too concerned."

"Sounds eager." Stella's chest heaves. "Here." She hands Kiki in through the driver's window. "You take her. I'll walk back."

"You're not sure a trade of office services for a seasonal site is the best idea." Nick's statement flies out of earshot and across the open stretch between two trailers, but she caught his words before they spun away.

"Alice took care of us, but she didn't run me—or the business. She supported my work with Aiden but didn't take over in my absence. She exercised balance—and I don't know if Cloris has the same personality." Stella shrugs. "Cloris convinced Duke to part with Kiki. She likes to be in control."

"You think I jumped too fast?"

"No, although I had no time to ruminate."

"The paint wasn't the issue." His words float out of the cab on another gust. "Hop in. She'll be here in fifteen minutes. If you're unsure, make the job sound demanding. Tell her what you want and determine if she's up to the challenge."

"I'll talk with her, but I'll walk back. See you at the house."

Chapter 4

Monday, March 15, 1982

The Players

Earlene 12:30PM

Refreshed and satisfied with her performance two hours ago in the Port Ephron Community Pool, Earlene steps out of her white walk-in shower. Her main winter exercises are attendance at a water aerobics class and a free swim afterward, where she accomplishes fifty lengths on a good day. She swims three times a week, the primary reason she schedules her bridge games for the afternoon. She prefers the ocean, but open water is certainly not practical in March. By June, the waters at the beach she frequents near Shale Harbour will be warm enough. She doesn't burn as many calories during a workout in the open ocean as she does in the pool, but the crash of waves and the caress of the salt spray justify the loss.

Earlene Marigold believes life has been good. She married well. Her husband came from a family with money and succeeded as a financial adviser in his own right. Although she assisted in his business and provided needed advice whether he asked or didn't, she ran her own life as she saw fit. They lived on an expansive property at the edge of town. The house rambled through multiple rooms and levels. The gardens were extensive. Earlene grew her own herbs, and with the help of Opal Painter, gained a considerable amount of expertise.

Opal Painter. Now she's a woman who let her need for control of the lives of everyone around her run amok. Earlene expects Opal to remain incarcerated for the foreseeable future. She shivers and knows Opal didn't consider her behaviour wrong. She protected her family.

After Richard died, Earlene hated her house. The building surrounded her with the final and painful memories of their marriage. She sold their home once she hired Fisher's Contracting. They built her the G-plex, which she designed herself. Away from the property she shared with her spouse, the herbs and flowers, and the scene of Richard's death, she strives each day to keep his part of her life snuggled in the past.

As she stands in front of her closet and debates what outfit is most suitable for today's game, her eyes drift toward the shelf reserved for her small collection of designer handbags, an indulgence she has nurtured since her husband died. Where did she leave her navy-blue leather Gucci shoulder bag, the one she uses when she has a meeting with her lawyer or accountant? The purse has a box structure, with a full flap and gold Gucci clasp. *What has happened to my bag?*

Her mind on the handbag, she chooses a grey pantsuit with tapered legs and narrow lapels to match her white silk blouse, and dresses in haste, which eliminates the pleasure she experiences when she admires her fit and shapely frame in cute and quality clothes. Afterward, she tears her closet apart. No Gucci shoulder bag. She knows she didn't misplace it. The thief must be Deena, but how does she access the apartment? Earlene searches spots where she has never left her purse. She understands her irrational behaviour stems from her inability to believe one of her tenants, specifically Deena—because it must be Deena—has entered units during an absence to steal personal items.

Deena is odd. Earlene wishes she had never rented to the woman who sports a permanent chip on her shoulder. She hides in her back apartment most of the time. Poor Patricia, at the Groceteria, is delighted to be rid of her, although she suspects Deena's injury is fake. The bridge game set-up in the common room today is Deena's responsibility. Maybe she's there now. Earlene grits her teeth, prepares for a confrontation, and marches out her access door into the lounge area. She sees the table assembled with cover, cards, and tallies. Deena's contribution to the afternoon passes inspection. The tablecloth is pressed, and she notes the woman remembered the pencils this time. As long as she doesn't bring those unpleasant lemon squares for dessert, the afternoon should go well.

Earlene returns to her unit, eats a few almonds, and drinks a glass of orange juice, before she brushes her teeth and applies a shade of apple red lipstick. Once she checks the security of her front door, she stomps through to the common room again, intent on a serious discussion with Deena. She's alone. The little clock on a side table says twelve thirty-five.

With a flushed face and a pumping heart, she knows her personality well enough to realize she must calm herself before the others enter. When did she last use her Gucci? *I'll just go check again.*

****

Velvet 12:35PM

Velvet Carmichael sits on the upholstered bench in front of the dresser which was her grandmother's and double-braids one long pigtail which is sure to please her fellow players. The completion of such a series of linear knots demands skill and focus. She nods toward her reflection. Today, she'll cooperate. She won't ruffle feathers. She won't rock boats. Adrift in a sea of clichés, she admonishes herself, while she weaves strands of course silver-streaked hair.

She glances at the alarm clock on her bedside table and then assesses her black linen trousers. Because of the colour, the wrinkles are hardly noticeable. She brushes crumbs, deposited while she ate her peanut butter sandwich for lunch, off her argyle sweater—another wardrobe choice Earlene will criticize.

"No need to accept their standards," she advises the woman in the mirror. She points her finger at the image. "You are your own person and much improved. You owe no one an apology."

Lunch with Mary Jo Frost on Friday was the best idea. They met at the Purple Tulip, Velvet's favourite lunch spot. Even in the middle of the day, the atmosphere always resembles the inside of a cave, with the cement floors, cheese grater chandeliers, and gas fireplaces embedded in the walls. It took her eyes a moment to adjust to the dim ambience before she saw Mary Jo snuggled behind a corner table in the back. She's a big-boned woman, with rounded shoulders when she stands or walks. She can be gruff when she talks and impatient with individuals she identifies as a waste of space. Velvet likes Mary Jo and, occasionally, believes the attraction might be reciprocated.

Presentation was important. Mary Jo is one of her favourite people and she wanted to look her best. Rosemary North's sister had complimented her on her enviable long hair and admired her deep cranberry-coloured sweater on another occasion. She wore her hair loose, held away from her face with a large plastic tortoiseshell clip. The top two buttons of her cardigan remained unfastened, confident Mary Jo would prefer this choice.

They laughed and talked together. Conversation never lagged. They ate crab cakes and salad, drank glasses of wine, and indulged in crème caramel for dessert. They requested the same menu items. Velvet revelled in what she perceived as their common ground. She wished Mary Jo lived at the G-plex instead of Deena but didn't express her desire.

The afternoon drifted, and they departed the restaurant near three o'clock. Mary Jo noticed the edgy wait staff who wanted to prepare for dinner service. Velvet didn't appreciate anyone besides Mary Jo. They lingered on the sidewalk before making their way toward separate vehicles. Velvet secured a commitment from Mary Jo to visit her in Shale Harbour soon. Mary Jo's plans depend on the ever-complicated Rosemary.

Velvet glances at the clock again. Time to carry her Death by Chocolate trifle into the lounge and place it in the bar fridge used for the convenient storage of drinks and water. She reaches for the four bowls which match the large one holding the dessert. *Now, where did I put my silver serving spoon?* It's not in the silver chest or in the utensil drawer. She checks she didn't leave it on the counter earlier. No spoon. Her hand flies over her mouth. Did someone—she suspects the someone is Deena—take her antique silver serving spoon? Although aware she has not reached the point of total incompetence, she opens the refrigerator, the cupboards, and the dresser in her bedroom, regardless. Her spoon is gone. She grabs a plain replacement and marches along her hall before she enters the common room, as Earlene's door clicks closed. Earlene always confirms the person assigned to set the table for the game has missed none of the preparation responsibilities.

After setting the glass bowls and the second choice serving spoon on the sideboard, she tucks her dessert into the fridge. Now, if Deena trots out those infernal lemon squares, she and the others can enjoy an alternative. She returns to her unit. With twenty minutes now left before their bridge game begins, she takes a moment to recover her composure, and decides she will search again. If the spoon remains missing, she'll confront Deena before they start their game this afternoon.

****

Deena 12:40PM

Deena Finch sits on the brocade and brass bench at the foot of her double bed. She admires the antique wardrobe which needed the strength and guidance of four vigorous men to fit the piece through the doors when they carted her possessions into this unit at the G-plex. Deena bought a pair of sneakers yesterday and pats the shoe box beside her before she rises and retrieves her Polaroid 1000 with the flash attachment, placed on the corner of her dresser. She opens the box with her free hand and removes the sneakers with care, sets them on top of the bench, then snaps a picture. The time drags until the damp photography paper spits out. She rips the square away from the camera and waves the magical paper in the air. The photo will take ten minutes to develop. While she waits, and with a flair for the dramatic, she throws open the cabinet to reveal five shelves of boxes, each with a photo of their contents taped to the outside. She determines she still has room for two or three more pairs after she settles this latest purchase on the second shelf from the bottom. Now, to choose the shoes she'll wear today.

Time to iron. She'll check the Polaroid picture again in a minute or two. No way to avoid the ironing board, but before she faces such a menial task, she opens her closet and digs out a cardboard office carton. The weight of the box surprises her when she wrestles it to rest on her bed. She doesn't remember the act of collection until she removes the lid and recalls, with elevated bliss, the antics required in the acquisition of the items selected because of their personal value to each owner. She fingers her most recently acquired objects—a Gucci handbag, a sterling serving spoon, and a photo in a silver frame. The picture has no useful qualities, but when she touches the frame, she shudders with pure pleasure while her breath catches in her throat. Yes, she nods at her imaginary audience. She's the culprit, the thief, but they aren't certain and sometimes accuse each other, which gives her no end of pleasure. The fact remains, she lives and interacts with three simpleminded women who are well below her station in life. They might suspect her, but they'll never know. She casts her eyes over the accumulated treasures and decides she'll take quiet time tonight and visit with her gatherings, for she considers them her gatherings.

Despite the pain which trips through the nerves in her shoulder and along her spine, she replaces the box at the back of her closet, avoids indulging further, and unlocks her vintage armoire collectible cabinet tucked into the corner of the room. The action reveals many pieces of costume jewellery she has amassed over the years. The unit remains secured at all times, and she avoids wearing specific items when playing bridge at home. She caresses a tortoiseshell bracelet but knows she can't flaunt the antique resin beauty amid today's company.

The lounge will be ready. Earlene, no doubt, did her inspection. Deena frowns. Their property owner is nothing, if not predictable. Deena grabs her trousers and trots into the kitchen. She'll iron them one more time before she dresses. She opens her refrigerator. The squares have set. She knows they aren't a favourite and can't figure out why. She admits the shortbread base is a challenge for the odd molar, but the lemon is tart enough to make a girl whistle.

With the ironing board assembled near an electrical outlet, and a hiss from the iron which signals temperature, she drapes her slacks and begins the tedious task of matching her press with an existing seam. The job proves difficult because she has chosen her St. Patrick Irish tartan trousers as an homage to the soon-to-arrive March 17. Her mind drifts toward a gold Bakelite bracelet that matches both the pants and her coordinated dark green cardigan.

Off with her housecoat and on with the pants. They'll each chirp across the table, discussing the items they've misplaced or lost. She'll enjoy the show. A noise attracts her attention as she zips her trousers. Standing still to listen, she hears a click, which sounds as if her door has opened.

****

Tess 12:55PM

Tess Boone munches on a banana muffin while she studies the pile of typewriter paper stacked across from her place at the table, which doubles as a desk. She imagines those pages covered with her words, and shivers. Grave responsibility.

After their bridge game last Wednesday, Tess called her friend Frances Ellis—the writer, whose husband writes, too. Tess suspects he's much more successful than Frances. She picks muffin crumbs off her blue corduroy dress. She loves her dress, which reaches mid-calf and makes her resemble an elf, but she doesn't care. Her reward is the warm and cozy comfort the garment provides. The common room can be cool on a March day. Frances effused enthusiasm when she described a joint memoir focused on Connie and Tess as girls and young women before Connie became afflicted with ALS. She threw out the option of someone else interviewing them and developing the manuscript. Tess admires her friend but ended the conversation with the distinct impression Frances didn't consider Tess to have the writing skills to cope with the task.

Her discussions with Connie proved more supportive. Connie thinks a memoir focused on the two of them is a fabulous idea and can't wait to see the outline. Tess took a course related to pacing a few years ago and knows the book must move from one chapter into the next without dragging. Once she has the concept developed and she reviews the details with her sister, she can focus on Connie and gather as many details as possible. Connie's afraid she'll die before they're finished.

Connie suggested they use a photo of the two of them, when they were teenagers, for the cover. She recalled one in particular—they were together at the beach and a friend took the snap. Tess keeps the picture in a silver frame on the oak drop-down side table by her new sofa. She turns to admire the photo, but sees only a coaster, lamp, and a space where the keepsake sat. She approaches and looks at the floor nearby. Did the frame fall? Did she move it? Why? This location is perfect. Deena. She knows Deena came in here and stole her picture. The thieving witch wants the silver frame. The photo is meaningless to her. Besides, she fully expects Deena will delight in exposing her secret today—a secret Tess has tried valiantly to keep.

Tess places her dirty dishes in the sink, brushes her teeth, and enters the lounge through her access door. She will confront Deena right now. She still has time before bridge. The woman has no scruples. Finding Deena's interior door locked, she hears nothing but the television when she knocks. She bustles out through the patio exit, without a coat for protection from the brisk March wind, and stomps along the back pathway to Deena's outside entrance. She knocks again, louder and with more determination. No response. She wraps her arms around her chest to guard against the chill and returns via the patio as Earlene and Velvet enter the common room ready for their bridge game.

They sit. She will play across from Earlene today. *Perfect. No pressure.* Sarcasm, even within her private thoughts.

"Deena prepared the table, but I see no sign of dessert. I brought my Death by Chocolate trifle." Velvet graces Earlene and Tess with a conspiratorial smile. "No need to eat those horrible squares."

Muttering her appreciation, Tess then spits her thoughts. "I don't know for sure, but I suspect Deena stole a picture of me and my sister. It sat on the end table beside my sofa and is gone." She has their undivided attention. "The frame is silver, and Connie suggested we use the photo for the cover of the book." Her eyes puddle.

"Well!" Velvet huffs her displeasure. "And you will miss my antique serving spoon when we break for dessert because I discovered it missing today, too." She glances toward Earlene. "Deena must be our thief."

"My Gucci handbag disappeared. It cost a fortune—plucked off the closet shelf and vaporized. If you agree, then we should talk with Deena. If she isn't our culprit, she'll invite us to walk around her apartment." Without waiting for a reply, she stands.

"I knocked on her front door before I came in here. She didn't answer. Let's bang on the inside access again." Tess jumps and runs toward Deena's suite. She knocks with unbridled vigour on the wooden surface.

"Here, let me. We can justify entry because she hasn't answered." Earlene waves the master key, affixed at the end of a long pink ribbon. Tess steps aside while Velvet hangs back nearer the bridge table.

Earlene shouts from the threshold. "Deena! Deena, where are you?"

Tess, her anger still bubbling, wedges past Earlene and enters the apartment, noting how Earlene, with no hesitation, created a rational excuse for accessing her tenant's suite. She walks along the hallway, albeit with less enthusiasm and annoyance than she imagined. She glances behind and determines Earlene has followed. With Earlene hovering nearby, she enters the main room. The ironing board is upset on the floor.

She turns toward Earlene and whispers, "Come closer." The two women approach side by side and spy the bloody iron and one of Deena's legs, awkward and crooked against the centre pedestal of her kitchen table.

"Velvet, call an ambulance! Deena has fallen, and she's hurt." Earlene's voice shakes.

"Okay," comes a faint answer.

Tess ventures further into the room. Deena's hair rests in a pool of blood. Her iron is nearby and bloodied as well. "I think we should contact the police, and it may be too late for medical help."

Earlene chooses her steps with care and makes her way around the body to avoid the blood pool. Deena's eyes are open. Tess watches as Earlene checks for a pulse in her neck. She meets Tess' gaze, then bows her head as if in prayer.

Venturing back along Deena's hallway, she yells for Velvet. "Call the police, too."

"The ambulance is on the way, Tess. The police, too. Did she fall?"

As Tess and Earlene offer Velvet their impressions, the emergency teams arrive. The three sit at the bridge table and allow the professionals room to do their jobs.

****

Stella 1:30PM

Before she returns to her office after lunch, Stella wanders into reception to assess the supplies needed for the 1982 season, eight weeks away. As she sorts through registration forms, pulls her lists of seasonals who provided a deposit, and those who will pay when they arrive, and counts the number of site maps she has on hand, her mind drifts to the conversation with Cloris last Wednesday.

Struck by Cloris' initial enthusiasm, she tried to discover why the woman might entertain the idea of running her registration office while helping inside the house when Stella isn't available. Two issues soon became clear. Cloris refuses to be at Duke's beck and call. She created the scenario where Duke cruises past her trailer on the golf cart one sunny morning, expecting her to jump on board and keep him company while he completes his rounds; then a cup of coffee and a muffin for his trouble. She said she doesn't want her activities and her life at Shale Cliffs revolving around Duke, as much as she enjoys him as a boyfriend. Apparently, Duke is often clingy in the romantic sense, which is news to Stella. Her second issue related to her previous role as caregiver to the sick and disabled. Stella struggled to avoid taking offence when Cloris compared working for Stella as a job within the same purview. She will run the office, make lunches as required, answer the phone, and complete light housework downstairs. She considers herself someone able to assess the need for an extra hand.

Cloris often patted her hair and smoothed her cardigan while she spoke—a nervous behaviour in Stella's eyes. Kiki is Stella's biggest concern. Cloris anxiously added she has no problem with the dog. She's fond of dogs, although she prefers not to host one in her home, trailer, or truck. She hates the hair. They decided to give each other a trial run, after Cloris stipulated that she won't dress in her best finery to avoid dog shedding on her favourite clothes. Stella will hold Cloris' deposit, but she won't pay any more money unless she decides the job isn't for her, in which case Stella promised to credit her for the time she worked. Stella will happily refund her deposit if she lasts the season.

Back in her office, doubts niggle. Cloris wants control and Stella sees the role as hers alone, as the owner / manager. Although she appreciates the act of being well-cared-for, she contemplates the thin line which separates an efficient caregiver from someone who runs your life—and frowns on dog hair. Maybe she'll clean more often than Alice. Who knows? Cloris made a commitment to Aiden. When Rosemary's discharge from the hospital is imminent, Cloris' loyalties will require review.

Startled out of her reverie by the phone, she jumps and curses under her breath. "Shale Cliffs RV…."

"Hi. It's me," Aiden interrupts the familiar salutation.

"How are you? Been a while." She states facts and doesn't admonish.

"I know and here I come, cap in hand, yet again. We received a report of a suspicious death within the last hour."

"Murder?"

"Well, I don't think the poor woman bashed her own skull in with an iron. Moyer is at the scene, along with uniforms and forensics. I'm on my way and I thought you might help."

"Where's Essie?" Essie Matkowski became Aiden's partner after the writers retreat murder of Owen Ellis-Thomas. Her mother's been sick, so Essie has been on leave, the reason Stella worked with Aiden on the nursing home cases.

"Essie resigned to stay home with her mother. Since we learned essential details about boarding homes and nursing homes, I suggested a reputable care facility, but I offended her. She was aghast and told me she has one mother and will resume her career when she's no longer needed at home."

Stella pauses before she answers. "I can't comment. We didn't keep Dad at home. I know he's happy at Harbour Manor—the routine, the other residents—but I often experience the guilt, anyway. No judgment from me."

"Are you up for another contract?"

Thoughts of earlier cases fly through her mind. Aiden North, a detective with the RCMP, first appeared on the scene when Lorraine Young, one of her park seasonals, disappeared in May 1980. With a mentally ill wife, he transferred back to home territory to finish out his career. Rosemary North has two sisters in Port Ephron. Stella helped him meet the locals. When Lucy Painter died and the police considered her death a case of misadventure, she pestered Aiden until the department took her suspicions into account. Paulina McAdams' execution required no such persuasion. She admits she crossed the line when they investigated Owen Ellis-Thomas' death. Aiden became ensnared in Rosemary's unstable condition at the time and she, a civilian, interviewed prime suspects and obtained a confession. Essie Matkowski sat in on the interviews and came away unimpressed by her tactics.

Now Essie has resigned. Stella can't fake disappointment. She enjoys Aiden's company and has treasured a soft spot for him ever since they were teenagers—her first love. They never reference their past, although they will admit to others they dated in high school. She expects Nick has figured out the convoluted history she shares with the detective but has harnessed any jealousy he experienced at the outset—for the most part. Rosemary views their high school romance differently. Aiden's wife considers Stella her nemesis, and she's convinced Stella will take Aiden away from her. When, and if, Rosemary leaves the hospital, the woman's threats and harassment may become an issue again. "Yes. The park is under control. Nick won't mind. Who died?"

"I don't know yet—one of the women we saw at the fourplex back in January."

"What? Someone at the G-plex?"

"Correct. Can you meet me in thirty minutes? I told Moyer I'd arrive at the scene no later than three."

✵

CHAPTER 5

Ample Opportunity

What does one wear to a murder scene? She's uncertain whether her attire has ever been appropriate for such a circumstance. She avoids the victim's remains. Her job isn't assessment of the dead, but in a more direct fashion, assessment of the living. She decides her current jeans and Dalhousie University sweatshirt will fit the bill, preventing her from wasting more time. Her conversation with Nick rattles through her mind once more.

After she heard from Aiden and consented to attend another death scene, she told Nick about her plans. The furrow between his brows and the way he rested his hand on her shoulder suggested his displeasure.

"Aiden hasn't called in two months," he emphasized, "or been out to the park, even for coffee, let alone a meal. I thought you were through with law enforcement consultations."

"Me, too," she answered. She explained how Essie won't return anytime soon. "The work is one contract at a time, and I expect Aiden's superiors will assign him a new partner soon." She stood on her tiptoes and kissed his stubbled cheek. "The case intrigues me." She revealed the location of the scene and provided Nick with a brief description of each woman.

"You don't know who's dead?"

"Nope. Aiden didn't either."

"Okay. Work is under control here. You understand I'll support you, regardless." He wrapped her in flannel-clad arms. "Call me as soon as you can."

The veranda door slammed ten minutes ago, so he's left for the workshop. "Kiki, are you still here?" No sound of nails clicking on the hardwood floor. She must be with Nick in the truck. Once she gathers her purse and keys,

Stella locks the doors and trots toward the Jeep. The driveway, despite a healthy layer of white gravel, generates a spongy sensation underfoot. Frost forces its way out of the ground.

She checks her watch, takes the extra time, and drives along the back lane to say goodbye in person. Although confident Nick understands, she translated the conflict which brewed behind his eyes as discomfort and wants to allay his concerns. She stops beside the old yellow Ford and opens her door before shouting, "Nick, I'm off!"

He materializes out of the gloom. Kiki, dressed in her fisherman's knit turtleneck, stands at his heel—the German Shepherd she believes herself to be. "Give us another kiss." He approaches, leans over, and reaches inside to caress her thigh. "I expect you home for supper," he teases. "I have a special menu in mind."

Maintaining a momentary straight face, she asks, "Chicken?" She grins while she navigates the lane way and leaves Shale Cliffs behind.

Earlene Marigold's fourplex sits near the town limits of Shale Harbour—a corner lot in a locale under steady development in recent years. Most of the new units are duplexes, built by contractors for those who crave seaside summers. Earlene's place differs from the others. Upon one's approach, the structure appears to be a traditional bungalow. Stella passes official vehicles on the side of the street before pulling into the generous driveway, also crowded with police and forensic cars and vans. She stops behind Aiden's sedan, after following hand signals supplied by Sergeant Moyer, who has saved her a spot. The lumbering police officer she considers a silent supporter stands poised at the right edge of the property, on the sidewalk. The cement path leads past Tess Boone's front door, the garden doors into the lounge, and around the end toward Deena's direct access at the back. If she walked in the opposite direction, it would lead her to Velvet's main entrance, which faces the side street.

"Hi, Sergeant. I gather Aiden arrived."

"He asked me to watch for you, Stella. The three other residents are in the lounge. He said he expected you to keep them company after you assessed the scene with him. I'd be happy to stay outside if that's okay. Those women are a weird lot."

"They gave you a tough time when you attended a burglary. Right?"

Moyer nods but doesn't elaborate.

She trots along beside the sergeant. "Aiden thinks I enjoy dead bodies." Her chest heaves. "Which one of them died?"

"The woman who lives at the back." He pauses and checks his notebook. "Deena Finch. She worked at Shale Harbour Groceteria but hurt her arm or shoulder, from what I heard."

The other three suspected Deena of stealing from them. When she and Aiden were here in January, their accusations were vague and without merit. As Moyer steps aside and allows her entry through the garden doors, Earlene, Velvet, and Tess sit wide-eyed and expressionless at the bridge table, as if still waiting for their fourth. A young constable stands nearby. She nods in their direction before she follows Moyer along the narrow hall into the primary living space of Deena's unit. She stops when she sees Aiden, the lower half of a woman's leg, twisted and visible from the corner of the table, and the ironing board tumbled on its side. The murder weapon isn't within her line of sight.

"Thanks, Moyer. You go back outside until our reinforcements arrive to cover the entries. Glad you're here, Stella." Aiden acknowledges her feet planted on the tile floor. "Do you intend to stand in the hall?"

"I thought you'd prefer me inside the lounge with the others," she replies.

"Come help me first. Forensics took pictures, but I want your impressions."

Stella inches her way through and stands four feet from the heart of the crime scene. She's careful to avoid any blood spots or pockets of spray on the floor and wall. "She didn't hit herself and the circumstances are no accident."

"Correct. I called the office in Port Ephron and one of the clerical staff ran to the hardware store and bought an iron for forensics, the same model as the victim owned. Is it heavy? It looks heavy." He glances at her from the corner of his eye. "I'm no expert. I send my shirts out, so don't press clothes."

"Not too weighty to be wielded at someone's head." Her tone contains an element of thoughtfulness as her imagination processes the actions which might have taken place inside the apartment. "Most women know their way around an iron."

He pauses, then meets her eyes. "Now, I can't permit any of the other three residents back in their apartments until back-up staff from Port Ephron arrive. I want a uniform in each unit to make sure they don't touch or remove relevant items before we take their formal statements at the office. Will you talk with them as a group, and individually as well?" His focus reverts to the scene. "Assess how shocked they are and whom they might suspect—the way you always do." He graces her with a quick look of admiration. "I'll instruct the service personnel assigned to allow each their bag and coat when we drive them to the station—nothing else."

****

The metallic smell of spilled blood lingers inside her nostrils. "May I sit?" She reaches for the back of the empty fourth chair at the bridge table and scans the faces of the three women. The young constable remains at the garden entrance. Moyer has returned to his post on the walkway. Earlene's erect posture and expressionless face focuses on Deena's door. Tess' cheeks are damp. Tears tumble unabated along her jaw. Velvet clenches a piece of her long hair like a person might grasp a rope to prevent a fall. She stares at her lap.

"Be my guest." Earlene starts. "Good God, Stella, do you have any idea what happened? And why are you here?"

"Thanks. I'll answer your second question first. I consult with Detective North and the Shale Harbour / Port Ephron RCMP when they ask. No, we aren't sure of exact circumstances, but her death isn't an accident, as you have probably surmised. Who found the body?" She encourages Velvet to lift her face. "You called the police and ambulance, eh, Velvet?"

Velvet manages a nod. Tess engages. "I wanted a conversation with Deena before our game." She glances at the clock. "We start at one." She closes her eyes for a second. "Her inside door was locked, and she didn't respond to my knock, so I trotted around to her main entrance. I didn't try the front door, although she didn't respond. The TV was on. I came back here with Earlene and Velvet. We used her inside door."

Stella expects Deena was dead by this time.

Earlene picks up the story. "I retrieved the master key from my unit, and we went in." She glances at Tess. "Tess walked ahead of me. At first, we thought she'd fallen, and I asked Velvet to call an ambulance. Then I checked her pulse."

Stella lifts her brows.

"Don't worry. I didn't step in any blood, and we left at once after we alerted Velvet. She contacted the RCMP as well. How long will the emergency people and the police be here, Stella? I hate their vehicles parked in front of my building." Earlene sits straighter in her chair.

"The duration, I imagine, Earlene. Be prepared. Each of you must make a formal statement at the station before day's end."

Earlene frowns. Tess' tears flow unchecked again. Velvet's focus remains glued on her lap. "Why did you want to speak with Deena, Tess? You expected her to play bridge, correct?"

Tess wipes her face with shaky and chapped hands before she explains. "On a personal matter. There was a picture of Connie and me when we were teenagers—in a silver frame on my sofa end table. Today, the photo and frame are missing. I'm convinced Deena stole them. I wanted a confrontation before the game." She makes eye contact with the other two women. "The issue isn't a secret. We're sure she's stolen from each of us. The police were here many times before." Recollection blushes her cheeks. "Why, you were even here once when we called. Earlene asked for Detective North."

"Yes, Tess. Everyone reported an article missing."

"Well, today my Gucci handbag has disappeared, and Velvet couldn't find her sterling serving spoon," Earlene huffs. "I decided we should ask Deena for permission to search her apartment. If she wasn't the thief, she should cooperate."

"What happened when you asked?"

"Stella." Earlene takes on the manner of a university professor with a dull-minded student. She continues in measured tones. "We found her dead. We never discussed her thievery. I thought you understood."

There are advantages in the portrayal of a potential misunderstanding. "You will hear the same questions often over the course of the investigation, Earlene." She turns toward Velvet. "And tell me what happened from your perspective."

"I made the phone calls. I did as asked." Velvet is hesitant and acts as if she bears a measure of blame, in some way yet undetected.

"Did any of you confront Deena in the past, and accuse her of theft in the fourplex?"

"Yes," Tess answers. "We each suspected Deena but couldn't figure out how she gained access. She often said Earlene has the master key and if anyone has free rein, the person is Earlene."

Earlene stands. "I refuse to stay here and feel accused. I'm going to my unit until summoned by the real police."

Stella lifts her hand and silently refuses to take offence. "Please sit. No one can go home until more personnel arrive. You may enter your apartment accompanied by an officer, at which point I will visit with you again alone. You'll each be driven to the station after Detective North finishes here."

Suitably chastised, Earlene drops into her chair. Two more constables shuffle into the lounge, led by Sergeant Moyer.

"Sergeant Moyer, let me introduce Earlene Marigold, the owner of the building, Velvet Carmichael, the renter who lives in the unit which faces the side road, and Tess Boone, who rents the smaller apartment you pass when you access via the garden doors."

Each woman nods while the three uniformed officers stand with feet shoulder distance apart and hands clasped in front.

"Please return to your own units. One of my constables will keep you company. Touch as little as possible." Moyer acknowledges Stella. "Ms. Kirk, here, wants a private word with each of you before we drive you to the station for formal statements. You may wear your coat and bring along your handbag. Are we good, Stella?"

"Yes." She nods in the general direction of the three uniforms. "I'll start with Earlene. Keep me posted on when Detective North leaves for his office."

****

Speculation suggests Earlene Marigold's age to be ten years her senior. She follows the erect and stoic woman along the short hallway from the common room into her pristine apartment. Every stick of furniture appears new. She nods toward the police officer, who assumes a position near the interior exit door, far enough into the unit to maintain full view of the open concept living area.

"Sit, Stella. May I make you a cup of tea?"

Stella glances at the overseer first, not sure if tea is permissible, considering the suggestion was to touch as little as possible. "Thanks, Earlene. I appreciate your hospitality under such difficult circumstances." She watches Earlene, who acts grateful for the task. She buzzes around, reaches into cupboards for cups and a teapot, a lower cabinet to retrieve the kettle, and drawers for silverware and napkins. Every item is new or seems new.

Earlene sits across from Stella at the kitchen table while they wait for the water to boil. "Officer, may I make you a cup as well?"

The young woman declines. "I'm fine."

"Show me around your apartment, Earlene. Did you buy your furniture and accessories when you moved?"

"Yes, I did. The people who bought my marital home asked if I could include the contents, since they live here six months of the year, and own another house in the city. I agreed with enthusiasm." She swings her arm and sweeps the air. "Time for a change."

They wander through the living room, two guest rooms, and into the main bedroom. Stella assesses. Each space gives the impression of a furniture store vignette. Even the bed linens are trendy and new. "I bet you enjoyed shopping. In my case, I still sit on the sofas my mother bought fifty years ago." Stella experiences a sense of personal pride—in her history? Or her frugality? She can't take time to analyze potential rationale.

"One's possessions offer comfort and solace. Occasionally, those same items are soggy with unwelcome memories. I'm afraid, after Richard's death, my furniture represented the latter." She turns on her heel with a surprising suddenness. "The kettle's boiling."

Once seated at the kitchen table with tea—a flowery variety—Stella begins. "Tell me what you think of Tess and Velvet, Earlene."

"Do you mean, did either of them murder Deena Finch? Someone killed the woman. Her death is no accident." She sips while she meets Stella's gaze over the rim of her cup. "They both enjoyed ample opportunity. I advised my tenants, on a regular basis, to keep their doors locked because a person or persons unknown—one of them—stole from us often. I suspected Deena, but I couldn't figure out how she accessed our units."

"Why do you suppose Velvet or Tess harmed Deena today, in particular?"

Earlene clenches her teeth. "I expect I'll repeat the same sentences a dozen times, but the operative word is opportunity. Velvet entered the lounge and deposited her dessert in the fridge. I heard her arrive as I left after I checked the table. She could have visited Deena. Even if the door was locked, Deena would have admitted her. Velvet could have carried out the deed and returned the way she came, locking Deena's entry behind her."

"There was a great deal of blood."

"Lots of time to change clothes." She leans forward. "My remarks don't represent an accusation, although she has a history of mental illness. I'm sure the police will check her laundry hamper. Mary Jo Frost, who spares for us when one of the four can't play, chums with Velvet." She pauses. "We may need her regularly now. As for Velvet, I've merely noted ample opportunity." Comfortable in her role as accuser, she continues. "And Tess, too."

"How do you suppose Tess killed Deena?"

"When I first saw Tess before our bridge game, she was racing from the direction of Deena's unit back into the lounge. She reported she knocked on Deena's main door but heard no answer. She said she wanted to confront her because she believes Deena stole a photo. I grabbed my key, and we entered Deena's suite." She frowns. "We've explained what happened already."

"Understood, Earlene, but be patient. I suspect we're in for a long day." Stella sets her empty teacup on the table and decides to change the subject. "Can you tell me more about the loss of your husband? After he died, you sold your big house and built the fourplex. Correct? The unique design became the talk of the town, but Richard's death must have been difficult."

"Dear Richard." Earlene's eyes mist. "The love of my life. I found him on the back step. He tried to reach me. I sat on the stoop and held his face in my hands as he died." One lone tear travels along her cheek and carves a path through her expertly applied foundation.

"Reports said he suffered a massive heart attack. Heart problems?"

"Not diagnosed. He told me he'd be out behind the garage, but he returned to the step before he died. Sheer horror. The experience changed me forever."

"You began a new life to erase reminders."

"Correct." She sits straighter in her chair, if such a movement is even possible. "I hope my lifestyle changes aren't held against me, Stella."

"I see no reason, Earlene. One more topic before I meet Velvet. I understand you and Opal Painter were friends."

"Yes. I imagine she will be behind bars for a long time."

"Fifteen years."

"Opal and I studied herbs. I often visited her. The youngest sister, Hester, acts unusual but knowledgeable in a wide range of flora. I hope you liked the tea. I concoct my own."

Stella glances toward her drained cup. "Tasted great. Thank you." She swivels in her chair and faces the constable, who has stood nearby for the last twenty minutes. "Please stay with Mrs. Marigold while she retrieves her handbag and coat, then wait with her in the lounge. I am off to find Miss Carmichael. Sergeant Moyer will fetch you when the time comes." She returns her attention to Earlene. "As I said, expect today to be a long one."

When she leaves Earlene's apartment, she searches for Moyer. "I'm off to Velvet's. Can you do me a huge favour and contact the station? Ask the desk person to call Nick and tell him I won't be home for supper."

⚘

CHAPTER 6

The Convenient Master Key

An assigned constable greets her inside the lounge entry to Velvet's apartment. "She's been in the same spot ever since we arrived," he whispers, while he jerks his thumb toward the living room. In contrast to Earlene, Stella finds Velvet curled into her lounger by the front window, her frowned attention focused on the side street, now lined with emergency vehicles.

"Hi, Velvet. May I sit?"

With her gaze still outside, she points at the couch.

"Detective North has asked me to discuss Deena's death with you. Let's start with the scene. Did you enter Deena's apartment?"

While nibbling on a strand of hair, she shakes her head.

Stella notices Velvet's waist-length mane now spills around her shoulders and against her face. The investigation depends on information from witnesses at this stage. She utilizes a familiar tactic and encourages Velvet's participation. "You and Deena were good friends, neighbours. Her death must be devastating."

Velvet abandons her hair-chewing and turns in her chair. "Deena hated me. We weren't friends, Stella. She could be a horrible person." She re-settles and her fingers search for the damp thread.

"Please explain how this horrible person, as you say, treated you."

"She stole, and she lied. An honest word never left her mouth. The police will find our stuff and prove we were right from the beginning. She couldn't stand me. I'm aware I need patience occasionally. Earlene often says, 'Velvet's an acquired taste'." She mimics Earlene with squared shoulders and a stiff neck.

"What does Earlene mean?"

"If people understand me, they'll know I'm smart. Those of us in this world with mental health issues aren't stupid. I react to situations differently than others." Her face muscles relax. "Just give me a chance."

"How long have you been here at the fourplex?"

"I was the first person to move in after Earlene. My apartment is perfect. I worked at the library and when I retired, the G-plex became available at the right time and satisfied my needs." She brushes invisible lint off her wrinkled trousers. "I finished work a year early. Computers overwhelmed me." She shifts in her seat to squint at Stella. "I understand my limits. The doctors' reports indicate I am 'managed'."

Stella takes a moment and assesses the space. The apartment isn't big, or doesn't appear grand, because Velvet's idea of décor comprises plastic tables piled with bric-à-brac in every corner. She obviously purchased her shabby furniture second-hand. Stella admonishes herself. She and Nick are encircled by shabby. "Will you show me around, Velvet? We're not allowed to touch your stuff, but you can give me a tour."

Velvet heaves herself off her recliner and rubs her hands along her pant legs once again. "My unit is the same size as Deena's—nine hundred square feet—but mine's a rectangle and hers is squarish. Earlene told me she wanted each apartment to give the impression of spaciousness. I can sit in my chair and still see the kitchen and my table and chairs. I preferred a spot facing the street." She frowns. "Deena often criticized my place and said she liked the privacy at the back because no one could find her if they didn't know the address."

"Your unit is cozy, Velvet. I understand. Will you describe what happened today?" They wander back into the living room and away from the untidy main bedroom.

Velvet claps a nail-bitten hand over her chapped lips. "I left my Death by Chocolate dessert in the lounge fridge. My bowls and a spoon, too. May I bring them back?"

"Not now. They're safe where they are. Let's sit and you can tell me every detail that occurred before you called the emergency teams."

She flounces across the room toward her lounger, sits, and directs a pout at Stella. "I'm craving a dish of my yummy dessert."

"Patience, Velvet. What happened today?"

"I prepared for our game as usual. I made a sweet treat because Deena bakes gross lemon squares when her turn rolls around, with rock-hard crust and too-tart lemon. The three of us hate them with passion, so we always offer a choice. I contributed my favourite chocolate concoction. I planned to pop out into the lounge early with the bowls and my sterling silver serving spoon." She yanks on a strand of hair. "The spoon was not in the drawer. My grandmother's. I have very few nice possessions, as you no doubt noticed but are too kind to mention. My spoon and six antique hair combs came from her." She wiggles deeper into the faded corduroy and takes a cursory glance out the window. "I remember I missed a silver comb when you were here last. I don't understand why Deena stole it. She has, or had, skinny, frail hair." She covers her mouth with her hand again. "Oops. Nothing personal," she adds, after a quick perusal of Stella's fine and wispy locks.

"None taken, Velvet. Continue."

"When I took my dessert out, I heard Earlene's door click shut. I suspected she checked to see if Deena completed her responsibilities and set the table for the game. The room appeared prepared, much to my surprise."

"Did you go into Deena's?"

"My word, no. I didn't want to confront Deena while we were alone. I wanted to talk before bridge when we were together." Her face flushes. "Deena scared me. She could be mean—even with strangers."

"Will you give me an example?"

"Ask Mary Jo Frost. She'll tell you. One day, when Tess couldn't play and Mary Jo spared, the subject of raising children came up. As you might already realize, none of us here at the fourplex are mothers, and the circle includes Mary Jo." She pauses and stares at the ceiling for a moment. "Funny, the women in our age group who bucked the trend and avoided family. You, too. Right?"

Stella expects Velvet to be fifteen years her senior, but no matter. "Yes, my sister Trixie is the parent. What happened?"

"The discussion centred around a story in the paper where social services took kids from their mother and placed them in care. I can't remember the details, but Mary Jo said the woman must have been incompetent to lose her children. Deena yelled at Mary Jo and said how you can't understand raising children unless you're a parent, and we shouldn't judge."

"A fair statement, Velvet."

"Our problem wasn't what she said, as much as how she said the words.

She hissed. The episode was hateful. Each of us felt upset afterward. I talked with Mary Jo later. She stayed for supper with me. Mary Jo blew the incident off, but I expect Deena hurt her feelings. No, we haven't kids, but everyone has a right to an opinion." She crosses her arms.

"Did you enter her apartment after Earlene unlocked her door?"

"No." She slouches in her chair. "I didn't want to see whatever happened. I did as I was told and made the calls, that's all."

Stella stands and turns toward the constable, who remains at the mouth of the hallway which leads into the lounge. "Velvet will collect her coat and purse. Afterward, the two of you come back into the main room. I am off for a visit with Miss Boone. Velvet, your information was helpful. I hope you won't find the time required to file your statement with the police too tedious. I'll see you again before day's end."

****

A young female police officer Stella imagines can't be much over nineteen opens Tess' door. She glances at the weapon on the woman's hip before she makes her way along the short hall and into the minuscule apartment. Easy to keep track of a suspect in a bachelor apartment with a bathroom. Stella sidles past multiple cardboard cartons. Tess remains seated at her kitchen table, strewn with scraps of paper, opened notebooks, and photographs. She displays the capacity for a limitless supply of tears. Even though their first conversation took place an hour ago, she continues to blubber.

"Thank you, Constable. Hi, Tess. May I sit?"

"Sure. Move my research aside. I offered our guard here a cup of tea, but she declined. You?"

"No thanks, Tess, but I appreciate your hospitality." Stella's gaze travels across the room. "Tiny but comfy, I see."

"Yes. I am not well off but enjoy enough income to support a place on my own. The books are a problem, as you probably noticed. I over-ordered my volume of short stories, and I still own fifty cookbooks which require selling. I never relish sitting perched on a hard chair at a craft market table, but such is the life of an aspiring writer." Her dramatic sigh catches Stella by surprise.

"I understood you hadn't completed a manuscript, Tess, let alone published one. I remember when we spoke at Connie's...."

"Well, I avoid details with Connie," she interrupts with a shrug. "My sister frets and worries that I'm afraid to author *any* book, but my problem is compiling *her* story. Now, my plan has changed."

"How?"

"Velvet, who often surprises me, suggested a valid idea. She said I should pen a memoir and tell the story of Connie and me as sisters. I ran the concept past Frances Ellis." She frowns.

"What did Frances say?"

"Oh, accomplished writers can be less than encouraging, and she thought someone else should write the memoir." Tess stares at a speck on her sweater sleeve for a moment. "She's afraid I'll be successful." When the phone rings, the answering machine takes the call.

The two women stay seated, listening as Theo Gorman leaves a message. He tells Tess he's thrilled to print another book for her, and she should come in at her convenience and discuss details. Tess blushes and titters while she listens, then adds, "The machine is a hand-me-down from my sister when she moved into Harbour Manor. I love feeling invisible while someone leaves a message."

Ignoring her reaction as best she can, Stella begins. "Tess, tell me what happened today, please."

"I'll cry again. I can't stop."

"Deep down, you were fond of Deena." Stella counts on her incorrect statement to force a further explanation.

"No. You're wrong. I've never seen a dead body before, except for when they're in a casket. I feel overwhelmed. The events of this afternoon muddled me. I hope I can remember."

"Take your time."

"When I noticed the picture of me and my sister gone, I felt sure Deena skulked in here when I wasn't home. She knew I wanted to write a memoir describing Connie and me and our story. The theft was vindictive and hurt me to the core." She touches her palm to her heart.

"You're sure Deena took the photo."

"Oh yes. Other items, too." She blinks several times in rapid succession and continues. "I hoped to confront her before the game—without an audience—to retrieve my picture, no matter the consequences."

"Did you?"

"No! No! Do you imagine I crept inside and walloped Deena before I grabbed my picture? She didn't answer my knock, on either door. I don't know if the front was locked because I would never walk directly in that way. As for the inside door, I tried the knob, but it was locked. I was freezing because I left without a coat, so I ran back toward the garden doors, came in, and met Earlene and Velvet. Earlene used her master key." Tess wipes stray tears and squints at Stella. "The convenient master key…and we went in."

"Understood. Let's focus on you. Are you retired, Tess?"

"I haven't worked in years."

"Injured on the job, I gather."

"Discussion of the details is a circumstance I avoid. I live a quiet and frugal life near my sister because I'm her advocate."

"Connie is a wonderful person. Her help on another case proved pivotal." Stella reaches for her keys and purse, accepting she will gain no further details regarding Tess' past, at least for the moment. "You understand the police will transport each of you to the station and ask you to make formal statements?"

Tess nods.

"I saw the pathologist's vehicle leave from Velvet's window. Forensics are probably on scene for the evening. I expect Detective North will be finished soon." She turns toward the door. "You grab your coat and handbag. Wait with the constable in the lounge and we'll talk again at the detachment. Questions?"

"May I return Theo's call?"

"You must refrain from any discussions with people until after your formal statement, okay? Once the death becomes public knowledge, you can contact Theo, and Connie as well."

"Oh my, yes. Connie will worry if she hears someone died in my building."

****

As her stomach rumbles, Stella waits in Aiden's office at the RCMP detachment in Shale Harbour. She doesn't expect they'll stop for supper. Aiden asked her, at the time they left the crime scene, for a debrief with him here before they take statements from each of the women. He's compelled to collect formal remarks today, before Earlene, Velvet, and Tess return to the G-plex and talk together with no official present. Her watch says six-thirty and her Monday should be over now. She imagines a cool glass of white wine and a snuggle with Nick and Kiki.

"I've settled them in different rooms, Stella. Did you tell Nick not to expect you home?" Aiden blusters into his office and throws himself into the chair behind his desk.

"No problem. Sergeant Moyer radioed the station, and someone called him for me. Earlene, Velvet, and Tess won't be happy, forced into sitting here over dinner hour."

Aiden tilts his head, and a lock of white hair dusts his brow. "I've isolated each witness—one in an empty office, one in the conference room, and one in another interview room. There's a constable assigned for company." He smirks. "We've provided tea and digestive biscuits."

"Keep them uncomfortable, but with little ammunition for the complaint department," Stella mutters. "I'd enjoy a digestive biscuit myself."

"We can order in—pizza from the hotel might be an idea." He sits straighter in his chair. "Tell me what you learned. We'll take time for a bite before we start with their statements. No one has asked for a lawyer yet."

"Okay. Earlene first. You're aware of the history of her husband's death and the subsequent construction of the fourplex?"

He nods.

"Part of her story doesn't ring true."

"What?"

"I can't isolate the issue, but Richard Marigold passed away without warning. Earlene knew he was behind the garage for a reason she never explained. He didn't tell her?" She lifts her brows. "Later, he crawled as far as the back door and died in her arms. She's an herbalist. Learned the tricks of the craft from Opal and Hester Painter." She lifts her brows for a second time. "Close friend of Opal's, I gathered."

"Did she poison her husband?"

"No idea, but puzzle pieces don't align. As for Deena Finch, Earlene had opportunity because Velvet heard her door click closed after Earlene entered the lounge and checked the bridge table. Earlene has the master key. She keeps it on a hook near her inside door, fastened with a long pink ribbon. Easy access."

"Easy access for anyone," Aiden adds.

"If one of them stole the key, the task requires Earlene not noticing and an unlocked door. No small feat."

"More?"

"When Earlene sold her marital home, she didn't even take a dinner plate with her. She claims she bought new furniture and accessories because the buyers wanted an equipped house. The result is an apartment devoid of any clues related to her history. There are no family pictures, no books on her nightstand, or dishes inherited from her mother. The décor gives the impression she's dropped in from outer space."

"Velvet Carmichael has a past. I often saw her when I visited Rosemary. She's enjoyed more successes than my poor wife."

In her heart, Stella hopes Rosemary remains in hospital, but she voices the obligatory, "How goes the battle? Discharge soon?"

"Toni and Mary Jo are convinced she'll be home in weeks, not months, but during her last episodes, she was out of control. Her sisters have reconsidered and want to offer care and supervision at my house with Cloris Kincaid on an on-call basis. I might manage if not faced with one murder after the other to investigate," he huffs.

"No chance of stepping back? You could retire, Aiden. Your staff won't think less of you. Your wife is sick, for God's sake." She avoids any conversation with Aiden related to Cloris for now.

"The work helps." He raises his finger as the telephone jangles. "Yeah, Constable. Sure. Send him along the hall. I'll open the door. Nick's fine—a friend of the force." Aiden rounds his desk. "The constable at the front says he's brought us supper."

"What?" Before she reacts further, Nick fills the doorway, an aluminum foil covered paper plate in each hand.

"Hi. I assumed you two might be hungry. I hope I've delivered dinner before you ordered takeout." His grin stretches across his handsome face.

Stella stands, takes the plates, and places them with care on Aiden's desk before she peeks under the foil.

"Chicken." Nick's grin turns into a rumbling chuckle. "You said chicken."

She blushes but says the words on her mind, in front of Aiden regardless. "The chicken was a metaphor," she stutters and blushes.

"Third wheel over here, you two." Aiden waves from behind his desk.

Stella covers her mouth with her hand and winks at Nick.

"What did you deliver for us, Nick?"

"Baked chicken breasts with coleslaw and potato salad," Stella answers.

"I figured the chicken could cool off, but I couldn't take the chance with mashed potatoes and gravy." He digs in his pockets and retrieves silverware and a plastic bag full of chocolate chip cookies. "Here you go." He hands the stash to Stella.

"Home by nine-thirty, if all goes well. Three statements to compile first, but a dinner delivered by you helps make the chore bearable." She touches his arm and hopes the act proves more intimate than their audience realizes. "Thank you."

"Okay. Must run. Kiki's in the truck."

"Thanks, Nick. I'll walk you to reception."

Aiden returns a minute later.

They hold paper plates and gobble Nick's offerings. "And Velvet?" Aiden mumbles with a full mouth.

"Opportunity, too. She arrived in the lounge with a dessert as Earlene returned to her unit. Time to do the deed, go home, and change. If one of the three women killed Deena, the forensics team should find bloody clothes someplace."

"You're right. They'll comb the building, inside and out."

"Deena took advantage of Velvet's history of mental illness and showed no compassion. I gather Mary Jo and Velvet are friends."

"Perhaps. Not sure." He inhales his food, as if he hasn't eaten in a week.

"Here. Eat a cookie. You're starving." She passes him the plastic bag. "Tess sustained her upset and tearful response but added anger as well. Before the game, she ran around the building and banged for entry on Deena's main door. She claims no one answered, and she met the other two when she returned via the lounge. I'm uncertain, Aiden. How does Tess make her money? She poor mouths, but doesn't work and has income, although not from book sales." Stella reaches for a sweet. "Possibility someone else killed Deena?"

"Are you suggesting three women sat in their respective units while a murder took place, and no one heard a sound or was aware an altercation happened?"

"First off, Velvet and Tess' apartments share walls with Deena's, but Earlene's doesn't. Tess said the TV was blaring. Second, there's the possibility they listened but ignored the noise." She pauses and squints. "Conspiracy?"

Chapter 7

We are None the Wiser

"Hi, Earlene." Stella inhales a deep breath when they enter the spare office, now occupied by their first witness. The constable moves to the hall. Aiden takes a seat behind the desk and Stella chooses her usual spot near the corner. An empty tea mug and digestive biscuit wrapper sit discarded on the surface between them.

"What did you two do for the last hour or more? Go out for supper?" She's perched on the front edge of her chair and her eyes flash with anger and impatience. "You people shouldn't treat an upstanding member of the community in such a fashion." She clenches her fists while she talks. "I am of the mind to write to your superior, Detective North."

"My apologies, Ms. Marigold. With a murder on your property, you are a primary witness. As you realize, our investigation will be extensive. The department, and I, appreciate your patience and cooperation—but if you must submit a letter of complaint, I'll make sure Sergeant Moyer supplies you with contact information for my boss. You are not under arrest or suspicion as of today. We are merely collecting statements and relationship details. We also requested a list of items you reported the victim stole from you. Now, shall we begin?"

Earlene leans back. "The name of your superior won't be necessary. Let's go ahead. What more can I tell you? I poured my heart out once." She faces Stella. "You didn't take notes, I noticed."

Aiden ignores her remark and starts the recorder. "Describe your day before the discovery of Ms. Finch's body, and your subsequent discussions with Stella."

She launches into a repetition of her earlier remarks. She avoids direct accusations of Velvet or Tess, but her comments show both women possessed ample opportunity and obvious motive. Her criticisms of Deena are blunt, and she's convinced the woman was their thief. She describes entering Deena's apartment and the discovery of the body in minute detail.

"Thank you, Ms. Marigold. Before we end our interview—a few questions regarding your history with Ms. Finch and when you accepted her as a tenant."

"Earlene," Stella begins. "I understand you knew Deena before your rental agreement. You were friends." Statement, not question.

"Not even close," she spouts. "Richard and I never travelled in the same social circles. I was aware of her from the Groceteria. She lived in a hovel one street off Main."

Brigitte and Trixie called a similar structure home before they moved into Yellow House, Stella muses. Now Trixie has her own place, a renovated and stunning Craftsman bungalow, five kilometres from the park. "Did Deena contact you?"

"Yes. Borden Fisher, my contractor, gave her my number. She appeared fine, could afford the rent, and acted excited to move in. I showed her the back unit and the bedsitter. She chose the former. She played bridge—my strict criteria. I want tenants who are single women and play my game." She pauses. "Velvet stretches the benchmark." She glances at each of them. "She muddles through, and we need patience. I met Velvet after I posted a notice at the café. I liked her." She shrugs. "Felt sorry for her, I guess."

Aiden harnesses the interview after he peeks at his watch. "In your estimation, Deena stole from you and the others."

"I'm certain. Deena's behaviour was often outrageous. She was rude, selfish, and brassy."

"What do you mean?" Stella needs clarification.

"She put on false eyelashes before noon, used sunglasses in cloudy weather, and wore wigs that disguised her appearance. One day, she pulled into the parking lot in her dented Biscayne, and I didn't recognize her when she stepped out of the car."

"Any other information you believe might be beneficial, Ms. Marigold?"

"I attempted fairness with Deena despite her personality challenges. Although ten years younger than us, I wanted her to take part in our group. Somehow, I failed. I experienced second thoughts after she hit Velvet." She clenches her jaw. "The details should be in one of your reports. Velvet forgave her. Deena had signed a lease, and I felt forced to accept the circumstances. I suspected she had a shady past, too, but saw no proof."

Aiden gives Stella a quick nod. "Ms. Marigold, the constable outside the door will drive you home. After the interview is transcribed, you'll be called in for your signature. Ms. Finch's apartment is now sealed by the police. Neither you nor your tenants may enter until forensics, and I, release the scene. Understood?"

"But what do I do in case of an emergency?"

"I'm sorry. We re-tumbled the locks. If you smell smoke or suspect a break-in, call the station. For two or three days, you will have no access."

"Fine, although your investigative techniques are intrusive, Detective."

****

"Intrusive, indeed," Stella says as they walk along the fluorescent-lit corridor toward the conference room. "What's this about physical violence?"

"Moyer detailed the calls and will make a report."

Velvet Carmichael sits with her back to the hallway window. An officer stands inside the door, hands clasped in front of her. Velvet appears to be chewing something. From her current angle, Stella observes periodic tugs, and the impression given suggests her hair is in her mouth.

"What is she eating?" Aiden's tone carries a layer of disgust. The packet of biscuits remains on the table untouched.

"Not sure from here. She holds a wad of her hair most of the time. The behaviour keeps her grounded, or focused, I guess."

"No matter. She's made more headway with her treatment than Rosemary. I expect she takes her medications for a start," he mutters. "Let's go." He opens the door, and they make their way around the conference table.

"Ms. Carmichael. Thank you for your patience."

Velvet drops the strand of hair and meets his eyes—without challenge or nervousness. "No problem, Detective North. I'm happy we've met before, though. Strangers cause me discomfort."

"Good. Good. We wouldn't want you to feel uncomfortable. You understand you aren't under arrest. Your formal statement and additional background information are needed for the investigation. Are you at ease with the recorder?"

"Sure." She leans forward, places her elbows on the table, and addresses

Stella first. "I should tell him what I told you earlier, right?"

"Correct, Velvet."

"Over the next fifteen minutes, the retired librarian repeats her story of her preparations for the Monday afternoon bridge game. She emphasizes she heard Earlene's door click closed when she entered the lounge." With the formality of the statement out of the way, Velvet adds, "I suspected Deena of criminal behaviour. She never discussed her past, and once she moved into the G-plex, she rarely left."

"She worked at the grocery store, Velvet. Deena wasn't afraid of the public."

"Except she avoided people. After her injury and move into our place, she crawled into a shell."

"Describe your interactions with Deena." His voice softens. "We understand she focused her impatience and unkindness on you. And then there was the issue where she slapped you."

Stella's breath catches in her throat.

Velvet sits straighter in her chair. "Make no mistake, Detective. My mental health history isn't a problem when I interact with friends and neighbours. Deena often suggested I'm insecure and unworthy, but I've grown past the stage where the opinions of others bother me. She slapped me because I wouldn't respond to her when she poked fun at me."

"You refused to lay charges."

"No reason to jeopardize my living circumstances. Earlene had no intention of renewing Deena's lease. I was certain." She leans forward. "Listen. I follow instructions, take my medications although I'm stable, and obtained my education despite the fact no one thought I could manage. I determined my limits and chose library work instead of the classroom. Detective, I grabbed a chance at life. I refuse to allow the undermining of my security by anyone like Deena Finch. I learned, over the years, to suffer the existence of those who cannot understand." She takes a deep breath and relaxes.

"Was Deena inappropriate in her attitude or behaviour with the others?" Stella expects their current interviewee to be more aware than her two neighbours.

"She didn't act hateful with Earlene in the obvious sense. She voiced apartment issue complaints and often reminded Earlene how people considered her husband's death suspicious. The man died of a heart attack, and she fell apart for a time. End of story. As for Tess, Deena picked at the poor woman because of her lack of a career as a successful author. She was merciless. If Tess put her work out into the public eye and let the world read the two books she's written, she'd land a publisher for her memoir. She claims she might upset her sister, but Connie, I bet, would be excited and supportive." She pauses. "With Deena no longer around to harangue her, she should spread her wings now."

"Did either Earlene or Tess play a role in Deena's death?"

Velvet nibbles on her lower lip, displaying a habit of self-consumption regardless of her claim that she's risen above personal loathing.

"I heard Earlene's door click closed. Tess came from Deena's main entry at the back of the building. What is the term you law enforcement folks use? Opportunity? I can't say, but I can tell you I'm not afraid."

"Good, Ms. Carmichael. The constable will drive you home. We appreciate your cooperation." Aiden rises and opens the conference room door.

"One more to go, Aiden. Velvet doesn't possess the fortitude necessary to beat her neighbour with an iron—not on her best day."

"Agreed. She has handled her condition well over the years. I wonder who convinced her to take her pills even if she felt better? If only the doctors could reason with Rosie and gain the same result."

They leave the conference room and cross the hall to the interview office, where Tess has been jotting in a lined notebook. Before they enter, Stella touches Aiden's sleeve. "I read an article years ago where someone compared mental illness and diabetes. Conditions without cures. You improve when you take the pills or the insulin, but if you stop, symptoms return. No cure— management. Velvet has accepted and managed."

****

Tess faces the entry, scratching notes. She lifts her face toward them. "I'm documenting my day in my journal. I hope you don't mind."

A quiet click signals the exit of the constable.

"Fodder for another book?"

The author with untapped aspirations titters at Stella. "Perhaps memoir number two. Who knows?"

"Ms. Boone, we are here to obtain a formal statement from you. You aren't under arrest, and we appreciate your patience after a long and difficult day."

Aiden repeats his mantra and switches on the tape recorder.

For the next twenty minutes, Tess describes the hours before their bridge game and her behaviour after the discovery of the missing picture of herself and Connie. "I don't mind saying I'm glad she's dead. The world lost a hateful woman who occupied too much space. She sucked the oxygen out of every room she entered."

No need to hold back, Stella ruminates.

"Although the wrong remark to make in front of people charged with the investigation of her murder, I can assure you of my lack of involvement in the crime. I voice my thoughts without fear of reprisal." Her manner, as she looks at Aiden, is direct. "At least I assume."

"Tell us your story, Tess. You said you worked for a time, but not anymore. You emphasized you're frugal, and not yet retirement age." Stella lets her point idle in mid-air.

"I laboured as a basic administrative assistant for the province. An incident occurred." She studies her pen for a moment. "I prefer not to discuss what happened, but I received a settlement. With interest rates the way they are, I manage basic survival without further exposure to possible abuse in another job." Her lower lip quivers. "I hope you appreciate my circumstance. The horrible experience is unrelated to Deena. I signed a paper which said I'm not allowed to disclose details."

"Okay, Tess. We understand." Stella soldiers forward. "You and Connie use different last names. I assume one of you has been married?"

"Simple answer. Connie and I share a mother, not a father. Such blended families exist." Her voice adopts a defensive tone. "We are as much sisters as you and Trixie, Stella."

"Without question. How did you meet Earlene and rent a spot from her?"

"Another uncomplicated answer. I imagine you have met the realtor, Cavelle Painter?"

Both Aiden and Stella nod.

"She searched for a rental property for me. I could no longer afford the house I occupied in Port Ephron and Shale Harbour is closer to Connie. She sold the piece of land Earlene built the fourplex on and was aware of the small apartment. My choice has worked out well. I appreciate Earlene despite her rigidity."

"Please describe." Aiden, who has been scratching notes even though the recorder remains on, requests further clarification.

Tess expels a puff of air. "She reprimands me because I often leave my inside door unlocked. I admit I'm forgetful, and slightly hard of hearing, but I hoped we could become a big, happy family until Deena appeared in my apartment unannounced."

Stella sits straighter in her chair. "What happened? Did she walk in and want to borrow sugar or give you a message?"

"I wish. When I came out of the bathroom and found her at my table, with my journal open, I was startled and screamed. She pooh-poohed me, said she dropped in for a visit, and immediately left."

"Did you tell Earlene?" Stella can't conceal her shock.

"No, because Earlene yelled at me after a theft episode earlier in the week. Another time, I woke and saw Deena seated at my table, staring at me. Don't worry, I lock my doors now. That incident frightened me. And then she hit Velvet, so I was more than a little scared."

"Ms. Boone, did Ms. Finch enter the apartments of the other two women when they were at home?"

"Neither has reported as much, although Earlene insisted each other's spaces were out of bounds unless invited."

****

"Well. Any new impressions?"

"Their collective calmness surprises me, for a trio who lost their fourth in such a violent way. And way too messy for a hired killer."

"A less traumatic option might have been poison in the dessert." Aiden examines his notes.

"Are they in on the murder together?"

"You're the one who suggested conspiracy. She tormented each of them. We need more information about Deena Finch. I've asked Moyer to compile details of the call reports which took place from the fourplex—those related to theft accusations." He nods to himself. "Forensics' report will be ready, and we'll compare the three lists of stolen articles with what we may retrieve from the deceased's apartment. Shall we regroup here tomorrow?"

She grabs her coat off the back of her chair, her handbag from the floor, and stands. "Long day. When will you release the scene?"

"Not soon. We need an opportunity to go over the place together." He raises bleary eyes to meet hers. "You always see what others don't."

Once inside her Jeep, and after a short debate with her inner voice on how much she yearns for a snuggle with Nick, she circles the outskirts of town and drives past the G-plex. As she suspected, light floods out through the two skylights in the lounge. Since constables drove each woman home separately, she assumes they're now congregated with their tea. She imagines they threw together a late supper and are exchanging notes in the common area. Velvet's Death by Chocolate dessert is surely on the ad hoc menu.

There are other interviews they'll need to conduct as they continue familiarizing themselves with potential suspects. She wants conversations with Mary Jo, Cavelle, and the owner of the Groceteria, Patricia Brooks. A manor visit with Connie Gee holds promise, as well.

Her vehicle crunches the gravel of the parking lot at nine-fifteen—earlier than expected. She climbs the veranda stairs, weary but thankful for home. Met with the soft glow of the living room lamps, she sees his form behind the screen door, no doubt alerted to her presence by Kiki's squeals.

"Hi, darlin'. You're early. Interviews went well?"

She bends and pats Kiki, lifting the little dog into her arms before she leans into the chest of the man she loves. "I'm uncertain. I spent my day in conversations with potential murderers. We are none the wiser."

Once settled behind closed doors, she basically explains the scene and the women. He doesn't ask many questions. She tells him what she can, and he never betrays her or Aiden's trust. He serves tea—her favourite black currant—and they cuddle together on one of the sofas in front of the fire. Stella assesses the space with fresh eyes. Yes, she guesses a stranger might assume their furniture came from a jumble sale or a junk shop. No more judgments on the fortunes or choices of others. She sips in silence.

After a moment, she further describes the experience. "They didn't come across as women who are killers, either individually or as a group. They took the idea of statements at the detachment in stride." She touches his hand.

"Maybe they hired someone. Not the first time in Shale Harbour."

Whenever circumstances cause her mind to drift toward Paulina, tears force themselves into the corners of her eyes. "Nick, a hit man—or person— doesn't plan an assassination and hope the victim has an iron nearby." Sarcasm spills into her tone. "The crime scene illustrated intense hate, and the assailant employed the nearest tool. Earlene, Velvet, and Tess each despised

Deena, but with the passion displayed at this murder?" She shrugs and yawns. "This could be another misunderstanding, like when Owen Ellis-Thomas was killed. Stranger circumstances have happened."

"Did you enjoy your chicken?"

The tease in his voice is unmistakable, and she plays along. "*That* chicken was okay for an appetizer. Is there more?"

He stands and pulls her to her feet. "We can avail ourselves of more chicken, my love." He wraps an arm around her shoulder. "You come with me."

$$\text{\Large ⚜}$$

CHAPTER 8

Long Time Ago

Fondness isn't the right word, but Stella and Moyer enjoy a mutual respect developed over the last two years. They first met after she tried to access Lorraine Young's trailer. Later, he followed her instructions, albeit with hesitation, when she confronted Lorraine's killer at the bank. He answered her call the day she found Paulina's body. She trusts him and her instincts suggest he supports her work with the department.

When he lumbers into Aiden's office to report on the calls from the G-plex, she notices his form has widened and his breath comes in quick gasps. "Busy morning, Sergeant?" Her question gives him an opportunity to regain his composure.

"Lots goin' on, Stella. Mornin' again, Detective." He glances at the chair across from the desk.

"Sit, Moyer. You brought a report for us."

"Indeed, Sir." He remains on his feet. "I compiled records of the three calls from Earlene Marigold's fourplex. The first call happened on Thursday, January 14, and you both attended. The second occurred on Wednesday, February 3. I responded with a constable to assist, and I can tell you, those women talk at the same time. We muddled our report, for sure. The third event occurred Friday, February 19, and you came with me."

Aiden nods, and swivels toward Stella, seated on his left. "The February 19 issue followed Deena's assault of Velvet. She didn't press charges. As Velvet repeated in her interview with us, she refused to be bated by the now deceased, who hit her in frustration." He returns his attention to Moyer.

"I've attached a list of the items noted as taken during each call. Forensics checked them off." He leans over the desk. "The women were right." He places the lengthy record within Aiden's reach.

"Good work, Sergeant. I see Tess reported two autographed books stolen. One by Elsbeth Strauss, signed at the writers retreat. The other described as a book of short stories by Maeve Binchy. When she revealed the theft, she was upset because she previously sent the volume to Ireland for an autograph."

"Hard imagining someone as frugal as Tess paying the postage and waiting for a signature." Stella doesn't hide her surprise.

"Tess also lost a silver-framed picture and gold hoop earrings; plus, a red Bakelite bracelet she claims to be both collectible and valuable."

"Every piece found?"

Aiden nods. "Velvet's combs—two of them—along with a French ivory brush, a silk scarf, and serving spoon are noted. I gather from the information that Earlene suffered the fewest losses. She mentioned an unused pottery mixing bowl and a collapsible reading lamp. The most recent item—a Gucci handbag."

"Deena picked on Tess. Most of the taken pieces were hers," Stella observes.

"And Deena reported, when police arrived on the scene, items stolen from her, too, but never of sufficient value to include in a statement." He frowns at Moyer. "Do you agree with my description of her behaviour, Sergeant? You went over after each of the calls."

"Right." He pauses. "If I may, Sir?"

Aiden waves his hand. "Of course."

"When Ms. Finch assaulted Ms. Carmichael, we avoided a fuss." He stands straighter and fiddles with his tie. "I understand she didn't want to rock the boat and lay charges, but police can do the job. I know you want evidence and not speculation, but maybe Ms. Carmichael found she couldn't tolerate the woman. She got mad and walloped Ms. Finch with the victim's own iron."

"Velvet had opportunity." Stella rifles through the documents on Aiden's desk. "I see no claim she's been violent in the past, despite her mental status." She directs her next statement toward Moyer, although she hopes Aiden listens, too. "We can't assume, because someone has a psychological issue, they could slip into violence with or without provocation."

"Understood, Stella. I never considered her personal challenges, but expect she was angry because Deena slapped her." He clears his throat. "On the flip side, the crew never found any blood anywhere but in the Finch apartment."

"Good point," Aiden inserts. "Thanks for your work, Sergeant. Let's hope we can figure out how Deena Finch accessed the apartments. By the sounds of the reports, she entered units even when the residents were inside."

"Women need to feel safe in their own homes," Sergeant Moyer mutters as he makes his way out, closing the door behind him.

Stella glances toward the report. "This good news will please the three when the police return their property to them. Earlene didn't lose items of sentimental value because everything she owns is new, but both Tess and Velvet lost family pieces and personal treasures. A serious search of the apartment, after your crew finishes, is in order. Remember what happened at Paulina's house when we found her diary?"

"I suppose you'll engage Hester Painter's help." He chuckles. "Not sure I can endure the public humiliation when she reminds me how I can't carry out my duties without her. She said as much when she assisted during the Owen Ellis-Thomas case."

"Swallow your pride, because the three of us need a walk-through in Deena's apartment. Hester has a method to her searches. You might find her valuable on staff," she suggests. Her eyes dance.

"Fine, but let's work through our suspects, Deena Finch's history, and interview people in the community connected to them. We can maintain the site for a week or more if necessary. First off, how did our victim access the other apartments?"

Stella sucks air in through her nose. "She duplicated Earlene's master. She stole the key somehow—our one option. Bacon Hardware makes keys. They'll remember."

"If she travelled to Port Ephron, I'm aware of a half-dozen places."

"Aiden, a thirty-minute drive was out of the question. If she saw an opportunity, she grabbed the key, ran out, made a copy, and sped home before anyone noticed. Earlene hangs the master on a hook in her access hall. If Deena waited for a time Earlene left the building and didn't lock her lounge door, she could take advantage of a short-lived set of circumstances."

He squints as he thinks. "Okay, lunch on me, followed by a trip to Bacon Hardware. We can discuss inside and outside doors—pretend we're an old married couple if necessary."

Confused, because Athena Bacon knows her, she snags a loose strand of hair behind her ear and ignores the obvious. "I'll call Nick and tell him I won't be home until teatime."

****

After they choose their favourite table near the rear of Cocoa and Café, Tiffany serves their coffee. She squares her padded shoulders, and in her high octave voice, rattles off the lunch special. "Andrew has made salmon salad bunwiches with coleslaw. The buns are homemade, too. For dessert, we have sticky toffee pudding." She bends nearer and winks. "It makes its own sauce in the oven."

Aiden nods his enthusiasm and, after a quick glance at Stella, replies, "Specials for both, Tiffany."

"I need another one of the café's desserts," she mumbles, with an element of self-loathing driven by her lack of discipline.

"You could always eat whatever you wanted, even when we were kids. You never change."

She appreciates the compliment and decides against further public and personal deprecation. Age has crept into her life unnoticed until now. Her body is changing. More exercise, she commits in silence. The answer is walking, and Kiki will appreciate her efforts.

"Each resident can lock both their front and lounge accesses. Even though they remain inside the building when in their common room, they should still secure their units."

"I understood from Earlene, and the others, too, that they imagined the idea of one big happy family. She designed the communal area for the enjoyment of each of them. They access the building's deck via the lounge." She stares at the wall behind Aiden and imagines such a lifestyle. "Earlene spoke as if she wanted them to play bridge, watch movies, and entertain in the common area. She never thought a tenant would use the room as a convenient way into a space other than their own. They found out our victim wasn't the ideal person to share their living accommodations."

"A robbery gone wrong. Another option. There's been no report, so far, of her purse or money missing, though. If the person who tried to rob her thought she was at her bridge game, then they would have been surprised to find her in the apartment." Aiden's grunt reverberates across the bistro and Tiffany, at the register, shifts her attention in their direction. "What a mess."

The saloon doors whoosh when Tiffany trots into the kitchen. "I'll be interested in hearing if Deena copied Earlene's master at the hardware store.

We'll never know exactly when she absconded with it, but she did."

"Or she rifled through Earlene's unit and discovered a duplicate. Here comes lunch, Aiden adds."

"Earlene never mentioned another key. Thanks. Looks scrumptious."

"I'll serve the pudding later. Refills?"

Brass bells over the front door tinkle as more customers arrive.

"When you find a minute, more coffee will be great." Stella knows the little café becomes busy as the clock nears one.

As expected, the toffee cake and sauce combo momentarily made life worth living. By the time Aiden paid the bill and they started their trek along Main toward Bacon Hardware, around the corner and next door to the Shale Harbour Savings and Loan, she regretted her dessert decision. She must make more effort. Nick could tire of a frumpy old lady.

More bells tinkle when they cross the scared wooden threshold into the antiquated business. Stuck in the 1940s, Bacon Hardware stands stuffed to capacity with stock ranging from small appliances to locks and pipes. Cluttered aisles run between shelves which stand seven feet high. Stella can't remember the last time she entered the premises. Hardware has become Nick's forté, and she's happy to leave such purchases in his capable hands. She tiptoes over hideous orange cracked asphalt tile floors, convinced they must be original, toward the counter near the rear. The checkout in the front sits empty.

"On my way," sings a voice from the back. Athena Bacon dashes forward. She stops and adjusts the cardboard display of furnace filters. "Now, what might I do for you two?"

"I'm Detective North from the RCMP and," he indicates Stella with his thumb, "my colleague Stella Kirk."

"Yes, yes. I recognize you, Stella. Your young man does most of the hardware shopping, doesn't he?"

"Correct, Athena." She ignores both the expression on Athena's face and the word "young" as she turns toward Aiden, thankful he didn't try to pass them off as a couple. "Please meet Athena Bacon, Detective. Ollie around today?"

"I can fetch him if necessary. Police. My goodness." She brushes stray hair off her plump cheek. Her mane flies in several directions—the obvious subject of high amounts of static.

"We want to discuss key cutting, Mrs. Bacon."

"Oh." The muscles in her face sag. "Talk to me. I don't let Ollie cut keys. He never gets them right and we lose money." She leans forward. "You can ask me whatever you wish up at the front. I try to stay close to the cash."

They follow her past more cluttered displays. Stella wonders if the fire marshal has inspected the business in recent memory.

"Athena, did you ever make a duplicate key for Deena Finch? She lived at the fourplex Earlene Marigold owns."

"My dear. The dead woman. The story was on the news. Did one of the other three kill her? People in town would disagree. They think she was a spy."

"We are investigating, Mrs. Bacon. Please answer Stella's question."

She squares her shoulders. "Roughly a year ago, as I recall, I made a key for the lady who died."

"How can you be sure, Athena?"

The proprietress huffs her annoyance. "First off, I am a fabulous witness because I never forget a face. I remember people's purchases as well." She furrows her brows. "One of us needs a functioning memory. In the second place, Deena Finch wanted a duplicate key, but refused to remove a long pink ribbon. I told her the task would be much easier if we untied the ribbon and reattached it later. She declined and stated if I knew my job, I could make a copy, regardless. I don't mind telling you, her rudeness put me off."

"You successfully created a copy?"

"No repeat visit, Detective. If their key doesn't work, customers readily return and express their annoyance. Believe me, there were times we dealt with recalls over bad keys every day." She focuses on a hangnail. "At least I solved one problem."

"Thank you, Athena. You've been a big help." As they shuffle their way through the abundance of stock, she yells out, "Don't open the boxes, Ollie! Put them on the shelf and leave the rest for me."

Aiden and Stella make eye contact but stay silent until they reach the street. The sounds of the entrance bells fade when they walk away. "Someone else who makes a living with a spouse who requires constant supervision." Aiden slams his hands in his coat pockets. "I sure appreciate her struggles."

She avoids discussing Rosemary for now. "At least we know Deena duplicated Earlene's master, although the forensics team never found a key suspected to fit the bill."

"Correct. They accounted for each one in the apartment."

"Another reason for a search of the place ourselves." She shrugs. "The mysterious intruder, if there was one, might have taken the key."

****

Nick has supper preparations well in hand by the time she arrives home for tea. They expect Duke and Cloris. Cloris called earlier and said she wanted a discussion, as she phrased the issue, "focused on options and unforeseen circumstances" regarding her work for the Norths. Stella suspects she talked with Mary Jo and Toni, who would be less than enthusiastic to hear Cloris is taking on another job over the summer. She invited Cloris and Duke to supper tonight, in the hopes a more informal visit helps ease any tension. They are still in the middle of March. If she needs a new hire, she can put the word out. No harm done, if Cloris changes her mind, and the idea might be for the best.

The house smells of basil, garlic, and warm bread. Her love has spaghetti sauce bubbling while an Italian hearth loaf, fresh out of the oven, cools on a rack nearby. "Hi," she chuckles. "The cook works hard and the dog snoozes." Kiki snuggles in her warm bed, opening one eye in a sleepy greeting.

He turns from the stove, a mixture of surprise and affection in his eyes. "Hi. Glad you're home. Time for tea before I make the salad. Long day?" He plugs in the kettle while she approaches the warm bread. "Don't touch. I experimented with a new recipe so will cut the loaf in half to inspect before I serve company. You can try an end piece, then."

Admonished, she collapses on a chair at the kitchen table. "Yes. In answer to your question, long but successful. We've identified Deena as the G-plex thief. We visited with Athena Bacon, who said Deena Finch asked her to duplicate a key on a pink ribbon. She remembered because Deena refused to untie the ribbon first. I imagine Deena didn't want to risk any telltale sign of tampering. Forensics found the items the other three reported stolen, along with pieces not missed by them—I guess our victim pilfered from others, too."

Nick pours their tea, places the pot and two mugs on the table, and folds into the chair beside her. "Who do you think killed Deena Finch? I mean, I've never met Velvet or Earlene, but could one of them be a killer?" His eyes widen.

"No idea. Until we recover more background information, Deena appears to have dropped out of nowhere. She worked at the Groceteria for a few years.

Aiden and I will interview her boss. I'll talk with Mary Jo and Cavelle, before I visit Connie Gee at the manor. You and Kiki can come with me and spend time with Dad."

His eyes reflect a deep sadness.

Visits with Norbert Kirk are more difficult these days. He may know one of them occasionally, but the chances remain slim. Nick never loses hope.

The Caesar salad chills in the fridge. Duke and Cloris arrive with chatter of what Stella suspects might be the tail-end of an argument. The minute she opens the door, they quiet. Although she senses tension, Stella carries on, offers and delivers their drinks, and settles them both on a sofa near the fire. "We'll serve supper in the kitchen tonight." She shrugs. "We consider you two family. The oven's been on, and the room is cozy." She assesses their expressions and shouts, "How long, Nick?"

"Five minutes."

"Okay," she addresses her guests. "Cloris, you said you wanted a conversation. A concern?" She sips her wine.

"After a chat with the girls, they insist I must be available at a moment's notice. I'm worried I might disappoint you." She runs her hand along her black slacks. Kiki sheds in the spring, a condition not appreciated by Cloris. She frowns at Duke, who clutches the dog in his arms, and scowls.

"I worked with Aiden most of the day." Stella apologizes. "Nick cooked supper. No time for a vacuum. I can find my lint roller," she mutters, as an addendum to her apology.

"Never mind," Cloris harrumphs. "I wish I'd worn lighter coloured clothes."

Stella blinks. "If you want to work here during the summer, Cloris, tolerating Kiki is part of the deal." *The best idea may well be to hire one more staff person to balance Eve's duties.* "And if your worry involves responsibilities to the North family, we haven't locked in our plans."

Cloris swallows a significant measure of her wine before she leans back into the leather of the sofa and closes her eyes. "You're right, Stella. I think we made our arrangement in haste. I brought my cheque book and want to pay you for my seasonal lot. No need to wait until May. I'll clear my bill with you now."

As they move into the kitchen, Stella experiences a relief she didn't expect. Better to hire someone new. Eve will help whenever necessary. Her offer letter suggests as much. Once they settle this case, she'll focus on staffing for the upcoming season.

Dinner, as usual, proves scrumptious. As a surprise, tucked away in the pantry beyond her prying eyes, Nick has concocted lemon tarts. He serves with a flourish before the discussion turns toward the most recent murder.

"What do you mean—lots of rumours circulating around town, Duke? I have no idea." She avoids any mention of Athena's remarks.

"You're too focused on the truth, or at least your search for the truth. Folks are sayin' Deena Finch was a spy, a secret agent. They say a hit man, or a lover, killed her. No chance of bein' bored in Shale Harbour." He chuckles. "There's even talk in Port Ephron. Not a soul suggests Tess, Earlene, or Velvet were involved, either alone or together."

"I can't comment—active investigation. We communicate with many people."

"You can interview me. I dated Deena and Tess—at different times, mind you, and not for long, but I know stuff."

"Must you go on, John? I find this conversation distasteful."

Stella grinds her teeth. "A good idea that you've decided against a job here in the house, Cloris. Much of the talk at our table centres around murder—at least lately." She glances at both Nick and Duke. "Tell me what stuff, Duke." She holds the last bite of tart in her mouth long enough to experience the sweetness of the pastry paired with the tangy smooth texture of the lemon, speculating that perhaps Deena needed baking lessons from Nick where lemon desserts are involved. She patiently waits for Duke's answer and reminds herself a walk will be necessary.

"Now don't misunderstand, Stella. I dated Deena twice. She refused to exchange personal stories and her attitude put me off. We ate in the back dining room at the hotel once, and another time we drank coffee at the beach. When someone said they thought she was a spy, I wasn't surprised." He snuggles the dog. "Kiki wasn't fond of her, either. You're an excellent judge of character, right, little one?"

"Will you speak to Aiden if he wants to hear about your experiences?"

Duke squares his shoulders. "By all means. Happy to assist law enforcement."

"And Tess?" Stella can't wait for his assessment of the aspiring author.

Cloris stares at the wall.

"Tess is a good person. She's into books and we related, but she was skittish, like I frightened her. I came out and asked if she'd ever had a boyfriend before and she told me our date was over and I should go home." He surveys his audience. "Sad. She lived in a rental house in Port Ephron back then." He pats Cloris on her hand. "A long time ago, my dear. Long time ago."

Kiki's appraisal of Cloris appears not to have influenced Duke's decision when Cloris entered the picture, Stella observes.

CHAPTER 9

Vagueness is Best

Toni Carr, one of Rosemary North's sisters, bustles through the living room of her Port Ephron bungalow with a tray of mugs, cream, sugar, and spoons. "Sit, Stella. I'll be back in a jiff with the coffeepot." She squints at her sibling. "Do you want me to stay? I don't play bridge, but I've met Velvet."

Mary Jo Frost flops into a recliner. "The one piece of furniture Toni allowed inside her house when I moved here with her to care for Rosemary." She pats the arm. "I stored my stuff, but I have an idea."

"You and your ideas, Mary Jo. Stella's come to discuss a murder, right Stella?"

She nods. "You're welcome to sit with us, Toni."

"Thank you." Her perm vibrates as she trots into the kitchen. "I'll grab the pot first," she replies over her shoulder.

"Toni won't want to hear what I say, Stella," Mary Jo whispers, "but I couldn't stand Deena Finch. I waited for her to make an appointment or be sick so I could play bridge with the other three, but never fail—each time they asked, I spared for one of them. Deena never left the complex."

"Here comes Toni," Stella unnecessarily contributes when Toni bustles around the corner. After the confusion of passing cups and adding embellishments, she begins. "Aiden avoided our interview today for obvious reasons."

"Not the first time he's seen fit to separate himself from family," Toni huffs.

"Let me ask you for your impressions of the four women at the G-plex, Mary Jo." She ignores the slur and turns back to Toni. "Good coffee. Your observations of Velvet will be welcome as well."

She nods. "Talk with Mary Jo first. I'll listen." She wiggles her rump further into her chair and holds her mug with both hands.

"Okay. Describe Deena, Earlene, Tess, and Velvet."

"Lots of tellin', Stella." She closes her eyes and sips her brew. "Let's start with my firm belief no one in Earlene's complex killed Deena Finch, although I expect each experienced the urge at one point or another. How did she die?"

Stella chews her lip. "I can't share those details, Mary Jo. You seem confident none of your bridge buddies are the culprit."

"The gals are the salt of the earth." She sips before launching into her spiel. "Earlene, for example. Her poor husband died in her arms." She pauses for a moment and checks on her sister.

Toni still pines for her spouse, dead for many years. She waves Mary Jo to continue.

"Earlene has suffered. She created her community family inside the G-plex. I think she's spunky. Her big mistake was approving Deena's lease. Have you turned up any of her history? Background? Relatives?"

"Not much yet." Vagueness is best for now.

"I suspect she had kids, but I saw no visitors."

"What makes you believe she was a mother?"

"Deena reacted badly one day when I made a stupid remark about raising children. She told me I had no right to pass judgment when I never birthed a child." Mary Jo glances at Toni. "I guess she had a point, but she flew off the handle for sure."

"I'll ask Aiden to double-check."

Mary Jo warms up to her audience. "Not researching Deena's background was Earlene's error. Then there's Tess. Such a sweet woman. Yearns," she bends at the waist, which emphasizes her point, "and I mean yearns, to become a famous writer. She's published two books on her own and they're not half bad. Velvet told me Tess is toying with the idea of a joint memoir with Connie." She leans back. "Good on her."

"And her career history? I gather she hasn't worked for a long time."

Mary Jo grimaces before she replies. "I think a terrible experience occurred at work. She gained money out of the deal but continues to suffer the scars. I never ask. Unlike you." She points an arthritic index finger in Stella's general direction. "I wait for people. I don't pry."

"The hazard of a consultation contract with your brother-in-law," she acknowledges, "although often I make statements and avoid direct questions while I try to find the truth."

A softness breaks through Mary Jo's stern countenance. "Understood. I harbour a weak spot for Velvet. Met her when she was in hospital at the same time as Rosemary. She's fascinating, Stella. She has a similar mental health profile and history as our sister, but she took charge and wrestled her demons. Rosemary never did. Although she can act like a normal person on occasion, she's never really made progress." Mary Jo stares out the picture window at the brown lawn. "Toni and I often wonder if we coddled Rosemary too much." She straightens in her chair. "Right, Toni?"

"Aiden coddled her, for sure, and hasn't been much help lately. We've tried strict rules, but no luck." Her eyes puddle. "I don't think she'll ever be better now."

Stella watches the interaction between the two women—broken hearts exposed when they discuss their sister's continual mental health challenges. "Has Cloris told you we decided against her employment in my registration office?"

Toni jumps and pours more coffee. "She called. We were glad, weren't we, Mary Jo?"

"Thanks, Stella," Mary Jo nods to her sister as she addresses their guest. "We appreciate you need staff, but neither of us could imagine Cloris' days if Aiden and Rosemary vacationed in their trailer and Cloris worked in your reception. At least, now, if Rosemary torments Cloris, her unacceptable behaviour won't be on your time."

"You think she'll be home soon?"

Mary Jo's eyes roll toward the ceiling. "I honestly hope not, Stella," she whispers.

After refreshing the coffee carafe from the kitchen, Toni adds, "Once you people solve this current case, the hospital plans to process her discharge. The doctors don't want her back with Aiden until he commits his ongoing support."

"Good idea." Stella believes that while Aiden continues to work, Rosemary's health management will be his biggest challenge. "Now, before I go, Toni, you've met Velvet. Can you give me your impressions?"

She pats her perm before she begins. "Mind you, a visitor never sees a patient at their best when they're institutionalized. Have you seen Velvet chew her hair? Gross habit, but Mary Jo says ignore her." She pauses and frowns at her sister. "I saw no evidence of violence in Velvet. I admire both how she rose above her diagnosis and her determination to lead a normal life. She practised as a librarian. Did she tell you? Librarians need a university degree. She's a smart cookie."

"Not capable of murder?"

Toni's soft chuckle bounces around her living room. "Not a chance. Mary Jo will argue with me, but I suspect Velvet has a big crush on her."

"For heaven's sake," Mary Jo blusters. "Let's change the subject. Did I tell you I sold my duplex? Toni and I are reasonably contented here, but I'm considering asking Earlene if she'll rent Deena's unit to me. I should negotiate a good lease if you consider the place was a murder scene." Her large bosom bounces as she laughs.

****

"Right on time. I see you brought your lunch." Cavelle Painter eyes Stella's brown bag while she remains behind the reception desk in the front room of Grey Cottage Realty. They decided on a meeting at the office because the owner, Farley Tompkins, travelled to Halifax for the day. Cavelle is stuck. Although more Trixie's friend, they became closer after Lucy Painter, Cavelle's sister-in-law, was killed in November 1980.

Stella has also rekindled her long-ago friendship with Cavelle's younger sister, Hester. Murder investigations have become a sideline occupation since returning to live in Shale Harbour, and Hester has a special mind—naïve, blunt, knowledgeable in specific areas, disinterested in others. She does not suffer fools, says what she thinks, and often hides from the public, thanks to her mother and the elder sibling, Opal, who sheltered her for most of her formative years. Circumstances have changed. Hester now accepts social interactions under limited conditions.

Stella glances out the window. "I hope clients don't arrive while we talk."

The realtor turns her heavy gold-linked watch around on her wrist and checks the time. "Nobody's scheduled before one-thirty. Let me grab my salad." She dashes toward the rear of the building—the kitchen in the cottage. "You said you want to discuss Earlene Marigold, right?" She returns to her desk. "I put the kettle on for tea. Shouldn't be a sec."

Stella unwraps her egg sandwich, carrot sticks, and chocolate chip cookies. She nods to Cavelle while she once again admonishes her choices, re-wraps the cookies, and replaces them in the paper bag which held her lunch. "Tea sounds wonderful, and yes, I want to discuss Earlene."

Cavelle pours a small measure of vinaigrette dressing over her salad and tosses the greens. "You understand I might run into confidentiality issues, Stella. This visit is informal and not an official police interview, right?"

"No real estate questions. The sale of her house, purchase of the property nearer town, and the construction are not relevant at this point. I don't think you need to worry. I want your considered opinion of the circumstances which surrounded the death of her husband, and what you might know regarding her interactions with Deena Finch."

"A few years ago, before Opal went to jail," she removes her attention from her salad and lifts her brows, "she and Earlene spent time together in the research of herbal remedies."

"Did Hester take part?"

"You could ask her, but I don't think she did. We were in the middle of one of Hester's withdrawn periods. I realize, now, she figured out Opal killed our parents, but Jacob and I attributed her behaviour to one of her phases—of which she's experienced many over the years." She stops, her fork in mid-air. "If we had been more alert regarding Hester, Lucy would still be alive." She digs into her salad. "No tears. Can't smudge my face."

"I heard rumours Earlene killed Richard Marigold."

"Lots of chatter. My goodness, people spoke as if she was guilty, but the police found no proof. Richard Marigold died two years ago. You might have uncovered the truth if you had been given the opportunity."

"The final report said an undiagnosed heart condition—fact, not rumour."

"Some might think his death was a suicide." Salad crunches. She doesn't make eye contact.

"Earlene told me he was behind the garage but appeared on the back step and passed away in her arms. Perhaps he wanted to kill himself but changed his mind and struggled to find her—or she poisoned him—and he dragged his way to the house before he collapsed for good."

Cavelle lifts her eyes away from her lunch. "I don't think poor Earlene killed Richard or Deena if you are in search of my opinion. How did Deena die?" Speculation related to Richard Marigold's death ends.

"Not at liberty to say, Cavelle, but not poison."

"Earlene didn't like Deena, but nobody did. I agree with the word on the street. Someone outside the fourplex murdered the woman. Now, are you interested in the Painter family's big news?"

Disappointed that Cavelle can't offer any added insight into one of her prime suspects, Stella refocuses her attention. "Sure."

"Hester has a boyfriend."

"You're joking, right?"

"No. My younger, and often weird, sister is dating someone. Please. I should be as lucky." She pushes her half-eaten plate of salad across the desk.

"Who?"

"His name is Angus Raspberry. He owns a farm around the shore from us. I guess you could walk to his place on the rocks, but the beach is dangerous at high tide. A person could become stranded under the cliffs and not be able to reach higher ground." She shrugs. "The drive takes ten minutes once you cross the isthmus."

"How did she meet him? I must admit, I find Hester and intimacy unimaginable."

"Jelly—she met him because he buys jelly. Hester asked him why he never bought her raspberry jelly. He told her his name. He said having the surname of Raspberry means he stays away from the fruit. Her reply was the best part of the story. She suggested if we adopted his philosophy, we wouldn't paint our house." She guffaws, a behaviour rare in the more dignified Cavelle. "His personality and quirks mirror hers in many ways, Stella. He lives alone since his parents died. Grows potatoes and doesn't mix much."

"Why don't I know him?"

"The family moved here from Ontario when Angus was twelve. He's six or seven years younger than Hester. We never attended school with him."

"Hester and a younger man," Stella muses aloud.

"Listen, my dear. When I mentioned their respective ages, she pointed out her friends Stella and Nick as her example. Besides, I'm not convinced intimacy plays a role. He comes over for meals. They sit in the living room and review potato varieties and crop rotation. He loves the dog and has offered to babysit, but with Jewel and Ken next door, a babysitter for Angel is never an issue."

Stella packs away the remains of her lunch. Her final stop is Harbour

Manor and a visit with Connie Gee, Tess Boone's sister. "I hope she can make room in her love life for Aiden and me. I need her help to search the crime scene before we release the apartment."

Cavelle stands. "She'll be thrilled. She wondered, last night at supper, why you hadn't requested her expertise. You know my sister."

****

Nick climbs out of the farm truck with Kiki cuddled under one arm. He's dressed her in a green turtleneck for St. Patrick's Day. The fur around her face forms a sunflower spray. Visits with her father are difficult and present increasing challenges. She expects he won't recognize them. Nick's patience provides evidence of his kindness and buffers her grief.

Harbour Manor sits near the edge of Shale Harbour. The organization runs well now, after Stella uncovered a scam which involved the unlawful burial and collection of pensions by Maura Martin, the former nurse supervisor and her husband, Hector Greene. She nods toward Nick. The case proved gruelling and spawned thoughts of their age and who might be their advocates in later years. Trixie emphasized there was no murder. Stella would argue.

"Hi. I called and said we were on our way. Olive Urback is the supervisor today. She's a gracious lady." Nick greets her with his update.

"Yes, and a big help with the boarding home investigations."

"I understand you aren't too enthusiastic, but let's check on Norbert together, okay?" He wraps the arm not clutching Kiki around her shoulder.

She waves at Olive, as they trek past reception and along the fluorescent-lit hallway toward her father's room. A knock on the door proved unnecessary because he swivelled his chair to face the entry as they approached.

"Well, hi, Kiki." He reaches out gnarled and veined hands.

"Here you go, Norbert." Nick places Kiki on his lap. "How are you today?"

His focus never leaves the dog. "And what are you doin' with two strangers, little one? Where's Duke? Shouldn't you be with Duke?"

His memory issues never cease to baffle her.

"Stella and I came for a visit. You remember me. I run the park."

Norbert believes Nick operates Shale Cliffs RV Park, and is married to Stella, whom he no longer remembers as his child. Until a few weeks ago, he recognized Trixie as his daughter, Brigitte as his granddaughter, and Mia as his great-granddaughter. Those connections, if Trixie is correct, are fast on the wane. "Yeah, Norbert, we're Nick and Stella Cochran. We run your business." Her lack of enthusiasm echoes in her voice.

He cuddles Kiki. "No. I don't know them, Kiki." He glances away from the dog. "My memory's muddled. I can't remember who folks are. Are you gonna sit a spell?"

"I'd love to, Norbert. Stella needs a visit with Connie."

"Who? Never mind."

Stella turns toward the hall and overhears Norbert remark to Nick as she leaves. "She's long in the tooth for a guy as young as you. What were ya thinkin'?"

Tears spring into her eyes, and she swipes them with the back of her hand. Losing her father while he's still alive remains her most painful life experience. In his demented fog, he recognizes the age gap between her and Nick, increasing her burden of loss for some untapped reason.

Olive leans across the reception desk.

"Lots of changes, Olive. The whole place hums with you at the controls. Looking forward to my visit with Connie."

The nurse supervisor nods her appreciation for the compliment, and whispers, "You may find Connie has deteriorated in the last couple of months, Stella."

"I need ten minutes with her, no more. What's happened?"

"Connie's in bed. The muscles in her back won't support her anymore. We strap her in her wheelchair for meals, but she's much more comfortable lying down. She sleeps most of the time, now, although her friends—Addie, Eula, Miriam, Dewey, and most importantly, Jasper—keep her company."

"Understood, Olive. Thanks. And how are you managing with your husband here?"

She reaches out and touches Stella's hand, which rests on the desk. "Our best decision. He loves Harbour Manor and I'm happy he's safe." She pats. "You're a hero around here. I bet you don't realize how you helped."

Stella blushes despite herself. "I appreciated your support. We did all we could under the circumstances. Okay. Off for a quick visit with Connie."

"Nasty business over at the G-plex, but Stella," Olive whispers, "no way Tess Boone killed anyone."

Connie lies stretched on her back in a hospital bed, her torso elevated, hands by her sides, and eyes closed. Stella taps on the door frame once she peeks in through the partially opened entry.

"I'm awake. Who's here?"

"It's me. Stella."

"Oh, hi. Olive told me Nick called and said you were on your way, and you wanted a word." She focuses on the end of her bed. "Will you come and sit at the foot? I can't turn my head anymore without help."

After Stella scuttles across the room and around Connie's wheelchair, fitted with a plethora of belts and harnesses, she perches where asked. "Better?"

"Yes. Thank you." She pauses, swallowing with effort.

Watching her struggle, Stella's compelled to ask, "What can I do?"

The clock on the wall clicks the seconds before Connie answers. "I focus to avoid drowning in spit. One of my many challenges."

"Let me know if you want me to help, okay? I'm here to discuss the murder at the fourplex where your sister lives." Stella pushes forward with their interview. Connie will stop her if necessary.

Another pause while eyes flash their interest. She doesn't waste breath if not necessary.

"Has Tess ever mentioned Deena Finch? Do you have any idea what she thought of her neighbour?"

"The woman frightened Tess." Pause.

"Tess told us Deena entered her apartment, uninvited, on two occasions."

"There were more. Earlene wasn't aware of every incident." Pause. Gulp. "Tess didn't want to rock the boat."

"Why?"

Patience while Connie exerts her energy to wrap her tongue around words yet to be said.

"Are you alright, Connie?"

Her response is a muffled gurgle.

"Shall I call someone?"

"No. Okay now. Tess needs a place. Spit."

Drool runs along Connie's chin. Stella jumps and dabs at the fluid with a tissue. The corners of Connie's lips lift. "Thanks. When I talk, I dribble."

"Tess hasn't worked in a long time. She watches her pennies."

"Raped at work."

"She never told us, Connie." Stella conceals her shock. "Tess said an incident occurred, and she received a settlement. If she's careful with her money, she can survive."

"True, but she never recovered in her head. Spit."

After leaping into service once more, Stella remains on her feet. "I'll go now, Connie."

"Okay. I hope Tess starts our book soon. I don't have much time."

"She will. Here comes Jasper." Tall, with white hair scattered in every direction, Jasper Nunn marches into the room, straight for Connie.

"Howdy, Stella." He turns his back and focuses on the bed. "And how is the most beautiful lady at Harbour Manor? Give us a hug."

As Stella leaves, she watches Jasper slide one arm behind Connie and pull the woman to his chest. He whispers in her ear, but she can't hear his words.

CHAPTER 10

On My Guard

Due to arrive at the RCMP detachment for lunch in Aiden's office, Stella sits at her desk balancing her business books, and startles when her phone rings. "Shale Cliffs RV Park. Stella speaking."

"Hi, Stella. How are you?"

Stella's heart sinks when she recognizes the voice. "I'm good, Eve." Will Eve say she won't resume her job this summer? "Are you home?"

"For a five-day break, and happy to accept your offer. I can't wait."

"Great news! Were you aware Alice isn't coming back?"

"I heard, which is the other reason I called. Have you ever met Merrilee Wild?"

"No, Eve. Tell me."

"Merrilee lives in the Port, but we attend classes together in Halifax. Alice told me she landed a permanent job, and I mentioned you to Merrilee. She has a car. When I come home, I hitch a ride with her."

"Does she study accountancy, too?"

"Yes. She likes indoor work." Eve tee-hees. "I guess I'll make an odd accountant because I'd rather be on the tractor instead of behind a desk."

Stella relaxes in the knowledge she made the right decision when she offered Eve her old job and not reception. "I should speak with Merrilee. I hired someone, but the offer fell through. What's her phone number?"

"We want to visit tomorrow morning. She and I could come over together. Are you busy? Mom said there's been another murder in town."

"Busy, yes, but I'll find time for my favourite gardener. Hopefully, Merrilee won't be put off by my sideline preoccupation," she adds with more nervousness than she expected of herself. "Come out to the park around nine and we'll chat." She pauses. "And thanks, Eve. You may have saved my summer."

"You and Merrilee will hit it off. I'm sure."

The line clicks in her ear. Stella checks her watch. She has a minute for a quick stop at the workshop to say bye to Nick before she meets with Aiden to report the contents of her interviews. They can plan to speak with Theodore Gorman, the printer, and Patricia Brooks at the Groceteria. No forensics until Friday. She grabs her lunch out of the fridge, trots across the living room, and runs down the veranda stairs toward the Jeep.

Nick fills the doorway of the workshop and wipes his hands on a greasy rag while he waits for her to navigate the bumpy trail which leads to the barn door, opened for the morning light. The sight of him still makes her heart, or stomach, or whatever, flutter—despite a slight change in the scene over the past months because of the addition of Kiki. As she emerges into full view, she sees the little dog perched on a tree stump Nick placed inside, to the right of the entry. Only Kiki, in a purple turtleneck, could own the place the way she does, balanced on the top of a stump. She watches Nick stand with a flat hand toward the dog, who remains quiet until her vehicle stops, after which he waves, and Kiki follows him. "I'm loving the look of you two," she spouts as she opens the door, which grinds under her effort.

"Deliver the Jeep back here when you come home. I'll grease her and give the old girl a wash before we go to the city."

"Okay. The noise is worse."

"We can't have a dirt-mobile with a squeaky hinge when we hand our keys to valet service." He winks but provides no more clues. "I found myself sidetracked yesterday and didn't tend to the issue. You'll be here for tea?"

"Yes. There's reception staff news to tell you later. I expect this weekend to be exciting." She smothers a girlish giggle.

He smooches her forehead. "I've planned Saturday and Sunday down to the last detail. You and I are going to paint the town." He pulls back and meets her gaze. "No Aiden North, okay? Not even a phone call for two days. Will you promise?"

She executes her most solemn nod. "I promise, Sir." She kisses him firmly on cool lips. "Is Trixie still on board as our dog-sitter?"

"Collecting the pooch tomorrow around lunch." He touches her shoulder. "I said don't worry. I've handled every detail. Now, go finish your meetings."

The drive into Shale Harbour proves uneventful. She tucked her notes, along with her salad and celery sticks, into her purse. No dessert today. Aiden suggested the hotel, but she opted for a bagged lunch, the same as they did at Grey Cottage Realty yesterday. She must admit, right now, she's more interested in Eve's friend Merrilee, followed by her surprise trip to Halifax. Who murdered Deena Finch ranks third. She expects the weekend off will do her good.

****

"An employee of a government department in Port Ephron raped Tess Boone at her place of work. Connie Gee, her sister, told me." Stella and Aiden are in his office. She stacks her notes in a pile in front of her and rummages for the plastic container of salad and a fork. "Can Sergeant Moyer search your records for a file on Tess Boone? Maybe he'll need to call the Port."

"I'll instruct Moyer, but how does a rape figure in our murder? We've observed Tess' skittishness ourselves. She feared the victim. Finch entered her premises without permission—often."

"Connie said many more times than Tess reported. Deena scared her. My speculation meter suggests Deena was aware of Tess' secret."

"Alright. Alright. If you feel a check will make a difference." Aiden clenches his teeth and rubs the back of his neck while he reaches for the phone. "Moyer, call the office in the Port and ask them to find a file on Tess Boone—a rape case. Probably take time. They store their records in the basement. Thanks." He returns his attention to Stella, who now has a forkful of salad wedged in her mouth.

"Sorry. I'm famished." She swallows and sets her container on the corner of Aiden's desk. Mary Jo is positive Deena has a past which involves children. She recalled a conversation where Deena spoke out on behalf of mothers, against those of us who never enjoyed the privilege. Velvet mentioned the incident earlier. Neither of your sisters-in-law considers any of the three women capable of killing Deena." She addresses her salad again and realizes the cookies from yesterday are still at the bottom of her bag.

"Changing the subject for a moment, I'm pleased you and Cloris decided against her working in your reception for the summer. Did Mary Jo tell you her scheme for moving into the fourplex once we solve this murder?"

"She mentioned the idea, yes. I told her our work will take more time, which didn't bother her."

"Not good for me. If Rosemary comes home and another case materializes, I'll be on the hunt all over town for one of them to cover me."

"No small task—your job coupled with Rosemary's return. I suggested you consider retirement when we discussed this earlier." She closes the lid on her salad, ignores the celery, and begins rooting for the cookies while avoiding his eyes.

"Stella, frankly, I can't imagine every day with Rosemary anymore. Life is stable without her at home." He leans across the desk. "I'll deny my deepest and darkest to anyone but you. Now, where were we?"

"Okay." She holds her first bite of cookie in her mouth for an extra second or two before she continues. The smell of the chocolate floats around her nose. "Mary Jo suspects a secret. Connie provided insights. Finally, Cavelle said Earlene learned lots of information related to herbal remedies from the queen of poison in her family, Opal." She frowns before she continues. "Deena figured out Earlene poisoned her husband and blackmailed her? Another theory."

"Richard Marigold's autopsy report suggested an undiagnosed heart condition."

"Perhaps he wanted to kill himself, but such an act nullifies insurance. They found a way for him to carry out the task, leaving the public none the wiser." She shrugs. "An idea, Aiden." The cookies are gone before she realizes.

"Too many theories and ideas. The report of his death wasn't suspicious—a plain old heart attack."

"I'm not finished—hair-eating Velvet. Mary Jo and Toni insist Velvet is harmless. They admire how she has risen above her diagnosis and created a decent life." She steels herself for his reaction. "They compared her to Rosemary and said the three of you coddled her over the years and gave her a pass. Velvet successfully navigated the world on her own. She listened to her doctors and therapists."

"Yeah. You and I discussed her history, and I admire the woman, too. I can't imagine Velvet walloping someone with an iron, either. Where do we go from here? Forensics will report to me tomorrow."

"Come for coffee at the park, then. I'm interviewing a new staff member, and we expect Trixie to fetch Kiki around noon. Will ten-thirty work?".

"Trixie's dog-sitting?"

"Nick and I are off to Halifax on Saturday, returning Sunday. He has plans, but a surprise for me. A break is just what I need."

"You and Nick are still good, right?"

She's known Aiden since they were fifteen. She reads his expression. "Yes, Aiden. Nick and I are lucky. We are good." She stands. "Gotta run. By the way, the first of next week, we should interview Theodore Gorman, Patricia Brooks from the grocery store, and a conversation with Frances Ellis might be wise, because she and Tess are writing friends."

Aiden brushes white hair off his brow. "And we'll go through Deena's apartment ourselves once they send the damned report, which has taken too long," he grumbles.

"The murder happened three days ago, Aiden. Once we receive clearance, I'll call Hester. Cavelle says your 'assistant'," she lifts her brows, "expects we need her help."

"Right," he drawls. "See you tomorrow." He reaches for the phone as she leaves.

****

Supper turns into a grand affair. Nick serves her his paprika chicken with the trimmings. She teases but cannot trick him into leaking weekend details. He clamps his lips shut. She knows he'll reveal no clues. After cleaning the kitchen, they curl on the sofa and catch an episode of *Perry Mason,* one of Nick's favourites, rerun or not. She startles when the phone rings, and wonders if she'd been snoozing.

Nick trots back from her office. "For you, Stella. Tess Boone."

"Oh, my." She checks her watch. "I wonder what has precipitated a call now. I hope Connie's okay." She touches his arm when she passes by.

"Hi, Tess. What can I do for you?"

"Sorry for calling after nine, but I spoke with my sister earlier and dithered. Am I too late?"

She settles in her chair. "No, Tess. Problem?"

"Connie told me she mentioned a four-letter word I never use."

"Rape."

"Yes. She revealed my secret."

"Correct. Your settlement and frugal lifestyle, plus the fact you don't work anymore, made more sense once I understood the truth, Tess. Lying to the police isn't wise." She frowns at the phone.

"I didn't lie, Stella. I used a term which doesn't imply my horrible experience. The assault occurred after hours in my place of employment. My ordeal was indescribable. He left, and I went home. I refused to go to the hospital because the staff must file a report with the police."

"Someone knew. You received a settlement." A statement can often prove more productive than more questions.

"My supervisor was the person I called. I stayed away from the office, and a lawyer telephoned. I signed a non-disclosure agreement before they deposited money into my bank account."

"Were you aware of similar incidents?"

"Suspicions, because my boss set the wheels in motion within hours. I assume I wasn't the first—nor the last."

"The man remains a government employee and was never charged." Another statement.

"For several years."

"What do you mean? Were charges ever laid?"

"No."

"Did Deena know about your history? Or was she connected to the rapist?"

"Good grief! I can't imagine her throwing such personal information in my face, even though I've never met a more unpleasant woman than her. Deena stole from me. She took personal and precious items. She entered my apartment uninvited, with me on the premises, at least half a dozen times. I lost track, but she never let on she possessed knowledge from my past."

She pauses, and Stella can hear her gulping for air. Tess still can't say the word "rape."

"She scared me every time. I didn't report each occurrence because Earlene was at her wit's end with Deena."

"Okay. Understood. Tess, I am sorry for what happened to you, although the crime needed to be reported. You never mentioned charges."

"Too late now. He died of cancer three years ago. Couldn't happen to a nicer guy." She titters. "Were those words in my outside voice?"

The sound emitted from Tess hovered between bitterness and glee. Stella imagines she experienced considerable solace when news of her assailant's death reached her.

"Any more information, Tess?"

"I guess I'm done. I wanted to tell you myself, but not in front of anyone."

Her relief is obvious, even over the phone. "Thanks for the call. I appreciate your forthrightness."

Before she returns to the warmth of Nick and the comfort of her sofa, she dials Aiden's number at home.

"Hello?"

"Hi, Aiden. Sorry for the late hour. Tess Boone called me."

"Moyer found no rape file." His voice sounds odd, sullen, and abrupt. She hears ice rattle in a glass but refuses to ask.

"She didn't report the assault. Tess is certain management created a routine protocol when this rapist attacked a poor unsuspecting office worker. A lawyer took care of the details and paid the victims' settlements. The perpetrator has since died. Deena wasn't aware of her experience as far as Tess knows. Deena never said as much, at least."

"Well, we're back to the beginning," he replies, his voice unsteady.

"We are. Tess emphasized Deena entered her apartment often and frightened the life out of her. She told Earlene after two or three of the incidents, but not each one. She felt sorry for her landlady, I guess. Maybe forensics will shed more light on the mysterious Deena Finch."

"Okay. Talk tomorrow."

The line disengages with a bang when he drops the receiver. She gathers her thoughts and drifts back toward Nick.

"Are you alright?" He reaches for her hand when she sits beside him.

"Yes. I spoke with Tess and her history troubles me. She experienced a violent rape, and her place of work paid her off—a routine procedure, she assumed, because of the speed of their actions. I called Aiden and told him what Tess reported. He may have been drunk. I heard ice tinkling in a glass."

"Unusual for him."

"Rosemary's discharge has him distracted. I reminded him of our next steps for the case this morning. He has problems. I suggested he could retire or take a leave, but he won't."

"Aiden wants a regular marriage where he can work and come home to a loving and sane wife."

"You could never classify Rosemary as normal, from what her sisters say. They protected and coddled her, as has Aiden, for most of her life." She heaves her shoulders. "Compare her to poor Velvet Carmichael. The same diagnosis, but she saw her therapists, followed her doctors' orders, and took her pills. As a result, she's a successful, retired professional. I admire her. Rosemary received too much attention because of her illness."

"Don't find yourself caught in the middle, Stella." Nick takes on a cautionary tone. "You're the layperson who conducts police business."

"I'm on my guard. Aiden can't drop the ball again. The RCMP clipped my wings after the Owen Ellis-Thomas case. No repeats." She strokes Kiki while they talk.

"Will you forget the fourplex and Deena Finch's murder when we go away on Saturday?" He wraps a flannel-clad arm around her shoulder. The tiny dog snuggles between them.

"You heard me promise. Are you sure you won't tell me your plans?"

"Not a chance. News and bed?"

"Yes. Tomorrow, Eve is bringing Merrilee Wild over and we'll discuss the reception position. Aiden said he would be here for coffee, and you scheduled Trixie for near noon. Busy morning."

CHAPTER 11

Dead Ends at Every Turn

"Meet Merrilee, Stella."

Stella has opened the door on this brisk Friday morning to two young women, although one doesn't appear as youthful as first surmised. Eve stands on the threshold, clad in overalls with her black curls piled under a dirty ball cap. The overalls propel Stella back to Ira Gold, found at the bottom of Mallory Gorman's grave last winter. "Nice to meet you, Merrilee. Come in. Come in." She stumbles over her words, confronted by the severity of Merrilee Wild's persona.

Merrilee extends her hand. "Nice to meet you, too, Ms. Kirk. Eve has spoken of you many times." She turns toward Eve. "More than I expect an employee should reveal," she adds with a vague expression Stella can't read, "but…."

"Please, come inside and sit, you two. Eve, how great to see you early in the year. We don't often cross paths before school wraps."

"A quick break." She wriggles until she finds a comfortable perch on the sofa. "Back to the grind on Monday, right, Merrilee?"

"Correct, Eve," Merrilee answers with an indulgent smirk. "I expect Ms. Kirk wants to speak with me regarding the position."

"Oh. Good idea. Stella, shall I make coffee?"

Stella waves her hand. "Sure, Eve. You can find everything. A big pot, okay? Nick will be back in the house by ten, and Aiden is due around the same time."

"You have a hectic day. We won't keep you long," Merrilee suggests.

Sensing reluctance, Stella comes right to the point. "Merrilee, first, please call me Stella. We stand on no formality here. Second, are you interested in a position as my assistant for the summer or are you here because Eve pestered you? I expect you've gotten other offers."

Merrilee touches the seam of her slacks, which match the jacket of her coral pantsuit from the 1970s. Her thick, straight, and grey-streaked bob frames her severe features. She's fit, well-groomed, and Stella expects she's in her thirties.

"Hopefully, we reach an arrangement. Eve has described Alice Morgan's work here. Alice was more flexible, but I expect I can do the job and become an asset."

"Okay." *Less flexible.* Eve rattles around in the kitchen. "Describe Merrilee Wild to me."

"I'm thirty-three," she begins, her voice hesitant and quiet. "Ten years after we married, my husband left because we couldn't have kids. My divorce was two years ago, and I invested my settlement into an education to become a productive member of society."

"Good for you. Goals and plans are important. You live in Port Ephron?"

"Yes. I rent a small studio apartment and drive into Halifax for classes each day. The gas for my Ford Fiesta is cheaper than the extra living expenses required in the city. I carpool another student, further assisting me to manage my money. Although I don't need a summer position in the financial sense, Eve convinced me I could learn much from you."

"I did, Stella," says Eve, upon her return from the kitchen. "Alice told me over and over how she learned people skills." She wiggles closer to Merrilee and pokes her arm. "Merrilee admits she needs a few people skills," she chatters.

Merrilee runs her thumb and index finger along a strand of hair which has drifted toward her cheek. "I concur, Stella, although with reluctance."

"Lots of people skills needed around here, for sure. While Eve pours us coffee, let me show you the office and describe the job. You can determine, and I'm not offended, if a position with me isn't the right fit for you."

Eve races back to the kitchen. Her friend stands, straightens her jacket, and states, "I'll leave my pocketbook on your sofa for the moment."

"Fine." Stella extends her arm toward reception. "Do you enjoy dogs?"

"Yes, I do. My husband, ex-husband, hated them. As a result, we never owned one, but I grew up with whippets."

"Nick Cochran, both my business and life partner, and I take care of Kiki, a Pomeranian. She has the run of the place and loved Alice. She'll hang out with you if encouraged. Duke—John Powell—our security man, owns Kiki, but he lives with Cloris, and she isn't fond of pets, so Kiki moved in with us."

"I've never visited an RV park. How does the business work?"

"Good question, Merrilee. Keep me focused," Stella blusters. She leads the way. "Campers drive to the front and enter through here. The property has one hundred sites. We'll finish the septic upgrade in a few weeks. We increased our seasonal sites to fifty from forty-five by decreasing the water only spots." She notes Merrilee's puzzled expression. "Seasonals are guests who lease from us for the whole summer. Their trailer becomes a cottage. We rent thirty-five overnight sites where we book folks in as they travel or visit for days or longer. These areas come equipped with water, power, and sewer hook-ups now. Finally, fifteen unserviced spots with water only make up the rest. These guests use our public bathrooms and showers. Each site has a fire pit and a picnic table. Paul, who is Alice's brother, Duke, and Nick will distribute those before we open. We accept reservations year-round and our seasonals arrive starting the Friday of the long weekend in May. Our start date falls on May 21 this year. I hire my staff to begin a week before, so you would start on Friday, May 14. You won't be too busy, but there will be calls with reservation requests. Reception wants a good spring cleaning and forms need to be ordered. We'll have time for you to learn my—Alice's—paperwork routine. We can walk the main floor of my house and explore the grounds."

"Do you have a map? I'm great with maps."

Stella reaches behind the counter. "Here you go. We provide a map to every guest who checks in. Now, let me show you around."

They return to the living room, where Eve has arranged coffee mugs on the table in front of the sofa. "I think I remember what everybody takes," she gushes.

"Thanks, Eve. We'll be a few more minutes." Stella turns her attention back to Merrilee and guides her toward the kitchen. "Most days are straight forward, Merrilee. You arrive by nine, grab a coffee and a bite of breakfast, if you choose. I check in with my guests often and may drive the park in the golf cart. Between the two of us, we assemble lunch for the staff—on a quiet day. Other days can be chaotic. Maybe someone needs a spot in a hurry and to accommodate, we move another guest. Storms happen or power problems, or, God forbid, our new septic system fails. Never fear, though. Nick or I will be nearby. When the weather is poor, Eve spends time in the house, as well. Light housework helps. Grocery lists are a great asset. What do you think?"

"Eve mentioned you're sometimes involved in murder investigations with the police."

"Correct. I'm working on a case with Aiden North of the RCMP right now. If an inquiry happens in the summer, you become my back-up here at the house. Most often, we'll share the workload, but sometimes I'm not reliable." She grimaces. "I hope you understand. Oh, one more piece of information. We work each day until five. If you need time off for an appointment or a wedding, or whatever, ask. As you can see from the wage, I compensate you for the seven-day-a-week inconvenience. Nick and I cover the office every night, and Duke closes the gate at ten." They return to the living room, and she acknowledges Eve. "Coffee smells delish."

Merrilee sits, studies the pay sheet, and sips her drink. "May I assume a job offer?"

Stella watches Eve observe her friend's expression. "Yes, Merrilee, but understand, I expect a great deal. Perching behind the reception desk each day won't be enough. Show initiative around the house and help when I'm called away." She has nothing to lose by being blunt.

With her eyes still focused on the paper in her hand, Merrilee bobs her head. "I'm reliable. I think you'll find me dependable." She first nods at Eve before she speaks. "For the second time today, I will shake your hand. You have a deal. Can we go for a walk around the park?"

Eve scrambles to her feet. "I'll give her a tour, Stella. Didn't you say you expected Detective North?"

"Thanks, Eve. Good idea."

****

"Eve made extra strong coffee a half hour ago. You might need a cup," Stella suggests. Aiden North appears overtired and rumpled. "Hung over, are we?" She musters a grin to go with the tease.

He glares. "Hard night." He reaches into the inside pocket of his suit jacket and retrieves a folded document.

"Let's sit in the kitchen. I'll pour you the coffee I promised."

Without a response, he follows her after he tosses his coat across the arm of a couch. He drops into one of Stella's kitchen chairs.

His overly dramatic and withered sigh doesn't impress. "What's the matter?"

"In my life right now, name a topic. As for the report, in terms of forensics, Deena Finch's death was because of a significant blow to the head with her own iron. A single hit with enough force to penetrate—well, you can read the gory details. They suggest she was knocked about and fell first. The poor woman didn't know what happened."

"Prints?" She sets the coffee before him.

"None except hers. I assume the killer wore gloves. Even if murder wasn't the person's intent, gloves aren't unusual in mid-March."

"I saw none when I met with the three other residents in their units. The constables who attended them didn't mention anyone disposing of gloves."

"And I asked for a search of the grounds with no luck." He sips his coffee. "Dead ends at every turn, Stella."

"Wait a minute." She rattles the paper in her hand. "Did you see how forensics mentioned Deena's probable OCD?"

"Yes—a neat-freak, but what's the relevance?"

"We found no master key. They say her clothes and shoes are in rows with pictures on shoe boxes and garments colour coordinated. They discovered each item reported stolen, which we knew. I want to search her apartment with Hester. I bet we'll find the copy of Earlene's master in a remote spot no one's noticed. Remember when we found Paulina's diary stuffed into her bedroom chair cushion? Are we cleared to go inside the unit?"

"You're the one who's off to Halifax for a romantic weekend."

She doesn't appreciate the slur in his tone. "I'll ignore your attitude for the moment. Nick and I arrive home on Sunday afternoon. If you arrange for interviews with Theodore Gorman, Patricia Brooks, and Frances Ellis for Monday, we can meet at the local detachment first. We'll start in Shale Harbour. I'll call Hester that night and plan a thorough search of Deena's apartment for Tuesday, since forensics is finished." She stops and inhales. "Will this atone for my trip away?"

"Sorry. I'm fed up."

"Right, but with no reason to take your annoyances out on me." She pauses, allowing her criticism to register. "Now, why are you in such a funk? Were you drunk when I called last night?"

"None of your business."

Rebuffed, she withdraws further personal comments and turns her attention to Rosemary.

"Her sisters expect the doctors will discharge her by Easter," he grumbles in response to her query.

"Good Friday is April 9."

"I'm not ready for the drama again. Toni says Rosie can stay with her and Mary Jo if the Finch case isn't solved, but I suspect Mary Jo to move as soon as possible, which complicates Rosemary's supervision. I'm tired, Stella."

"You suggested I consider your behaviour none of my business, but…."

"I said my drinking doesn't concern you."

Translating his expression proves difficult when he holds his mug in front of his face. "Okay. You need a new plan. Borrow a page out of Velvet Carmichael's book," she asserts.

He frowns. The action knits his white eyebrows together.

"Be direct with Rosemary. 'You must take these medications. These are the directions you must follow. These are the doctors you must see. No exceptions.' No excuses—no more coddling. If she cannot, or will not, focus on the maintenance of a stable treatment plan, she risks permanent institutionalization. One chance, not two. No coddling," she repeats. "And Mary Jo and Toni need to be on board."

A shock of hair falls across his brow when he makes eye contact with her. "You are a taskmaster."

"Whatever. I'm right. You crave a normal marriage. Yours can be a version of normal if she follows the rules inspired by Velvet. You can't make her want the same life you do. Either she follows the rules or suffers the consequences." Stella leans forward in her chair. "You, my friend, must quit coddling—sorry if I've over-emphasized the word—and convince your sisters-in-law to do the same."

****

Pack dress-up comfy clothes for tonight, he said. What the hell comprises dress-up comfy? Stella stands in front of their closet and assesses her wardrobe selections. Such decisions haven't been necessary in months. For the trip, she'll wear a long jean skirt and a cotton sweater. As Trixie's voice reverberates at the back of her mind, she grabs a scarf to wrap around her neck. When her sister arrived yesterday and fetched Kiki, she reminded Stella to present her best self, and suggested slippage in that department has occurred since she and Nick became partners in the business. *Am I too relaxed? Do I take Nick for granted? Trixie thinks too many murder investigations and not enough attention to my partner.*

Okay. Focus on the task at hand. She grabs another sweater for the trip home on Sunday. As for Saturday evening, she expects a fancy dinner and doesn't know what else he has in store. A blush travels from her neck toward her cheeks. He's planned events besides supper. She reaches into the back of the closet and retrieves palazzo pants, the ones with the cranberry pattern, folds them and adds the winter-white angora sweater she's worn with them in the past. One more scarf and another pair of earrings will suffice. She snaps her case shut and trots into the bathroom. Nick wants to leave by noon. He said the check-in time at their hotel is three o'clock, which provides no clue as to their destination.

"Are you ready?" He shouts from the foot of the stairway. "We can eat lunch before we leave. I made fruit salad and thawed buns. Don't lug your suitcase. I'll grab it afterward."

"On my way. Hard to choose clothes when I don't know what or where." She hopes he hears her enthusiasm and not criticism in her tone, while she navigates the stairs.

"Beautiful, as usual. Let's have lunch and go."

Impatience shows in Nick because he hops from one foot to the other when he's excited. Dressed in a white shirt and khakis, he acts every bit the part of the world traveller, although the drive into Halifax, if that's their ultimate destination, is a mere two hours.

****

They arrive at the hotel before check-in time—typical for Nick, but their room is ready. The old and posh Brunswick, with valet service and bellboys, exhibits cool marble floors and elevators trimmed in brass. Stella has never been inside the business and feels she should whisper in the hushed atmosphere.

Plush carpets and a king-size bed greet them when the attendant opens the door. Their room, shrouded with dark draperies, surrounds them in subdued luxury. Nick hands him a bank note.

"Enjoy your stay," the young man spouts while he doffs his hat.

Nick bustles. He sets their travel cases on luggage racks. He pulls back the heavy curtains and inhales as he watches a cargo ship navigate the harbour. Dust motes float in the afternoon sun, which floods the moody space. "I'll make tea and tell you what I've planned." He grabs the miniature kettle and trots into the bathroom, which rivals the size of theirs at home.

Stella examines the choices and decides on a berry blend for herself and a chamomile for Nick. The cups and saucers are china, not paper. The tea will taste better.

While they wait for the water, she hangs her clothes in the closet and sorts her toiletries. Nick pours. They sit across from one another in coordinated tub chairs upholstered in gold brocade. Stella forces her thoughts away from Paulina McAdams and where they found her diary.

"Okay," he huffs. "I made reservations at The Cleaver. We can walk, enjoy supper, and afterward take the Jeep downtown to the theatre for the premier of Victor/Victoria! What do you think?"

Her eyes widen. "I heard, on the radio, Victor/Victoria released yesterday."

"I know. Julie Andrews and James Garner. He's one of my all-time favourites. I ordered tickets last month and we will see the movie at the old Bedford Theatre. Four hundred and fifty seats and I managed two front row balcony spots." He bounces in the tub chair. "The show starts at nine. I made reservations at the restaurant for six. He glances at his watch. Do you want to shop, or go for a walk, or visit a museum?" Enthusiasm twinkles in his eyes.

"No, Nick. I'd rather sit here with you, drink my tea, and luxuriate in the fact no one knows where we are."

"Not totally true," he pouts. "I told Trixie, in case of an emergency."

She nods. "No matter. Trixie won't disturb us. She's concerned I don't give you enough attention, and the world will need to be ending for her to interrupt our weekend."

"You give me lots of attention, Stella." He sets his teacup on the coffee table between them. They find a way to occupy their time before dinner.

****

He holds her arm while they walk to The Cleaver, a steak and shrimp restaurant a city block from The Brunswick. Stella has never eaten there before. Her eyes take a moment to adjust to the dark wood, dim lighting, and labyrinth of passageways which connect multiple dining areas. They follow their hostess to a table a mile from the entry, where they're seated, and a single candle is lit.

Once alone, Nick covers her hand in his. "Happy birthday."

"I love the fact you created a special occasion."

"What looks good? Sky's the limit."

He's reverted to being a teenager on his first fancy date. "I think I'll have the grilled shrimp with jasmine rice and roasted vegetables. Have you decided, Stella?"

"Let's order wine. I know they won't approve of white, because I want a steak, but what the hey?" He lifts his eyebrows in mock scorn as she continues. "I'll ask for the Teriyaki sirloin with a loaded baked potato and the veggies."

He pats her hand. "Save room for dessert. I hear they serve the best."

On their return walk, Nick wraps his arm around her shoulder. After their scrumptious meal, they take time to freshen up before their drive to the Bedford Theatre. "I forgot. I managed reservations for The Brunswick Hotel's Sunday brunch, too."

She lifts her face and meets his eyes. "How long did you wait to land those?"

"I went on a list until someone cancelled. They called two days ago. Lucky, eh?"

The movie fulfilled their expectations and more. They walked an actual red carpet, and one of the producers spoke before the velvet curtains lifted and the show began. They slept in on Sunday morning, enjoyed a decadent brunch at eleven, and returned home before tea.

****

While Stella unpacks, Nick is off on the five-minute drive to Trixie's place to retrieve Kiki. With Nick gone, she reflects on her two-day gift from the man she loves. Maybe her sister's observations are correct. Once the investigation into Deena Finch's death wraps…. The phone bleats.

"Are we on for tomorrow?"

"As promised, Aiden. Hi."

"I booked Gorman and the Groceteria for the morning, at ten and eleven, plus Frances Ellis for one-thirty and a doctor at two. I'll buy you lunch."

"Okay. What doctor?" Before hearing an answer, she adds, "Must go. I hear Nick on his way in with Kiki."

CHAPTER 12

Routine Inquiries

The bell over the door jangles after Aiden and Stella climb the two steps and enter the foyer of the business, where a wide counter separates any customer from the print facilities in the rear. A curtain serves as the back wall. Theo pops out from behind the fabric before the tinkle of the bells stops.

"Good morning. Right on time." He leans on the worn and faded beige onyx patterned laminate top. "And to what do I owe the honour of a meeting with you two today?" The shop owner is a reserved man of normal build and stature. His sandy hair has more streaks of grey since the death of his wife late last year. He watches them over reading glasses perched on the end of his nose.

Aiden takes the lead. "We hear you publish Tess Boone's books for her."

"Not exactly. I print hard cover copies. She's a good customer."

"We're interested in your assessment of Tess as a person, Theo." Stella encourages him.

"Tess is a fine woman. We connect," he blushes, "but Mallory...." His voice fades. He blinks and continues. "As an author, she produces her own work. Having never found a legitimate publisher, she sells a few or gives copies as gifts. The writers retreat last fall excited her—an opportunity to meet a contact or two—help guide her on her journey."

"Are you acquainted with the other women who live, or lived, at the G-plex?"

"Richard Marigold and I were business colleagues. He often requested brochures printed. I never met Earlene." He pushes closer across the counter and lowers his voice, although no one else has entered the premises. "Few people are aware of the details, but Marigold Financial experienced money troubles. Earlene suffered no monetary challenges after Richard died, or no obvious ones. She paid off his outstanding account with me." He shrugs. "His family is wealthy, though. Maybe someone helped. Not the first time, eh?"

"And the others?" Stella pushes for more.

"I saw the dead woman often when she worked at the Groceteria. She acted nice enough. I have no personal knowledge regarding the fourth person, although her name inspires me." He stares at the ceiling. "Velvet—soft and smooth, with texture, right?"

Stella nods. The man is certainly more expressive since Mallory's death.

"You don't suspect one of the three women killed her, do you? Good grief, Tess wouldn't hurt a fly. As for Earlene or Velvet—far-fetched."

"We collect information on every player, Mr. Gorman. Routine inquiries. Thank you for your time today." As they turn away from the counter, the door opens and Pepper Ferguson breezes through on a gust of cool air. "Hi, Mr. Gorman. Gotta minute for a review of our menu changes? Eugenie needs them yesterday." She smirks in Stella's direction. "You understand my boss and her demands, right Stella?"

****

No matter how often she enters the local grocery store, the smell of cabbage assaults her. Time of year bears no consequence. Cabbages may or may not be within sight. Even in the dairy aisle, the pervasive odour hangs in the air. Today proves no different.

Patricia Brooks, the charitable and reliable owner of the Groceteria, putters behind the cash. "Did you contact her for an interview?" Stella asks Aiden, puzzled the woman isn't in her office.

Aiden huffs his response. "Mrs. Brooks," he elevates his voice above the din of overhead music and random chatter. "Detective North and Stella Kirk. I called earlier?"

She glances in their direction, not fazed by the interruption. "Right. I'll find someone to take over, although we aren't busy. Mondays never are."

Dressed in a pair of jeans and T-shirt covered by a flowered bib apron one might don while working in the kitchen, Patricia has tied her short hair with a wide blue bandanna. She wears hospital-style white orthopedic shoes. They squish with every step. When a staff person arrives behind the checkout, she leads Aiden and Stella into a cluttered and windowless office at the rear of the store. Once they sit on dilapidated oak chairs which probably furnished a board room somewhere in a former life, she states, "You want to discuss your murder victim."

"Yes, Mrs. Brooks." Aiden produces his notebook and turns toward Stella before Patricia begins.

"Happy to help." She crosses her arms over her chest and inhales. "Deena Finch arrived on the scene about two years ago. She said she needed a job, and she acted nice enough." Patricia continues in a rehearsed staccato. "I hired her. I prefer the more mature types. She fit the bill. Oh." Patricia stops and frowns. "She told me her SIN was in her ex-spouses' name—Greer—so I should file her deductions under Greer instead of Finch. Odd, eh? She filled in the paperwork, but the next day, I went into the Registry of Motor Vehicles with her and vouched for her identity, because she lost her wallet after our interview."

"Deena applied for a new licence with your help?" Aiden squints as he reviews his notes.

"Did you see her social insurance number, Patricia? They're necessary to accept a job with you, right?"

"She completed an application form and provided her SIN, birth date, and address at the G-plex. When she complained of an injury, I happily turned the mess over to my insurer. It was my best excuse to let her go."

"Can you tell us why?" The problem isn't difficult to imagine.

"She was a mean-spirited woman, made unkind statements, and demeaned staff and customers alike. I removed her from cash, and she stocked shelves. She wasn't happy and claimed she hurt her back and shoulder at work."

"Did she?" Aiden sounds unconvinced.

"Couldn't care less," she insists. "Luckily, the insurance paid her, and she left without a fuss. My premiums haven't risen. As a result, the business didn't suffer. Was someone angry enough to kill her?" She shrugs and avoids eye contact.

"Anyone who works here at the store?"

"No. We were happy when we saw the hind end of Deena Finch walk out the door. We are a family here. I take good care of my girls, and she didn't fit in from the start. Poor judgment on my part." She peers at the clock on the wall behind Stella. "I'm needed back out on the floor now. People want their breaks. Are we done?"

An assessment of Patricia's gaunt frame suggests she rarely takes time for her own breaks.

"Can I be of more help, Stella?"

"May we take a copy of Deena's application?"

"No problem." She reaches into a dented metal file cabinet. "Here you are. I made extra copies when insurance got involved."

On their way toward the hotel for lunch, Stella mutters, "I must admit, I never encountered Deena at the grocery store." She sighs. "Staff and Nick do most of the shopping, I guess. Who knows? Deena Finch might not even be her real name. Your folks must have found her wallet, right?"

"As far as I know, they located her driver's licence, but no other official cards, like a SIN or provincial medicare. I recall a credit card."

****

Pepper Ferguson guides them into a smaller dining room in the back and pours ice water into two glasses. She appears to be working alone, although Stella can never be sure. "Here are the menus. Nice seeing you earlier. Coffee?"

They nod.

"Chef made creamed lobster on a homemade biscuit for the special. He says the dish is to die for." She covers her mouth with her hand. "Oops. Poor choice of words." She titters. "Substitute swoon for die." She turns on her heel and races away from their table, ponytail swishing.

"I see Pepper's handling both the desk and the lunch patrons—again. What is Eugenie Charlebois hoping to accomplish when she leaves the poor girl with no help?" Stella grumbles.

Aiden sips his water. "Didn't you tell me Pepper expects the manager position will be hers soon? I bet the owner wants to test how well she juggles the work. Or Charlebois is taking advantage of Pepper's good nature." He sets his glass back on the table. "I sense you believe the latter."

"Eugenie Charlebois uses her." She frowns. "I must suggest to Cavelle that she approach Pepper and encourage a move into the real estate business. Meredith Tompkins offered her a job before going to jail. They're in desperate need of a third agent at Grey Cottage Realty and Pepper fits the bill."

"Anybody ever tell you not to meddle?"

From the twinkle she glimpses in his eyes, Stella expects he's not waiting for an answer.

They followed Pepper's suggestion, enjoyed the special, and then made the thirty-minute drive to Port Ephron in discussions focused on the authors, Frances Ellis and Edward Thomas. The latter carves out a living as a successful science-fiction writer, although presents as docile and quiet. Frances writes romance novels and the consensus, discovered during the investigation of their son's death, was that Edward's publisher handles her books to garner Edward's favour. Frances' romances aren't great, in Stella's opinion, and since they've shown no commercial success, bookish types might well be correct.

Stella first met the Ellis-Thomas couple as plans took shape for the inaugural Shale Harbour Writers Retreat. The family stayed at the Shale Cliffs RV Park cottage at the time of the event last fall. The four-day function was disrupted when their son, Owen, died at the hands of one of the workshop authors.

Frances Ellis and Tess Boone are friends. Today's visit will assess Frances' opinion of Tess, both as a writer and as a person capable of murder.

Their home has changed little in the few months since Aiden and Stella made frequent visits to the bungalow in the shabby neighbourhood. Frances, as expected, waits at the entrance, behind the dented and screen-torn aluminum storm door. "Welcome, you two. Haven't seen you in a while." Her pudgy face crumples. Strands of hair, loosened from her braid wrapped in a halo around the crown of her head, wobble as she attempts control. She waves her hand in front of her eyes, as if swatting a fly. "Sorry. I mist with the least provocation. Come into the kitchen. Edward has gone to a meeting with his publisher." She turns, expression now alight. "They are releasing his latest book soon. He's excited."

Thankful she can avoid Frances' flowered sofa, the seats of which feel a bare two inches off the carpet, Stella happily follows their hostess.

"I've made tea. Sit." She bustles—the norm for Frances. "Detective, you said you wanted to discuss Tess Boone."

"Correct, Ms. Ellis. You are friends."

Aiden's taken a page from Stella's playbook and given Frances an opportunity to agree or not.

"Not friends, exactly, Detective. Tess has sought my writing advice often." She distributes tea, adds cream, sugar, and spoons around the table before she joins them. "I consider Tess a writer who scratches out stories for her own pleasure. She has never secured a publisher. Gorman Printing turns her manuscripts into books, and she flogs them at various markets." She pats her braid. "My dear, I can't imagine sitting in a booth smelling sausage from across the way, or staring at someone's knitting creations, while I discuss my work with strangers. How demeaning." She touches her hair again. "Poor Tess. She has gumption, I'll give her credit."

"Tess told us she discussed a potential book idea related to her sister, Connie Gee, and ALS."

"Yes. She had a notion that a story focused on the two of them as children and how ALS has changed the lives of both sisters might sell. Although the concept has merit, I suggested a ghost writer—a competent person who will listen and document their life experiences," Frances explains. "With professional writing, the manuscript would have a chance of attracting a contract."

"And Tess' reaction?" Stella suspects Frances' interpretation to be enlightening.

"She disagreed with my idea." The author props her elbows on the table. "I sensed she wanted an introduction to Edward's and my publisher. She can be forward." Frances tilts her face and leans closer. "Now, I have no information connected to the murder of Deena Finch, except for what I read in the papers, but if you consider Tess Boone a suspect, I'm skeptical. She may have a high opinion of herself and her writing, but she's not capable of killing anyone, mouse that she is."

"Frances, you have been very helpful. We appreciate your time, don't we, Stella?" Aiden stands.

Surprised, Stella follows his lead. "And your frankness, Frances. Thanks for the tea."

On the drive toward the local mental health clinic and an appointment with the psychologist who sees Velvet Carmichael, Aiden blusters. "No news of any consequence. Honestly, Stella, one of the three women must be our culprit."

****

"I received permission from my patient, Ms. Velvet Carmichael, to speak with you in relation to her treatments. I advise you both, though, that although Velvet was generous with her consent, my time is precious."

Duly advised and alerted, Aiden begins his questions for Dr. Bram

Visser, a psychologist at the Port Ephron Mental Health Clinic. When Aiden secured the appointment, he first asked that Velvet contact the clinic and give permission for her therapist to talk with them.

Formidable in both his height and build, Dr. Visser gives the impression he lifts weights and has the capacity to toss either of them out of the second-story office window. Stella instantly dislikes this abrupt and impatient person, who taps his foot, checks his watch, and interrupts before he hears a complete question.

"A picture of your professional interactions with Ms. Carmichael, in terms of how long you've treated her, and the structure of her treatment plan, are of interest." Aiden ignores Dr. Visser's behaviour.

"Ms. Carmichael requested my services soon after she retired from her career in education. She required support to avoid a trip into Halifax and the hospital where she spent time earlier on in her life."

"Why did she seek help at this stage?"

"My patient needs routine. While she worked in the school library, her hours and activities were pigeon-holed, and she felt safe. Without those rituals, she expected to experience mental health drift and needed guidance with reorganizing her purpose. I helped her—with considerable success, I might add."

"Has Velvet ever exhibited violent tendencies or expressed concerns related to a particular person?" Stella jumps to the crux of the matter.

"I'm sure your reference relates to the murder victim, Deena Finch." He pauses and squints. "I encouraged my patient to move into the communal setting where she now lives. I considered the organizational skills of the owner, as described by Ms. Carmichael, beneficial." His broad chest lifts when he inhales. "Predicting the personality challenges of the other tenants didn't enter my recommendations. Your victim bullied Ms. Carmichael non-stop. We worked, with great diligence over the past many months, on the improvement of her coping capabilities."

Stella wonders. She glances at Aiden, who nods. "Did she cope, Dr. Visser?"

"The woman who died was mean and thoughtless, in my patient's estimation. Ms. Carmichael reported Ms. Finch even stole from her neighbours. We analyzed her anxiety and I have confidence she isn't your culprit. I gather I've answered your ultimate question—whether or not she killed your victim." He sweeps his shoulder-length blond hair off his collar.

"Appreciate your time, Doctor. We will be in touch if we need more information."

Dr. Visser stands. "In case you're interested, although you didn't ask, based on my patient's observations, your assailant likely isn't a resident of the building where Velvet lives. She has a keen sense of the humanity in people. Deena Finch's murderer may be a person further afield." He waves his dismissal.

"Again, thank you, Dr. Visser."

Stella shakes his hand before they leave.

On the return trip to Shale Harbour, they discuss the interview. "He's confident Velvet has risen above her psychological issues and managed the challenges of Deena Finch." Stella muses. "A psychotic episode didn't push Velvet to kill her neighbour, in Visser's opinion."

"And he suggested we were on the wrong track if we pin Deena's death on either Tess or Earlene, too." Frustration permeates Aiden's tone. "What a mess," he ruminates aloud, repeating his previous assessment of the matter.

"I'm interested in Earlene and her husband. If Earlene murdered Richard, she's capable of a repeat performance with Deena, although whacking someone with an iron can't compare to using poison as a weapon. She might have helped Richard commit suicide or killed him outright."

Aiden's eyes jerk away from the road. "You think we should open another investigation? Seriously?"

"Not this minute. What I want now is time with Hester Painter in Deena's apartment. We should examine every shoe box and every pocket of every piece of clothing. There's more to learn from Deena Finch. I'm certain."

"Okay. Okay. You contact Hester and plan for tomorrow, if possible. I expect she will reprimand me since you asked for her help," he smirks. "Are you sure you and I can't search the unit without Hester?"

"The woman has a sixth sense for the art of the hidden."

"You found Paulina's diary."

"Yes, but Hester inspired me. Let's include her. Besides, she has a gentleman friend and I want to hear about him—every detail."

Aiden pulls the police issue Caprice into the back lot of the RCMP detachment in Shale Harbour. Stella's Jeep is nearby. "Come in with me for a moment. I'll instruct the front desk to copy Richard Marigold's file and you can read the contents to your heart's content at home. If she killed him, we'll need to find out, eventually. You make more work for me, Stella," he mutters.

"Sorry."

"No, don't be sorry. My instincts aren't as reliable as they should be these days. I blundered Lucy Painter's death in the beginning, and we might have overlooked the subtleties if not for you. The complete debacle with the boarding homes went unnoticed for years until you insisted on following your gut. Take the file. Do a review and we can discuss."

After fifteen minutes, a constable on desk duty produces a copy for her. She's late for tea but finished for the day. Tonight, she'll call Hester and arrange for a trip to the G-plex tomorrow. In the meantime, the thought of supper with Nick and a cuddle by the fire is all she needs to propel her to the park.

Chapter 13

Suspicious Circumstances

"Hello."

"Hester, you answered the phone. Wonders never cease. How are you?"

"Stella." The lightness in her voice disappears. "I expected someone else."

"Sorry. Might his name be Angus?" Stella teases.

"Yes, as a matter of fact. He didn't come over for supper and when he stays at the farm, he calls me and says good night," she huffs. "Now, what do you want?"

"Is that any way to talk to a friend?"

"We haven't spoken since New Year's Day when you honoured us with your presence for the sole purpose of scrounging vegetables."

"I've been busy, Hester. There was the nursing home debacle Aiden and I investigated."

"You spoke with Cavelle, but not me. A missed opportunity for my valuable aid."

Good segue. "We need your guidance in our current case. Your expertise could prove pivotal." *Flatter her.* "Forensics released the murder scene over at the G-plex and now we can conduct a thorough search. You're the one person I trust."

Silence.

"Hester. Are you still on the line?"

"I'm here. Although interested in assisting you and Detective North, the morning is better. After three o'clock, I help Jewel cook supper. Angus will dine with us since he didn't come tonight."

"Sure. Sure. I'll buy you lunch."

"Appreciated. Are you finished?"

"No, Hester." Stella lowers her voice, as if someone might overhear. "Describe your friend, Angus."

"If I must. Angus Raspberry owns the farm he inherited from his parents, around the cliffs from us. I can see his property, but the beach path is treacherous. We promised each other not to travel the rocks as a shortcut."

"Sounds serious."

"Angus is a potato farmer and smart, too. He has a vast knowledge of plants. We share mutual interests. He plans an expansion of the varieties he grows, and I help him with choices."

Stella leads. "Why haven't I met him?"

"He's younger than you, and shy. He's younger than me, as well. You never went to school with him."

"Other family?"

"No. His parents are both dead. They moved here from Ontario when he was twelve." She's quiet for a time. Stella refrains from interrupting. "We are a good fit. We both have social challenges, although I've changed since Lucy died."

"Opal held you back, but now you've improved, my friend. I hope I can meet Angus soon. Here's another question."

"Okay, but I don't want a busy signal greeting Angus when he calls."

"I'll be quick. Do you remember when Earlene Marigold visited with Opal and studied plants and herbs?"

"I recall the time, and I felt offended because Opal thought she could teach Mrs. Marigold without my participation as the expert. They spent hours discussing poisonous species one could grow at home."

"When we are together tomorrow, I may ask you more questions, alright?"

"You cannot study and expand your horizons if you don't seek smart people for answers to your queries. Please arrive at eight-thirty. I will pour you a cup of Jewel's excellent coffee before we start our workday. Now, say goodbye and make the line free for Angus."

****

She's unsure if Nick considers a cuddle on the couch, while she scans a photocopied file of a person dead two years, to be romantic, but when she rounds the corner from her office and spies Nick curled with Kiki, she figures she has a chance. "Hi. I'm meeting with Hester tomorrow. We'll search Deena

Finch's apartment before the police release the scene to Earlene."

"Okay. I've planned a few machinery checks, and the truck needs an oil change. Duke's supposed to arrive later in the day and help me repair picnic tables. I bought the materials to build ten new ones." He moves his long legs and makes room for her. "Are you back home for lunch?"

"No. I promised Hester that I'd treat her. I'll stop for supper takeout if you like."

"Not on your life. There are egg rolls in the freezer." He widens his eyes. "I will make us honey shrimp and fried rice." He smacks his lips. "What's with the file?"

Frowning, she opens the manila folder. "Aiden gave me a copy of the police record of Richard Marigold's sudden death two years ago. Although Aiden insists my review is a waste of time, I wanted to see for myself."

Nick straightens on the sofa, rearranges the sleeping Kiki beside him, and closes his book.

Stella recognizes the cover of one of her mother's old cookbooks, faded red and worn on the spine. She can imagine her mother's hands on the cover but refrains from voicing her observation.

"What do you think, Stella?"

"Earlene and Opal were friends. Theo Gorman said few people were aware, but Richard's financial business was failing." She squints. "No wonder, with interest rates these days. She told me he was out behind the garage for an unknown reason. He stumbled, gasping, on to the back step before he died in her arms."

"Sounds sad."

"Yes," she winces. "I wonder if she gave him an herb concoction so he could commit suicide, or if she poisoned him without his knowledge? Opal explained poisonous plants to her, and Hester felt offended the women didn't ask for her input—suspicious circumstances." She reads the contents—two sheets of paper. One shows a diagram of a man's body with no external damage, except a scar on his shoulder from an earlier surgery. The other addresses a massive heart attack. "He was soaked in urine and vomited before he died." She lifts her eyes and meets Nick's. "Do people wet themselves and hurl during a coronary?"

"God, I hope we never find out, Stella."

"Yeah. Me, too," she shudders. "I'll ask Hester tomorrow. I think Earlene poisoned her husband, or perhaps he wanted to die, and she helped. Either way, she collected his insurance."

"Do you consider your dark mind a blessing, my love?"

She smirks. "Yes, sometimes I assume the worst in people, don't I? Sorry. No more murder discussions tonight. News and bed?"

"No need for news." He lifts his brows and grins.

****

Wind whistles around the Jeep while she parks in the lot at the front of the Painter property. She suspects Hester waits inside the house, behind the screened-in porch. She's correct. Hester sweeps the oak door open with a flourish.

"You are on time, Stella. I take full credit for your acceptance of the advantages of punctuality."

Arguments and corrections are a fruitless exercise. "Good morning. Shall we investigate Deena Finch today?"

"I will provide my assistance as promised, as long as you buy me lunch and we are home by three." The slightest ghost of a smile brushes her lips.

Hester is smitten. "How serious are you and Angus Raspberry? May I meet him?" She tosses her coat across the banister and follows her friend into the kitchen at the back of the house.

Jewel, the family's housekeeper and Hester's companion, lifts her hand in a quick wave as she runs after Kenny, her little boy who appears more mobile than the last time Stella saw him.

"Hi, Jewel. Kenny's grown." She laughs.

"Yup," Jewel grins as she grabs her son and wedges him under her arm. "Back in the playpen for you, Buster." She sits him on a blanket and offers a stuffed giraffe, which solves her problem for the moment. "Coffee?"

"Thanks." Stella settles at the scarred kitchen table.

"We will examine a crime scene and victim's apartment today. They've asked for my expertise, since neither Stella nor Detective North can find clues on their own," Hester addresses the young mother.

"Harsh, Hester." Stella stares in her friend's direction. "Forensics has been through the place for traces related to the actual murder. We want to study Deena Finch, the person; use her possessions as a window into her personality. We are first on the scene after the police. Detective North will meet us at the apartment. Um. Great coffee, as usual, Jewel."

Once they're settled in the Jeep, Hester avoids any preamble and remarks, "Angus and I are serious, Stella, and I need your advice. Cavelle worries me."

With her eyes maintaining focus on the road while she tries not to betray her shock, Stella replies, "Tell me your concerns. You have my support, Hester."

"If I live with Angus at Raspberry Farm, Cavelle and Jacob will be without my help. I thought I could maintain our little market garden in the summer—do the planning, plant, harvest, and preserve. My family always appreciates my efforts."

"Are they aware of your intentions?"

"No. Angus and I are in the initial phase of our proposed living circumstances. We want to wait until after spring planting, a critical time for everyone, and reveal our arrangements when life quiets. I expect to move in the fall." She pats her skirt. "After we complete the harvest," she adds.

She turns. Stella watches Hester's movements in her peripheral vision. "Sounds fair. Can I help?" She's sure the answer will be "no."

"We require your support when we tell Jacob and Cavelle. If you explain how society accepts that you are older than Nick and haven't considered marriage, they are more likely to understand. Angus and I want a partnership like yours."

As various thoughts fly around inside her brain, Stella agrees to accompany Hester and Angus whenever they speak with her family. "Whatever works, Hester," she says as they pull into the parking lot at the G-plex.

"Such a peculiar structure. I'm interested in the interior layout."

****

Aiden stands in front of Deena Finch's outside entrance. He holds a fist full of latex gloves, unnecessary as Hester carries her own bag of investigative tools.

"Good morning, you two."

Stella accepts Aiden's offer.

"Let's follow the same protocol as Paulina's house. We'll each take an area."

Hester frowns. "Stella and I worked together on clothes and on the upstairs areas, Detective. You searched downstairs."

While his face flushes at the reminder, Aiden adds, "You're right. One couldn't describe this space as big. You two manage her bedroom and bath. I'll handle the kitchen and the living room. We can go in now."

Focused on moving further into the apartment, Hester avoids the marks left on the floor by forensics. She folds her coat and places the garment across a kitchen chair before she makes her way forward with Stella close at hand. She sets her drawstring bag on the bed and removes gloves, a notebook, a pen, and her flashlight. Her eyes scan the room as she mutters, "I'm happy the poor woman didn't die in here. You check the bedside tables. I will start with her armoire."

They both startle when Aiden materializes at the door. "The search team found a box inside the closet which contained items she stole from the other residents. I don't expect you'll find any spoils. More clues into her personality and background are my goal."

"She exhibited obsessive, compulsive tendencies," Hester remarks, her tone flat and factual as she pulls shoe boxes out of the cabinet and arranges them on the bed.

"Yes, as noted in the forensics report." Stella watches her friend. "Will you open every box? They are full of shoes, for heaven's sake."

"A carton with a Polaroid picture of sneakers taped on the end does not confirm footwear inside," she admonishes.

"The camera she used." Stella points at the Polaroid 1000 perched on the corner of the dresser.

They work in silence for fifteen minutes before Hester comments, "Stella, call Detective North. I've discovered a wedding picture and the bride might be the victim." She offers the photo for inspection. "You check."

Stella reaches for the snapshot, faded with age but still readable. The bride is Deena Finch, without a doubt. "Aiden! Hester located a photograph."

Study isn't required. The image reflects their victim.

"Move nothing, Hester." Aiden snaps pictures of the outside and contents, along with the photo and the place in the armoire where the carton sat. Hester stands nearby, hands clasped. Stella remains seated on the side of the bed with a second bedside table drawer yet to be examined.

"Okay. Great. Obviously, the forensics team didn't open every box." He drops the picture into a plastic bag. "Keep up the good work. She ran a sparse kitchen, by the way."

Both women search methodically, as they hold, examine, remove lids, and replace contents.

Incensed, Stella mutters, "We should have found out she was married. My interview with Mary Jo suggested she identified with the challenges of motherhood." She mutters self-admonishment. "Aiden, did the checks completed by your people find no evidence of family?"

"No report yet." He stands in the doorway. "I expect tomorrow. And the federal government isn't cooperative with SIN details, even when the police ask." His chest heaves.

In ten more minutes, she clears the bedside tables. The inside of the armoire reveals no more secrets. Hester searches each item of clothing in the closet. She turns out all pockets and checks every hem and cuff. Stella focuses her attention on the treasure cabinet, which stores jewellery. "My Lord! No wonder she needed a special cupboard. She owned masses of stuff!" Stella's mouth hangs open. "Aiden, come check out her accessories."

He returns to the bedroom again, scraping a shock of white hair off his brow.

"Are any of the pieces stolen?" Stella notices the antique Bakelite in particular.

Reaching for a crumpled piece of paper from his pocket, he scans his list and inspects her findings. "A few of these items could be from reports of items lost or stolen in the last year. I'll take pictures and we can bag the lot."

"The obvious question, Aiden, is why didn't the forensics team check her jewellery cabinet?"

"No idea. They found the cardboard box full of stolen pieces at the back of the clothes closet. Obviously, the murder happened elsewhere, which means only a cursory overview of the bedroom."

"Your employees need a lesson in comprehensive searches." Hester, who has the annoying habit of pointing out the painfully obvious, pulls a key from the waistband of a pair of trousers.

"You may have found the master, Hester. Good job. We've discovered the items she pilfered from her neighbours, but finding the key confirms our theory. I'll ask Mrs. Marigold for permission to check the other doors. Thank you." Aiden extends a gloved hand, accepts her discovery, and places it in an evidence bag.

"There isn't one item out of place in the kitchen." He glances toward Hester. "And yes, I opened and searched inside every box and cookie tin."

"Good job, Detective." Her eyes twinkle as she returns his earlier compliment.

Stella watches Aiden but remains quiet.

"Detective, did the victim line her drawers or use utensil trays?"

"As you noted—compulsive."

"Check beneath."

"Sound idea. I should have thought of that."

"People tuck notes, recipes, or menus under a drawer liner or silverware tray for safe keeping," she replies in a matter-of-fact monotone. With the closet cleared, and the shoe boxes searched and placed on the floor and on the bed, Hester returns her attention to the armoire. She runs her gloved hands along the back and shelves, feeling for any potential hidden compartment. Aiden stands and watches. Afterward, flashlight at the ready, she kneels and peeks under the massive piece of furniture. "Detective, before you leave, there might be a wallet or billfold under here." Aiden retrieves the item after he takes a photo of the location.

"I see a SIN card for Deena Greer," Aiden notes as he pulls another plastic item from a slot. And here's a Visa card and a driver's licence in the name of Deena Onslow. Deena Finch identified herself both as Deena Onslow and Deena Greer.

He returns to the kitchen, and within five minutes, he locates a note tucked under the liner of the drawer which holds potholders and wax paper. "Hester, you were right. I found a letter."

The three of them stand at the counter while Aiden reads the words written to Deena from someone named Odette. *"Your son questions me. I told him I don't know where you live or work. I lied about the work part. Finn wants to see you. He says you owe him. He says he deserves to learn about his mother, and I want to help him. Call me and we'll talk. Odette."* Aiden looks up. "The word 'Deena' is printed on the envelope above 'Groceteria'."

"This letter was probably dropped off at her workplace because Odette didn't have a mailing address for Deena," Stella speculates.

"I'll contact Patricia Brooks once we're finished and find out who delivered this. We've completed a productive morning. I'm off to speak to Mrs. Marigold and call Mrs. Brooks. What about you two?"

"I owe Hester a lunch on me. We'll discuss the side-effects of poisonous plants you can grow in your yard, right Hester?"

"Although I often impart what knowledge I possess, Stella, you only absorb a portion." Hester retrieves her coat from the kitchen chair.

A titter escapes Stella's lips. "Sometimes I wonder how I tolerate you, Hester."

"I regularly think the same, yet here we find ourselves." Her expression remains blank. She shakes Aiden's hand, says she's happy she could be of assistance yet again, and turns toward the door.

Settled at the café, they order the turkey salad bunwich and potato chips before Stella asks her questions. "Hester, what type of poison, when taken at home, causes someone to wet themselves, vomit, experience a heart attack, and die? The coroner said death was because of a massive coronary from an undiagnosed condition."

She sips her tea before she responds. "Foxglove is the obvious answer. Foxglove is the plant used in the manufacture of a medication called digoxin. If you grind the flowers, seeds, and stems into a powder, and ingest the mixture, you could overdose and bring on a heart attack."

"Are you sick first? Not a pleasant experience."

"Yes. I expect a victim would endure serious cramps, shortness of breath, vomiting, and, as you mentioned, excessive urination. Did someone kill themselves with foxglove?"

"Not sure," she sighs. "Maybe Earlene made the poison for her husband to help him, or she decided he was worth less than his insurance. Claims don't pay out after suicide and aren't any use if you're in jail for murder, but a surprise heart attack is another matter. Enough of such talk for today. You and Angus. Tell me more."

CHAPTER 14

Forensics Botched the Job

"I promise I'll be home both Thursday and Friday."

"Yeah, right," Nick snickers, his mouth full of toast. "I scheduled the plumbers and landscapers, and expect Duke, too. I promised Trixie I'd make bread as my contribution for dinner Friday night." He bends and feeds Kiki a piece of crust.

Stella hesitates. "What can I do?"

"Take the next few days off, like you said. The weather doesn't sound good—late season ice storm forecast for Saturday into Sunday."

"Really?" She's out of touch. The thought of a visit to Trixie's, with the entire family, provides a distraction. "Okay. Aiden and his staff have the tools to research the photo we found and find Odette, who must be Deena's sister. They won't need me." She reaches for the jam. "We'll take a kitchen day on Friday and prepare for a storm."

He frowns. "Sort of. I'll start with bread, but will you cook a chicken and boil potatoes and eggs? We'll want food readied in case we lose power. Remember when we were without for three days two years ago? Not fun. I can load wood into the house. Our emergency water jugs are full. I expect the landscapers to cancel, but the plumbers and electricians are coming. I need to supervise."

"No problem." She scrunches her shoulders. "Tucked in for the weekend. Can't wait."

She races upstairs to prepare for their interviews in town. Her first stop will be Aiden's office. She's interested in the story of his encounter with Earlene and the key found with Deena's possessions. He said he scheduled a re-interview with Patricia Brooks at the Groceteria to discuss the letter left for Deena. She's curious to understand why Mrs. Brooks didn't share the information initially. After coffee, they've planned meetings with each of the G-plex residents in their own unit.

****

"Detective North is in his office, Stella." Sergeant Moyer greets her with a wave. She feels welcomed even when his ear is glued to the telephone receiver.

"Hi, Aiden. Busy?" She nods toward the stack of paper on his desk.

"Too much paperwork." He jumps from his chair and grabs his topcoat off the hanger in the corner. "I will tell you my news once I find a decent cup of coffee."

"Nick says there's a storm on the way for the end of the week, on Saturday into Sunday." They walk along the side street, cross Main, and turn toward the café.

"Wasn't aware. Too busy at work. I arrive home and collapse." He opens the door for her. "What kind of storm? Rain?"

"The weather guy on the radio stressed ice. Hard to predict in March." She looks at Tiffany as she approaches.

"Did you say ice storm? We need another day closed," she pouts. "Shall I fetch you both coffee?"

"Perfect," Aiden gushes with an enthusiasm Stella hasn't detected in his voice in weeks. "Hester Painter can find the proverbial needle in a haystack. I give her full credit. I should hire her as a search supervisor."

The scent of coffee intensifies as Tiffany approaches.

"Drink your brew, which you've obviously been craving, but did the key fit, or what?"

"Yes, yes," he nods while he sips. "All three women now know the victim duplicated the master and entered their units at will.

"You're kidding, right?"

"Forensics botched the job. I talked with them yesterday. With such a gruesome scene, the team focused on the spot near the kitchen and front entry, where we found Deena's body. They looked for stolen goods and lucked-out in the closet, but once they discovered the box, they didn't bother with the rest. Hester saved the day—and you, too," he acknowledges.

"Right," she mutters. "Hester can design an orientation workshop where she instructs new hires on proper search protocols over a contrived crime scene."

"Good idea. I wish I could make such a course happen, but budgets are tight." He stares at the acoustic tiled ceiling, missing her intended sarcasm.

Once Tiffany finally moves out of earshot, she prods him for a second time. "Did you talk with Mrs. Brooks?"

"Uh-huh. She introduced two noteworthy pieces of information. First off, a woman dropped off the letter with the cashier on duty, but since Deena no longer worked there, the employee directed her to Mrs. Brooks' office. The description provided isn't useful unless we assume the writer and deliverer are the same person. She's around the same age as Deena."

"And the other?"

"Patricia Brooks said a young man appeared the next day and asked for Deena Onslow. The cashier told him no Deena Onslow worked there. She added the Groceteria employed someone called Deena Finch, but she left after an injury. They didn't reveal an address because of Deena's specific request at the time of hiring. She wanted her apartment location kept in absolute confidence, no matter who enquired."

"What was her reason for not telling us this when we spoke with her two days ago?"

"Witnesses are funny. Sometimes people answer the exact question and won't volunteer more. When I wondered aloud why she didn't mention the note earlier, she said the incident seemed unimportant. Someone delivered a letter—nothing more."

"The guy who nosed around must be her son."

"Yes. Brooks suggested he appeared to be the right age and could be a child of Deena's."

"I bet Deena's married name was Onslow."

"Staff will dig into marriages and births related to the surname Onslow. If there's a connection, they'll find one within the next few days. Let's go. Mrs. Marigold expects us by eleven, and the other two interviews are afterward."

****

"Come in. Come in." Earlene Marigold swings open her front door as they approach. "I kept watch for you."

They enter the stark unit, and Stella thinks again of room vignettes at a furniture store. She seats them at her dining table, offers coffee, which they both refuse, and clasps her manicured hands together once she sits.

"We appreciate you two accommodating our bridge schedule today. We play after lunch." She makes eye contact with them both. "Will you release the apartment soon, Detective? I contracted a new tenant, but the floors need replacement, and the walls require both repair and paint before she moves in."

Stella doesn't ask if Mary Jo Frost is her renter. Aiden must be aware if his sister-in-law has already leased the space, as she intended.

"Forensics requires one more sweep, Mrs. Marigold, before you schedule your trades. We're here today because we discovered information which suggests Deena Finch once used the surnames Greer and Onslow. Are those names relevant to you?"

She covers her mouth with her hand. The gesture strikes Stella as contrived.

"No idea, Detective. She was Deena Finch to me."

Aiden pushes forward. "Did she ever mention an earlier marriage or the existence of a child?"

"Married? I didn't suspect."

"You listened to her defend the lot of mothers during a bridge game."

"Yes, Stella. She admonished Mary Jo because of her remarks on motherhood. Mary Jo can be critical, but I never assumed Deena was a mother."

"Thanks for your clarification, Mrs. Marigold."

"Are you off to see the others now? I'll take you through the lounge."

"Yes. Ms. Carmichael expects us. We appreciate your time, and my office will notify you as soon as we release the unit."

****

Velvet bustles around her small space. She perches on a flowered footstool and directs Aiden and Stella toward chairs. "How may I help you both today?"

Aiden repeats his query related to the names Greer and Onslow. Stella can tell by the flush on Velvet's cheeks she has held back information.

"I'm friends with Deena's sister, Odette Greer. I met her in the waiting room at Dr. Visser's. She visits another physician. We see each other every two weeks in the waiting room. I told her who lived in the G-plex." She inhales. Her cheeks remain flushed, and she tugs on a strand of hair while she speaks. "When she found out her sister was my neighbour, she acted twitchy and uneasy. She said she couldn't come visit me here because she never wanted to run into Deena. She added that if I ever mentioned to anyone that we were acquaintances, she would deny our friendship."

"When we've spoken in the past, you never suggested you were aware of Deena's relatives."

"I didn't want any trouble. I enjoy Odette. We meet at the doctor's office and go for lunch or dinner afterward. She lives in Port Ephron."

"And the name Onslow? Familiar?"

Velvet's face blanks and she clutches her hair. "No. Why?"

"We think Deena was married to someone whose surname is Onslow. We also suspect she gave birth to a son."

"Yes!" She bounces on her perch. "Mary Jo and I figured there was a kid in her past somewhere."

"What else can you tell us, Velvet? We need every detail you're able to remember."

"Odette hated Deena." Velvet lowers her voice and stares at her lap. "She had no idea where Deena lived until she met me, and I spilled the beans. Funny. Odette refused to visit me here to avoid a chance meeting with Deena. She said someone could follow her." Her chin quivers. "I never asked questions. I didn't want to know details."

"She understood Deena hid herself away, and although they hated one another, she was eager not to blow Deena's cover," Stella surmises aloud.

"I wanted Odette as my friend." Velvet ignores Stella's statement. "I detested Deena. Odette felt the same and said she would never reconcile with her sister. I hoped not."

****

They sidestep their way along the box-lined corridor into Tess' bedsitter. The book-peddling business must be slow, since they see as many stacked books as they did the last time they were here. Tess seats them at her kitchen table.

Stella begins. "How's your memoir work with Connie progressing?"

A frown transforms every muscle in her face. "Not well, I'm afraid." She sits straighter in her chair and closes her eyes for a moment. "I will persevere, but Connie isn't why you two are here today."

"No, Ms. Boone. We wonder if you recognize the surnames Greer or Onslow related to Deena Finch."

Her brows lift. "Does she have family? She never suggested she did."

"She may have been married, had a son, and a sister. We haven't connected every dot, but thought you, one of her neighbours, might offer important details." Aiden watches her.

"Detective, as you and Stella realize, Deena Finch was a closed book. I found her distasteful and preferred limited interaction." Her eyes narrow. "If she had relations of any sort, or in any form, I have no insider information. I'm sorry I can't help you further."

"Thank you, Ms. Boone. We're aware of your bridge game scheduled for this afternoon, and we won't trouble you any further."

On the way to Aiden's car, Stella reminds him she won't be available for a few days. "I need family time. The park is swarming with workers, and I expect the ice storm to slow their progress. We're invited for dinner at Trixie's house on Friday night. Call me if your people discover any details on Odette or Deena's in-laws."

Aiden nods but offers no comment.

"I will surprise Nick and be home before noon."

"We could go for lunch."

"Nope. Homeward bound. Call me, though," she repeats.

His hooded eyes remain focused on the road.

****

Her walk with Kiki turns into a chaotic adventure for which she's unprepared. Ahead of the approaching storm, the plumbers, electricians, and landscapers, which are a surprise, pepper the property, completing connections and laying sod. Forecasters describe the in-coming system as fast and brutal, resulting in ice-coated trees and wires, coupled with a swift melt the following day. She overheard a plumber say, "one bad Sunday on the way", and as a result, they want to tie any loose ends. Nick went to the pump house. She expects he's shocked that the landscapers are here. When asked if there would be consequences from the ice, a worker suggested Stella wouldn't need to water right away.

She watches Kiki struggle against the wind while they wander near the cliffs and decides the time has come for a pivot back toward the house. She snuggles inside her collar and lifts the dog into her arms. You'd think the bad weather was already on the doorstep.

Over the next forty-eight hours, they secure the systems on the property while workers complete most of the landscaping. Nick has used the phrase "buttoned-up" a dozen times while he describes his pre-storm work. He and Duke finished the picnic tables and they're safe in the workshop. Between Stella and Nick, they made food ahead, and he baked bread for Trixie as promised. The break from the RCMP detachment, Aiden, and various witnesses has given her necessary rumination time.

While she dresses for their evening at Trixie's, she reviews what they know so far. Deena had a sister named Odette Greer and Deena also appears to have been the mother of a young man named Finn. She must have in-laws—both Finn's grandparents and her ex-husband's parents. She thinks Deena's married name could be Onslow, and she was a Greer before marriage, but both conclusions are assumptions based on the cards in her wallet, the note from Odette, and Velvet's acquaintance with an Odette Greer. Stella's sure Deena hid from her nearest relatives. She may have faked a shoulder and back injury because her sister discovered where she worked, and she couldn't chance visibility in the store every day. More assumptions.

Although over twenty-four hours until the predicted storm nears the coast, the wind rattles the old windows, and she shivers in response. She chooses soft navy velveteen trousers and a turtleneck sweater of fine white cotton for tonight. Nick loads wood into the living room. He took an hour and piled more on the veranda for easy access. They'll complete another check of the property tomorrow. Surely, the weather system can't be as powerful as the news continues to report.

Their drive to Trixie's Craftsman-style cottage-turned-home takes five minutes. They climb the wide porch with the stone pillars while Stella admires the lights, the foggy grey/green colours, and the traditional oak door. Val Reguly, the caretaker for both the Presbyterian Church and the Shale Harbour Community Hall and Playhouse, answers their knock. "Hi, Stella, Nick. Come in."

The main living and dining rooms buzz with voices and laughter. Trixie sashays around the corner, resplendent in a floor-length black skirt paired with a lime green angora sweater. "Welcome, you two. Nick, you are a man of your word." She reaches for the bread.

Stella sets Kiki on the polished hardwood. She bounds toward Mia, Trixie's four-year-old granddaughter. "Is that Dad's voice?" Stella furrows her brows.

"Yup. Carter collected him from the manor." She pats Stella on the sleeve.

"After they met the first time, when Carter went on a visit with Brigitte, Dad believes Carter's his own personal lawyer. Too funny." Her laughter bounces around the entrance hall.

Trixie has embraced Russ Harrison's, or the hit man Harry Russell's, home. Despite the history associated with the property, Trixie used her buy-out money from the park wisely. She's surrounded by her people, which has always been her goal. Besides Val, who has become a permanent fixture, Brigitte and her fiancé, Carter Stephens, are here. Trixie helps care for Mia most days at Yellow House in town, while Brigitte runs the little bookstore and children's reading room. Norbert Kirk, their father, doesn't spend as much time with the family as he did even two or three years ago. He lives at Harbour Manor and feels safest at the complex. He ventured out tonight, which pleases everyone.

With wine in hand, she wanders into the kitchen and asks if Trixie needs her help. "Great gathering. Special occasion or an excuse for a loaf of Nick's bread?"

Her sister leans toward her and whispers, "I hope Carter and Brigitte will announce their wedding date. I expect June, but she won't say. She asked Val to book the community hall, but plans change, and besides, Val knows how to keep a secret."

"I guess we wait and see. What's for dinner?"

"Good grub. Not fancy. I made ribs and baked potatoes. You'll find a big Caesar salad and a bean salad in the fridge. Cheesecake for dessert—Brigitte's contribution."

"Sounds yummy. What can I do?"

"Toss the salad for me, okay? The dressing is in the jar on the counter." She opens the oven and pokes a fork into one potato. "We'll be ready in ten minutes." She stands. "I'll alert Val to refresh drinks before we sit."

Alone in the kitchen, Stella gazes around at the tall cabinets with lighted units near the ceiling. She appreciates the large island and the solid surface countertops. Russ spared no expense. She wonders if her sister uses the combination safe they found in Russ' office. By the time Trixie returns, she's tossed the salad and taken a sip of her wine.

"Any headway on your latest investigation? Did one of the three women over at the G-plex kill Deena Finch?" She lifts the ribs from the oven and plates them. "If I'm honest, the scenario is far-fetched."

"Agreed. We believe we've discovered she had relatives—a sister named Odette Greer, and a son, so even an ex-husband and in-laws. We think the in-laws would be Onslows."

On their way into the dining room, Trixie whispers again. "No murder talk at the table. Let the kids share their news, Stella."

Suitably admonished, Stella falls into line. Before the evening ends, Brigitte and Carter announce they will be married on June 26. Mia claps as they gush with details.

Carter broaches the forbidden topic.

Stella glances toward Trixie, who stares at the medallion trimming the ceiling around the chandelier. "Well, we discovered two names outside the G-plex and we're in search of relatives."

"Names?" Norbert loves names—backwards names, rhyming names. No one knows why.

"Greer and Onslow, Dad. Sound familiar?" Stella strives to humour her father and include him in the discussion, despite his memory issues.

Callin' a boy Finn is a sin," he cackles.

"What on earth is he on about?" Trixie frowns at Stella.

"Finn who, Dad?" Stella's heart pounds.

"Old guy, a grandpa called Hermie, took care of a kid named Finn. Camped at the park. Mean feller. Didn't like him. Are they dead?"

"I hope not, Dad, but you're always a big help when we mention names. Describe mean."

"Yelled at the boy. Grabbed him by the ear. Lotsa Onslows around. Common name from down the shore, and into the city. Any more cheese pie?"

"Sure, Granddad. I'll cut you another slice." Brigitte hops from the table and reaches for her grandfather's dessert plate. Mia scrambles off her chair and follows.

With her elbows propping her chin, Trixie leans across toward Carter. "You felt compelled to mention murder?"

Stella recognizes the softness in her tone as a gentle tease. "We accept help from everyone. Thanks, Dad." She pats her father's flannel sleeve. "Is the manor prepared for the storm?"

"What storm?"

Chapter 15

No Power is Often a Gift

Cool sheets greet her outreached hand. Nick's side of the bed is empty. No Kiki either. Ice shards pummel the roof and distract her from her family's absence. She sways for a second, with the shock, as her bare feet hit the frigid floor. No power. In the gloom of Sunday morning, she deciphers the shadows and remembers not to flush. The pumps won't work without electricity. She drags on sweatpants, a Mount Allison University hoodie, and slip-on sneakers, before she thunders down the stairs in search of Nick.

"Anybody home?" She yells from the kitchen door.

"Hi. Kiki and I are out here on the veranda making coffee. The temperature's risen enough that the ice on the trees is breaking off and hitting the roof. Come out. Crazy times."

She trots through the living room, past the warmth of the crackling fire, and toward his voice. Kiki, with her tiny face pressed against the screen, watches her approach. "You two abandoned me," she accuses, her tone full of affection.

"The noise probably scared her, because she woke, couldn't roust you, and came over to my side of the bed. We used the front lawn this morning, didn't we, Kiki? Falling ice at the back of the house," comes the unnecessary explanation.

Stella bends to pat but changes her mind and lifts the Pomeranian into her arms. "Rough start, little one? What a racket."

"Yeah, the thermometer shows right on zero, which means we're graced with both the ice and the melt. Thank God for the veranda and the Coleman I moved from the cottage yesterday. Cowboy coffee on the way!"

Water boils in a copper saucepan. Nick adds heaped spoonsful of grounds and lets the mixture return to a boil.

"Prepare for strong," he warns. Two mugs sit beside the stove. He holds a kitchen strainer in his left hand and pours, with impressive expertise, through the mesh into a mug. "For Madam." He bows as he places her brew near the edge of the table. She sets Kiki on the deck floor and reaches for the cup.

"Great coffee," she mumbles after her first sip. "I still need milk, though." She returns in a moment with the jug. "Let's go inside and sit by the fire. I imagine we'll eat peanut butter sandwiches for breakfast, right?"

He lifts his brows in mock shock. "No way! I've made plans. Drink up. Surprise coming. I'll lug a bucket of water upstairs for the toilet. Won't be a minute."

Stella and Kiki settle on the couch after she warms her coffee with more from the saucepan. Kiki's snorts, while she cuddles into the blanket Stella pulled from the back of the sofa, interrupt the quiet. No power is often a gift. Without the normal rhythms of appliances, showers running, or other activities which require electricity, she has room in her brain to live in the moment. Nick joins her. They sip together and watch the crackling flames.

Before long, he jumps to his feet. "I'll make another one each and boil more water for us to wash."

"Great." She offers her empty cup. "And breakfast—you made a plan without peanut butter sandwiches?"

"Anticipation counts as half the fun, my love." His eyes twinkle.

After he prepares more coffee for her, he successfully carries two pans of heated water into the kitchen, where they splash faces and hands before resuming their posts near the fire. "You stay here. I'll fetch the platter."

"Breakfast by ten. A great Sunday morning start." She hears him chuckle on the way.

He returns with a large, handled wooden tray, crowded with sliced brown bread, strawberry and plum jams, and peanut butter. After he places his offering on the coffee table, he adds another log to the fire. He holds his finger in a mock freeze signal, dashes into the kitchen again, and comes back in a moment with an iron contraption she's not sure she's seen before, although the design has a vague familiarity.

"What in the world did you find?" Odds and ends often surface on the property—in the cottage, the machine shed, or even the pantry. Nick is great at ferreting out a utensil or cookbook long forgotten by her parents.

"A hand-forged bread toaster." He drops on the sofa beside her and waves the gadget in the air between them. "You stick the bread into one of the upright holders which provide support on both sides. The tip swivels. Ingenious. See? You can place the business end where you want above the fire, and the long handle guarantees you won't burn yourself. I found it in the machine shop and showed Matt Savioli at Parlour Antiques. His research confirmed it's an eighteenth-century hand-forged wrought iron rotary fireplace toaster. I don't know where your parents discovered such a tool, but Matt says the value is in the hundreds of dollars, maybe thousands." He stops for breath. "I've cleaned each section and we'll enjoy our toast without power! I considered a fire outside, but the fireplace will be as much fun and safer, given the ice."

"And the dangers of eating food cooked on antique wrought iron?" She's half serious.

"No idea." He shrugs. "One time can't hurt." He points at the heart-shaped holders. "While the bread cooks, the toaster impresses a design on the sides."

"Well, if hearts are the goal, let's get busy." She leans into him, much to Kiki's discomfort.

Results are better than she expected. Smothered in Hester's jam, and chased by cowboy coffee, they enjoy their unique Sunday morning breakfast, before a raucous knock on the veranda door brings them back to reality. They stare at one another, momentarily startled. Not a day for unexpected company. Nick sets his plate on the table and answers.

****

Duke peers around Nick into the living room. "Mornin' folks. You've made the most of nasty circumstances."

"Cloris. Duke. Come in out of the damp."

They both step inside, although Duke waits for Cloris to enter before him. Her curls poke past the raised collar of her faux-fur coat, which gives the impression a large raccoon has swallowed all of her except her head. Duke braves the weather in typical Duke fashion, clad in his leather jacket with the fringes on the sleeves. "Wet and cold. No power in Port Ephron. Cloris figured we'd drive out here and see how you two were gettin' on." He squints at the breakfast preparations. "Pretty good, by the smell of your livin' room."

"I'll take your coat, Cloris. Please sit. Coffee? I'll light the Coleman again. Ready for you in no time."

"Thank you, Nick." She turns toward Stella. "Don't let him lead you astray. John has information that he assumes will prove pertinent to your investigation. He insisted we drive through the mess and come see you, regardless."

"The roads must be horrible, Cloris. I admire your driving skills. I refuse to venture out today." Stella's surprised they made the trip.

"Good truck and good tires. I've been through worse." She pats her perm.

"Any more toast?" Duke asks, while he makes himself comfortable in one of the leather chairs which frame the fireplace.

They settle. Nick serves them coffee and Stella works the newly discovered modern convenience toaster. Duke and Cloris both devour whatever they're offered as if they haven't eaten in days.

"Power's been off in the Port since supper time last night."

"Don't talk with your mouth full, John." Cloris tut-tuts her impatience. "Honest to God."

"Kiki, come visit with me." Duke ignores Cloris and eyes the dog.

Stella doesn't encourage her to crawl out of the blanket nest. "She'll show more interest once she moves off the couch, Duke, which might be a while, eh, Kiki?" She ruffles the dog's ears. "Now, what information needs sharing?"

"I guess we're gonna talk murder and dead girlfriends," Cloris mumbles in Nick's general direction.

Nick reaches for the toaster and crouches in front of the fireplace. "Fine with me. We often discuss criminal behaviour at Shale Cliffs, as you might imagine."

His support doesn't go unnoticed.

"Deena Finch was mother to a son. Did you know?"

"We've pieced together basic information, Duke. Tell me."

"She mentioned havin' a kid—positive she said a boy. She hadn't seen him in a long time. Seemed scared of her in-laws. They were raisin' him. I don't remember anythin' else. She kept her business private. I forgot, what with the excitement of her murder and stuff." He wipes his mouth with the back of his hand before Cloris offers him a napkin.

"Aiden will call you, I'm sure."

"Great. Nick, are you cookin' more toast for me?"

They linger for an hour. Cloris decides the power might be on in Port Ephron and they could start the treacherous drive home. The temperature hovers around zero Celsius. Hopefully, road conditions have improved.

After Nick locks the veranda door and returns to the comfort of the couch and the fire, the house suddenly hums. Electricity graces Shale Cliffs once again.

****

"Hi. I assumed you'd be home, but thought I'd try the Shale Harbour office first and there you are. Travel still isn't recommended, according to the radio, by the way."

"Emergency vehicles are exempted, Stella. I'm a police officer."

"Okay," she answers. "Point taken. I won't be in town any time soon, but I've learned details you might find useful. Has your team uncovered any information?"

"They've found Odette Greer in Port Ephron and continue to dig for weddings."

"I can provide a shortcut. Dad helped."

"Good grief, Stella. Really? Has your father cracked another case?" Aiden emits a half-hearted snort. With his random thoughts last summer, Norbert reminded Aiden of a gunman named Harry Russell. Everyone was together one night at a family and friends party, when her dad became fixated on people whose names were reversible. The solution to this riddle began with the reversible names of Edward Thomas and Frances Ellis, then ended with Russ Harrison. Known as Harry Russell, a hit man Aiden tried to arrest many years earlier, they uncovered his identity after Norbert triggered a memory for Aiden.

"Dad rattled off: 'it's a sin callin' a boy Finn'."

"Come on," he encourages. "You've caught my attention. What happened?"

Stella launches into the story where Norbert recalled a child named Finn who camped with his grandfather, Hermie Onslow. "He described the old man as mean. He recalled, probably because of their interactions. Dad has always hated seeing children mistreated by adults. Mom often needed to discourage him from intervening. Back when we were kids, you didn't interfere with other people's families. I remember how Dad felt bad because the Painters locked Hester away and didn't allow her to go to school."

"I'll instruct my staff to search for a Herman Onslow and see what we can uncover."

"Duke and Cloris arrived yesterday despite the conditions. Because of the ice dropping from the trees, Duke said Cloris held her purse over her hair while she ran for the cover of the veranda. He teased her by suggesting she needed a bigger handbag."

"They shouldn't have been on the road."

"Understood. Or under my trees, either, but Cloris prides herself on the fact she can drive her truck through any, and all, conditions." She pauses to refocus. "In any event, Duke remembered a conversation with Deena when they went out on a date. She told him she had a son but didn't see him anymore. Duke described her as acting afraid of her in-laws."

"I must call Duke and hear his recollections for myself. We may find ourselves blessed with suspects besides the three residents of the G-plex. Are you able to interview Deena's sister with me? I expect we'll schedule her in on Wednesday."

"Okay."

"Staff will locate the boy and his grandparents now, thanks in no small measure to Norbert."

"Before I let you go, tell me the latest on Rosemary. Discharge soon?" She wonders if Aiden is ready for Rosemary's homecoming.

His moan rattles along the line. "Not imminent, but not distant, either. She's regressed. Her habit reversal therapy, as they call her attempt at normal behaviour, flew out the window."

"What's happened?" Stella cringes at the idea of Rosemary living at home again after the threats the woman made toward her in early January.

"Well, the last time I saw her, a week ago, she greeted me at her door and called me Big Daddy. Annette Funicello might be back."

"Honestly, Aiden, you've always preferred the prom queen compared to the empty shell she becomes with too much medication on board, or when she avoids the pills and fakes normalcy." She stops and doesn't add how the "not-medicated" Rosemary scares her.

"She can't live with me anymore, Stella."

The hard edginess and determination in his voice comes as a shock.

"No amount of support from Toni or Mary Jo will help. I could retire, but the work gives me purpose. If I'm honest, spending my retirement babysitting a mentally ill woman who cares little about herself, or me, would be hell on earth based on my years of experience. Do I sound harsh?"

"Yes, but no. You've spent your married life with Rosemary's challenges. Everyone has their limits. What will happen if you don't accept her home?"

"I've spoken with Toni and Mary Jo. They've never abandoned their sister, although Mary Jo is on the edge. They accused me of desertion, and they're right. Financial support is no problem, but I refuse to provide direct care anymore. My plan is to list the house for sale, if she can't live by herself, and move into Shale Harbour. Cavelle Painter is helping me find a place."

"You've moved fast and considered every variable. I'm sorry, Aiden. No one can accuse you of not doing the best you could do. Listen. Come for dinner on Wednesday night, after we conduct the Odette Greer interview in Port Ephron. I'll persuade Nick to cook a chicken. Nick's chicken dinner will cure whatever ails you," she inserts as an afterthought.

"Invitation accepted, but Nick's prowess in the kitchen won't do the trick for this issue. May I bring a guest?"

"Do you expect Rosemary to be home on a pass?" She winces at the thought, but will include Rosemary, if necessary.

"No. Someone else."

"Sure. Anyone I know?"

"Ask Nick to plan for four, okay? I'll contribute the beer he likes."

After they say their goodbyes, she leans into the back of her chair and closes her eyes. He avoided her questions. She assumes Aiden must have a colleague he wants along so they can discuss the case. She leaves her office and trots into the kitchen.

****

"Hi, little one. Why are you here by yourself?" Kiki's alone, curled in her fluffy bed tucked into the corner near the table. Stella hears the crunch of a metal scraper and realizes Nick has gone outside to remove ice from the doorsteps and walkways. She should help. She pats the dog, trots through the living room, and opens the veranda door. "Do you need me?"

"No. Not right now." He glances toward her and lifts his brows. "Finished for the time being. Did you plug in the perk?"

"Yup."

"I'll be in." He points at the ice-coated lower stairs. "I'll let Mother Nature take care of the rest. The radio said the temperature will climb well above zero today."

"Great." She's relieved she won't be required to manhandle a chisel. "I want to discuss news and ask a favour."

"On my way." He drops his tools on the veranda floor with a clatter.

Once seated, with a warm drink and a banana muffin at hand, he asks, "What's your request?" He then snickers. "I'm at your service."

"Can you make dinner on Wednesday, a roast chicken or another concoction?"

"Right," he munches. "Do we expect guests?" He reaches for a second muffin.

"Aiden and a friend. He and I scheduled an interview with Odette Greer in Port Ephron in the afternoon. His people located her without too much trouble. He asked if he could bring a guest to dinner."

"No problem. I found a new recipe for cranberry chicken in one of your mother's old cookbooks. I'll experiment. No pressure." He snickers again. "What's the news?"

"Aiden doesn't plan to accept Rosemary back. He wants to end their marriage and explained how he'll support her. He says she can live with Toni or by herself, because he can't take care of her anymore. Frankly, I was shocked."

"Surely he's accumulated enough service years by now to retire and be home for her."

"Yes, but regardless of his time on the job, he loves the work and refuses to exchange policing for care giving. He's talked with Cavelle and said he's interested in a place in Shale Harbour, so will put his Port Ephron house on the market, if Rosemary doesn't want to live there alone."

Nick's silence unnerves her. He stares across the table. Muffin crumbs hang from his fingertips. When he eventually responds, she's surprised.

"He's dumped his mentally ill wife and plans to move closer to you." His eyes narrow.

She sways in her chair and stutters her fierce denial. "Nick, Aiden has no influence over me. The man's a troubled person with mountains of baggage. I'm not interested in him. We resolved any issues related to Aiden ages ago. Besides, the man keeps a trailer here in the park."

"The Norths lived in Port Ephron, Stella."

His voice thuds its dullness.

"Now, he'll be single and live in Shale Harbour—permanently. You may not even realize your affection for him. He's always been with Rosemary," he mumbles.

"I don't care for Aiden North as any more than a friend. You and I are a team." Her eyes soften while she studies his troubled face. "As much as I often wonder why you stick around with this old gal, I love you, Nick. We're partners. I want my life no other way."

He tips his cup and drains the last few drops. "I'm back outside. Let's see how Wednesday night goes before you decide he isn't interested."

While she rinses the dishes, she can hear the scraper bang into the ice. He's taking out his frustrations, rendering Mother Nature's help unnecessary.

CHAPTER 16

Wednesday, March 31, 1982
The Players

Earlene

She runs her fingers across her new yellow quilted bridge cloth before she arranges the cards and the score pad on the table. Earlene expects Mary Jo any minute. Previously scheduled as Deena's rotation, Mary Jo promised dessert if Earlene set up the room. Her thoughts wander to Deena Finch's murder. Although the police released the scene, the ice storm over the weekend put a crimp in her plans. She's hired men to move Deena's possessions into the ample basement of the G-plex, accessible only via a locked door in her unit. Since Detective North and Stella Kirk suggested the poor woman did, in fact, have family, they will eventually return her belongings to someone as yet unknown to her. No harm in keeping Deena's property in storage here. The weather delayed the painters and flooring installers, but serious activity starts before the end of this week. She glances at the clock. Mary Jo taps on the patio slider while she balances a covered cake plate in one hand and her handbag in the other. Pleasure crosses Earlene's typically stern countenance. She likes Mary Jo, with her gruff and opinionated personality. She speaks her mind.

A gust of cool, damp air invades the lounge when she slides the door open. "Come in, Mary Jo. What did you bring for us today? My goodness, what a big cake plate."

"Can't take the credit," she blusters. "Toni offered an angel food concoction with lemon filling and boiled icing because she thought I should create a good impression." She sets the milk glass pedestal server on the side counter and lifts the lid. "I couldn't build a cake, for sure." She turns and faces Earlene. "When I move in here, I'll make you pumpkin cookies each time my turn for dessert comes along. They're all I know how to bake." She snorts.

Earlene frowns as she opens the refrigerator. "Put your offering in here, if you want—and I'll be on the horn with Toni, if you don't produce," she teases. "I assume our lease agreement can be made public today and we can share our news with the girls. I expect the painters tomorrow and the floor installers on Friday. Move in by Monday, April fifth, if that suits you."

"Perfect. My house closes the end of April, which leaves three weeks to ready my old place once the tenants move out." As they walk toward the bridge table, Tess and Velvet enter the lounge via their access doors. "Hi, you guys." Mary Jo waves. "Guess what?"

"When do you finally take up residence?" Velvet bounces on slippered feet. Her loose hair flies around the shoulders of her black and gauzy dress, which resembles a nightgown.

"I hope soon, Mary Jo." Tess' soft voice soothes and supports. "It's wonderful you're to join us."

"Okay, everyone. But before she moves, workers will be in the unit the rest of the week—movers, flooring installers, and painters. The noise might be an annoyance, but for a few days, at most. Mary Jo arrives for good on April fifth. Now, let's play a hand or two of bridge."

Partnered with Tess, who can be reticent, Earlene soon has the perfect hand for a finesse opportunity. With Tess as the dummy, she leads the Eight of Spades from the board but doesn't know who holds the King. She has the Ace and Queen in her hand. Mary Jo offers the Ten of Spades and covers the Eight. Earlene plays her Queen and hopes Mary Jo held back her King. She expects she's correct when Velvet plays the Seven of Spades, which enables a successful finesse. She leads her Ace before she switches suits. If anyone holds their King to play later, she'll trump Spades because she's void. Fate deals the cards, but one's success is in how you play the hand.

After four consecutive rounds, they break for tea and coffee. Mary Jo produces and serves her contribution. Earlene notices how the dishes tremble when she sets plates in front of Tess and Velvet. Surprised Mary Jo might be nervous, she helps, and whispers, "We're friends here. Relax."

"No one on the face of the earth ever relaxed because someone told them to, Earlene," she hisses her reply, "but thanks anyway."

Over dessert, which proves light, refreshing, and decadent with thick boiled icing, discussion turns to Deena and her personality. "Her continual barrage of unsolicited advice and 'why' questions bothered me most," Velvet stutters. "Did anybody else notice?"

Earlene nods.

"Tell me what you mean, Velvet." Mary Jo's voice encourages her with both interest and kindness.

"She asked stupid questions." Velvet mimics Deena's confrontational tone. "'Why don't you cut you hair? Why don't you volunteer at the library? Why don't you sell your old chair?' I felt uneasy and hesitant to answer. She forced me to qualify any decision I ever made—to her."

"You're right. She expected me to justify my life choices, too." Tess nibbles her lip. "She said, 'Why don't you ask your friend Frances for help? Why don't you find a real publisher, instead of Gorman Printing? What will you do with your stock of books?' On and on. She never held back. As is often mentioned, one hates talking ill of the dead, but I won't miss her questions."

"Toni's cake tastes scrumptious." Velvet wipes crumbs from her lips and eyes Mary Jo with affection. "I'm sure I can represent everyone when I tell you how happy we are because you will be Earlene's new tenant."

Mary Jo rests her elbows on the table, which trembles under the force. "I expect I'm the one person prepared to live in a murder scene, but the idea of a unit here pleases me." She folds her napkin with precision while she connects her gaze with each woman. "I decided not to stay with Toni, and my sister Rosemary, after she's discharged from hospital. Need some separation, but they're bound to visit with me here in my apartment occasionally. I hope that won't put any of you off."

She didn't expect Rosemary North to be welcomed at Mary Jo's, and the revelation shocks Earlene. Too many stories involving the sister who has controlled both her siblings and her husband for most of their lives have circulated over the last months. She hopes Mary Jo will use her sister's home as the meeting place instead of the G-plex but keeps her concerns to herself. "Okay, ladies, let's get back to our game. And Velvet was correct, Mary Jo. Delicious cake. Toni can bake for us anytime."

"Before we start, Earlene, congratulations on your finesse earlier. Good job. I'll be more alert next time." Mary Jo winks at her new landlady.

****

Velvet

"Shall we begin? I want to play a solid ninety minutes, people." Earlene takes charge, and whenever she does, Velvet becomes distracted. She grabs a tendril of her hair but forces her hand away from her mouth. Earlene will yell if she chews.

They sit in silence for a full round of four hands. Velvet's mind wanders to other issues. Stella said they found indicators at Deena's. She assumes pictures or other mementoes made them assume she married at one point and gave birth. She wanted her past kept secret, but hid telltale signs of her former life nearby.

As if the words can no longer stay inside her brain and must fly out into the world, Velvet places the deck of cards on the table beside her before she deals, and blurts, "I suffered a miscarriage at twenty-five. The father never knew and there's no evidence. I can't prove my story. I saved no mementoes."

Three pairs of eyes stare at her in stunned silence.

"What has brought this on, Velvet? How awful." Tess, positioned at her left, places her right hand on Velvet's arm. "My sympathies, dear."

"I'm sorry, too, V. You never said." Mary Jo wipes moisture from the corner of her eye. "You poor soul."

"And the reason for your revelation today?" Earlene rests her elbows on the table and her chin in her hands.

She accepts Earlene's formal, yet clumsy, sincerity. "We've discussed Deena and how she birthed a child but didn't tell us. There could be multiple reasons. Maybe the kid died. Maybe her husband stole their baby away from her. Maybe someone else did the stealing. Horrible events happen. I can understand why a person avoids revealing life-changing issues in their lives." She stands and wanders over to the counter, finding a napkin, and blowing her nose. "I don't want to die and afterward, you three discover I experienced a miscarriage. You'd think I lied throughout our friendship. You are my friends and deserve the truth. My one stab at romance failed, and I said never again."

Earlene's questions persist. "Was there a chance to keep the baby if the poor child had lived?"

Velvet returns, sits, and focuses on the tablecloth before she answers. "I expect authorities would have insisted I surrender a live birth, because I had a hard enough time caring for me. I had started steady work three months earlier, and my entire world risked being upended."

"Was the loss for the best in the end?" Mary Jo leans across the table.

"Yes," she replies in a soft voice. "Funny. We've often said that we are the bridge ladies who never bore children. Deena became the exception. Although mine died, I guess I'm an exception, too."

"We can discuss your experience whenever you want," Mary Jo adds before she pulls back to her side of the table.

"Thank you for listening and for your kindness. I feel better because I've been honest. Shall we play?" Velvet inhales deeply and calms herself, a technique learned years ago in the hospital.

Her palms sweat when she wins the contract, but she expects her cards to provide the resources needed to make the bid. Can she remember what they have played so far? She leads her Three of Diamonds. The King of Diamonds, from Mary Jo's hand, sits exposed on the board. If Tess has the Ace of Diamonds, she may save the King. Tess plays a Ten, Velvet jumps in with the King from the board, but typical for Velvet, Earlene slaps the Ace of Diamonds on the trick and Velvet's effort to advance her King fails. She frowns, but soldiers on. Down two.

"Don't be ashamed, Velvet," comes Mary Jo's kind response. "Did you know fifty per cent of finesse attempts fall flat?"

"Thanks, Mary Jo. Tess deals next. Anyone else want more tea or coffee?" Velvet hops from her chair and dashes toward the counter. She avoids contact for a moment. Finesses are confusing. She can't keep her options straight. Chances are, there's a face card split. The same circumstance has happened many times. Bridge might not be her game.

When she sits at the table with her tea refreshed, she finds Earlene has laid out the hand just played. "See, Velvet? There was no chance because of the way the cards fell. Tess and I held the Ace, Queen, Jack, and Ten between us. Whenever you offered the King, I could cover with the Ace. Don't fuss. You tried."

As Tess deals, Velvet senses Earlene's gaze - hot breath on the side of her face. She turns.

"Velvet, when I first accepted you as a tenant, I must admit I worried. You're a quirky person, and your history sounded troubling. Understand how pleased I am you're living here. You can talk with anyone or all of us whenever you need."

"Thank you," she mumbles from behind her hair, which now shields her face from everyone's view, except for Mary Jo. "Let's be honest, though. We each possess a measure of quirky, in our own way." Her eyes meet Earlene's and twinkle. "Don't you agree?"

****

Tess

Tess doles out the cards. The heavy silence around the table, after Velvet's revelation, presses down on her. "Pass," she says.

Mary Jo mutters, "Pass."

"Pass," says Earlene.

"Oh, for heaven's sake," Velvet blusters while she throws her hand into the centre. "One of you three held points."

"Not enough for a bid," Earlene replies. "One more time, Tess."

Earlene shuffles while Mary Jo slides the deck made earlier toward Tess. Velvet cuts and they repeat the ritual.

"Was anyone as scared of Deena as me? She appeared in my apartment unannounced on countless occasions. I contemplated leaving the building and moving away."

"Yes, I was aware." Earlene remarks with quiet authority.

"I stayed because I trust you. Honestly, I trust each of you. Since the discovery Deena has relatives, we might not be suspects anymore."

Velvet lifts her face and gazes around the table. "I often have lunch with her sister."

"What?" Tess gasps. What has motivated Velvet to keep such information private? "Velvet, you never said a word."

"You mentioned fear. Odette was afraid for, and of, Deena. She told me if I ever revealed we knew one another, our friendship was over." Her eyes puddle. "I levelled with the police when they asked. Didn't they question you regarding the names Greer and Onslow?"

"Certainly," Earlene replies, "but Tess and I," she glances across the table for confirmation, "didn't recognize either name."

"They said they expected she had in-laws, a son, and a sister because of evidence they found in her unit," Tess contributes. "Big surprise to me."

"Describe Odette."

Mary Jo is always encouraging. Tess pauses her deal for now.

Velvet reveals her history with Deena's sister. She tells them how Odette didn't want Deena to be aware she discovered where her sister lived. After Velvet's revelation, Odette visited the Groceteria. Velvet's voice trembles when she recalls how she spoke of Deena as a tenant at the G-plex because she discussed her personal living arrangements with Odette. She was unaware Deena kept her location a secret. Her privacy mattered to her, but lots of people prefer their own space. In Tess' limited experience, such a case isn't unusual.

"Was Deena afraid of a person or persons? Was she in witness protection, or hiding, I wonder?" Tess frowns. Odette could have murdered Deena. Sisters often find themselves angry at one another. The iron became a weapon of opportunity. Unknown to Velvet, Odette might have visited her sister. "I don't think the murderer is after any of us. We aren't hateful." She gazes at her friends for confirmation.

"From what Odette has said, Deena cut herself off from her family, which included her son." Velvet's voice trembles. "I can't imagine abandonment of my child by choice. Odette called me and told me the police will interview her around three today." She turns toward Tess. "Could we play bridge now? Let's focus on Diamonds and Spades instead of babies and murders."

"Fine with me." Tess distributes the cards.

Tess has the contract, and she holds her breath while she eyes the Queen of Hearts from Earlene's dummy hand on the board. She hopes Mary Jo, on her left, has the King of Hearts and plays the card, which will make the Queen good in the next round. Trumps are out and she still has her Ace of Hearts. Mary Jo offers the Ten of Hearts and covers the Six which was led. Tess plays her Queen from the board, expecting Mary Jo held back her King, but in the end, Velvet slaps the King of Hearts on top of her Queen. Another failed finesse.

"Good grief. I was sure I could make use of your Queen, Earlene. I suspected Mary Jo held the King."

"I never hold back a card when it beats the highest one on the board, Tess. Not when you've sloughed a low one. The trick was a loser regardless of the Queen." Mary Jo huffs her annoyance.

"Mary Jo, please don't be cross," Velvet admonishes, much to Tess' relief. "We avoid criticism. We turn errors or mistakes into teaching moments, okay? You can't change the hand, just how you play."

In a spontaneous and magnanimous decision, Tess leans toward Mary Jo. "Playing the Queen was a mistake. Lesson learned, ladies. Now, who deals next?"

****

Mary Jo

"My round." Mary Jo reaches for the deck and slides the pack along for Tess' cut. The women of the G-plex hold expectations. Toni reminds her regularly of her gruff exterior and judgmental attitudes. She distributes the cards. "I'm excited." She glances toward Earlene. "I'll be over in a heartbeat once the workers fix the floors and walls." She wants to reinforce her pleasure with the move.

"I understand you said the idea of a murder in the apartment doesn't bother you, but don't you care someone you knew died in the living room?" Tess' eyes widen.

"Not in the least. I didn't kill Deena…and neither did any of you. Toni asked me the same question."

"And transportation, Mary Jo?" Velvet is aware the Mustang she drives belongs to Toni.

"Part of my arrangement with Toni was I'd buy a car if I moved over here. She can't give up the 'Stang. I'm purchasing a VW Rabbit—last year's model. The dealer was selling his demonstrator. I gave him a deposit." She glances at each woman. "I'll be happy to drive anybody anywhere. Bad weather and roads don't bother me. Anytime."

Velvet and Tess both nod with enthusiasm. Neither drives much, and they share Tess' 1975 Toyota Corolla when they need a vehicle. "I'm excited you'll be here, Mary Jo." Velvet blushes while she picks through her cards. "When do you expect your sister's discharge this time?"

"Within weeks." Mary Jo makes a spontaneous decision and confides in her soon-to-be neighbours. "We aren't sure of her release date, but she won't be moving back with Aiden—Detective North, to you guys—because he's decided on a separation. He'll sell their house in the Port if Rosemary doesn't want to live alone, and he wants to settle over here, too. He told Toni he'd cover her expenses, but not cohabitate with Rosemary anymore."

"Both you and your brother-in-law will abandon your sisters, Mary Jo."

Earlene's face remains blank, but her words carry a sting.

"I'll help," Mary Jo sputters. "One Heart. I promised Toni I'd come whenever she needs me. Listen. Toni and I have reassembled the pieces, which are our sister, countless times—since we were children. We hoped, if I rented my duplex and moved in with Toni, we could create the perfect solution to assist Aiden. I sold my property when the time was right and Rosemary's ready for discharge yet again. If she became a permanent patient, I would stay put, but I can't handle her anymore on a steady basis. She's often violent and smacked me once." She studies her cards.

The table remains quiet, with no reaction to her remark or counter to her bid. They might not be supportive of Rosemary coming to visit. She should not have mentioned the violence. Mary Jo must honour the contract for one heart. The group quiets while Earlene places her first card on the table, and Velvet arranges her dummy hand. Mary Jo stops and sets her cards face down. "Please understand how excited I am to live here. I need the space. Stuck under the same roof with my sisters isn't for me, and I admit my mistake. Now, can we play?"

At the end of the last round, Tess apologizes again. Earlene closes her eyes in an obvious attempt at patience. "Listen, Tess. As we said before, fifty per cent of finesses fail. Our odds were below average today, but there'll be a next time." She reaches across the table and pats Tess' hand. "Mary Jo, you've over half a cake left. None of us want Toni to feel we didn't appreciate her dessert. I, for one, will fetch a plate from my apartment and cut a slice for later."

Velvet claps her hands. "Me, too."

Before Mary Jo suggests the dessert can return home because she'll be happy eating the rest with Toni, the three women scurry into their respective units. She fills the bar sink with soapy water. They keep a set of plates, bowls, mugs, and cups and saucers, along with silverware, in their shared room for communal use. She washes the dishes and reflects on her new housemates. No, she won't live with them, but they'll be nearby. Tess, with her books, her nervousness about each element of her life, and her sick sister, needs constant support. And sweet Velvet—who has a crush on her. Mary Jo admires Velvet, understands her struggles, and appreciates her progress through a mental illness similar to Rosemary's, but a romantic involvement with Velvet is out of the question. She frowns. Good friends. Just good friends. Earlene presents a different story. She strives to assess Earlene, a decent person, but with an impenetrable shell. *I'll fit in. No choice. The deal's struck.*

When they return, with a symphony of closed doors and various exclamations because she's washed the dishes, she reaches for the clean knife and pulls the dessert from the refrigerator. She cuts three pieces of cake but leaves enough to share with Toni tonight. They determine the date of their next game and who will prepare the room.

"Despite our many discussions and revelations," Earlene acknowledges Velvet with a brisk nod, "we're finished ahead of our four o'clock schedule today. Most games run later. See you soon, and remember to lock your inside doors, girls. Must race to the grocery store. The list for our next game is on the wall." Earlene breezes into her unit.

"Thanks for being my partner, Mary Jo—and for the cake. May I invite you for supper at my apartment tonight?"

She remembers her steadfast commitment and declines. "Promised Toni I'd be home by five."

Chapter 17

The Beginning is Good

"Must look your best for 'the man'," he says as he watches her change for her three o'clock interview in Port Ephron. Nick can't get over the idea of Aiden's potential move to Shale Harbour, and his planned separation from Rosemary. Any attempt to focus her thoughts on Odette Greer becomes impossible.

Lunch turned into a disaster. They included Duke because he came to the park and helped with landscape work needed before the season begins. She made salmon salad bunwiches, coleslaw, a veggie platter, and scrounged chocolate chip cookies from the freezer, for when the two men appeared. She expected them to be hungry. Duke plowed through while Nick picked at his food. The air hung damp and motionless with what she interpreted as his anger and jealousy.

"Guess what? Did you know the 'great detective' plans a relocation into Shale Harbour?" He asked Duke an unnecessary question as he pushed coleslaw around on his plate.

While he glanced at Stella, Duke lifted his brows and mumbled, "Hadn't heard. What's wrong with poor Rosemary? Are they keepin' her in the loony bin?"

"Oh, no." Nick draweled his reply. "Detective North will ditch his wife of twenty-five or more years to live nearer Stella."

"Come on, Nick." Exasperated, and with an urge to run, her face burned. "His move isn't because of me. He wants out of Port Ephron, and he spends half his time in the Shale Harbour RCMP office, anyway."

"You're the expert," came the sullen retort.

Duke took Kiki for a walk and Nick followed her upstairs after they washed the lunch dishes in silence. The back of her neck prickled. She's never appreciated the jealous version of Nick, which has appeared on rare occasions over their time together.

Flattery tickles a sliver of her mind, but not enough to ignore his unacceptable behaviour, especially the idea she might be dressing to impress Aiden. "Shall I expect a similar attitude when he and his mystery guest arrive for dinner tonight? I'm shocked." She throws a sweater on the bed, tears off her sweatshirt, and stops to face him in her bra and blue jeans. "You and I are a team. We've discussed the subject more than once. Aiden and I have a history. You said you understood. I love you."

He interrupts her tirade and points out she might mention the love part more often, but his eyes shimmer. He's seated on one of the wingback chairs flanking the balcony door. "You're not the problem, Stella. I worry Aiden will put the moves on you when he sees you as vulnerable. You represent his safety net."

She finishes dressing, relieved he's harnessed control of his initial outburst. "Aiden and I dated thirty years ago. We had no contact after high school until he arrived here in Shale Harbour." She stops and frowns. "If you recall, he didn't come near until Lorraine Young died. He never even telephoned to say hi."

"Yes." He watches her while she pokes earrings into her pierced ears. "I remember now. You were as shocked as anybody when he appeared."

Nick's right. He didn't reach out to her when he came back to Port Ephron, which was surprising. Since investigations have brought them together, she's ignored Aiden's occasional remarks when he's mentioned their high school romance. She has no room for Aiden in her life but has often wondered if her lover imagines another scenario. "End of the jealousy, Nick. There's no spark, and there will be no spark, between Aiden and me. You don't wear green well, and I, for one, am not appreciative." She avoids a stomp of her foot, but the urge remains.

"No more, I promise." He stands, approaches, and wraps his arms around her shoulders.

"I felt embarrassed in front of Duke," she mumbles into his chest.

"Understood. I'll apologize. You finish or you'll be late."

****

Another crisis averted. Focus on the task at hand is necessary now. She pulls the Jeep into the parking lot at the Port Ephron RCMP detachment office and checks her watch. If she breezes through, she might make their appointment, but by the time they call Aiden and she's forced to wait, she won't. The last circumstance when she was tardy for an interview, Nick was the cause, but the reason was considerably more amorous.

"Go right in. Detective North is waiting in the meeting room."

The civilian on duty glances in her direction and waves her in—an uncommon occurrence in this location. She races along the passage and sees Aiden through the hallway glass, seated alone. "Hi. Am I late?" Her watch shows five minutes past three.

"No problem," he huffs. "We'll speak to Odette in a minute. I wanted to prepare you for my date tonight."

"Prepare me? Date? I said we'd welcome a guest. I assumed you were bringing a staff member who has worked on the case."

"I'm involved with someone. She knows you, but I want her identity to be a surprise."

Nick will be the one surprised. She struggles for a supportive response. "You are exercising your options, Aiden. Marriage doesn't complicate another relationship in the least." She punctuates her sarcasm with a smirk.

"You and Nick are the first people we'll tell. I've bought a house, but I'll save the details for tonight as well." He winks, as if in possession of the best-kept secrets in town. "Now. Odette Greer, younger sister of Deena Finch. She agreed to meet with us today, to share Deena's true history and the nature of her estrangement from her family. She's not here as a suspect at present. We need more information."

A young constable enters the room. "Ms. Odette Greer, Detective."

****

Stella had glanced at the file earlier. Odette Greer is forty-five, a pharmacy technician here in Port Ephron, and the murder victim's younger sister. She watches the woman approach without fanfare, take the seat Aiden offers, and sit with her handbag clasped in her lap. For a moment, Hester crosses Stella's mind.

Odette Greer's medium build supports shoulder-length brown hair peppered with blond streaks. Although no authority, Stella figures the colour doesn't appear professional. She cuts her nails straight across and her hands are without rings, likely because of job requirements coupled with personal taste. Her clothes are tidy and clean. Odette would fade into any crowd today.

"Good afternoon, Ms. Greer. I am Detective Aiden North and," he nods toward Stella, "my community consultant, Stella Kirk."

"Happy to make your acquaintance." Her soft voice projects a whisper-like quality. She meets his gaze before she turns and smiles at Stella.

"First off, we are sorry for your loss, Ms. Greer."

"Please call me Odette. The formality makes me nervous." She scratches a patch of mottled red skin on the back of her hand.

"Describe your sister, how you interacted, and any family background. Details you offer will be helpful in our investigation."

Odette places her pocketbook on the seat beside her and leans into her chair. "Where should I start?"

"The beginning is good." Stella smiles encouragement.

"Okay." She inhales a gulp of air before reciting. "Deena and I are five years apart. She was older. Mom and Dad tolerated big trouble from Deena most of the time. They said we were hard girls. Deena was hard to handle while I was a hard worker. Different versions of hard, Dad joked. We lived outside Halifax. Deena wasn't interested in school or a good job. She finished grade twelve by luck. She was boy-crazy. I'm shy and I wanted a career. There was no money for university. I took a technician's course in pharmacy instead. I worked for Fuller's Pharmacy until they closed. Now, I work for the new chain, Pharmasave, here in town. Mom and Dad died in a car crash right after I turned twenty. They went on a brief vacation." She stares at the wall behind them. "And never came home."

"I'm sorry, Odette. Their sudden deaths were traumatizing for both of you." Stella states what might be true, allowing Odette space for further explanation.

"More for me. Deena was married to Rupert Onslow, and Finn had been born. They lived in the apartment above his parents, Herman and Isla, in Halifax. I was alone." The hollow sounds of her words palpate the air between them.

Despite the recorder, Aiden scribbles in his notebook, as usual. Stella studies Odette's face. She wants more descriptions of Deena's in-laws but focuses on Odette for a moment. "How did you manage?"

"Work. I work—and I knit for the hospital—baby blankets, hats. Never

156

enough. Enjoy the luxury of a few good friends." She shrugs, as if her self-assessment is unimportant.

The expression Aiden shares with Stella suggests her questions have drifted too far afield, but she wanted Odette to see they're listening, so she's comfortable in the interview. Back to the plan. "Will you describe Deena's in-laws, please?"

"I'll tell you what I can. I've met them a few times. They are raw people—rough, often out-spoken, coarse language. Do you understand? They make me nervous. I called and told them Deena had died. Herman said he didn't care. Rupert is out of jail—yet again." She frowns. "The fourth or fifth time, by my calculation. Finn will be thirty soon, but still lives above Herman and Isla. They raised him."

"Deena left the marriage and her son when he was what? Five years old?" Aiden sounds surprised. He knows Deena hid from the world.

"She ran the last time Rupert lost control. He broke her arm. She disappeared but came back this way three years ago. I found out by accident from Velvet Carmichael. She sees a psychologist at the same office where I meet with my skin specialist." She scratches the patch on her hand again.

"Continue."

"Velvet told me she lived in a fourplex with Deena and two other women. She called her neighbour Deena Finch. She said Deena worked for a while at the local grocery store but hurt her shoulder so received disability payments. I dropped a note off at the Groceteria because I expected she shopped there and was familiar to the staff."

"Was a reconnection with her important?" The story makes little sense. If Odette understood Deena's fear of her husband, especially since she changed her surname, why did she risk her sister's exposure?

"Not for me." Her eyes widen. "Deena and I were never close. I was afraid of her most of the time. I wrote the note for Finn. I take him out for supper every couple of weeks. He's a lost young man. Herman, his grandfather, has been hard on him ever since Deena left. Finn struggles." She leans toward the table. "Herman bashed him around from the time he was a wee tyke, and I'm convinced the guy's scared for his life, although he won't leave—no education, no way to support himself. He pestered me because he wanted to talk to his mother. He didn't even know what she looked like. I gave him a picture of the two of us. 'Can I find her? Do I have her address?', he would ask over and over. Deena always frightened me. I never trusted her. She belittled me. My life was fine without her. No, a reunion with my sister wasn't my motive."

"You dropped the note off at the store where Velvet said Deena once worked." Stella doesn't reveal the fact they found her message in Deena's apartment.

"Correct. I told her Finn needed her."

"Did she call you?"

"No."

"Can you provide us with contact information for," Aiden consults his notes, "Herman and Isla Onslow?"

"Yes, Detective. I have noted the details for you. They are hard people," she repeats as she slides a piece of yellow foolscap across the table.

"Stay in the area. We will speak with you again," Aiden directs.

As a constable escorts Odette out of the detachment, Stella squints at Aiden. "Such a meek and thoughtful woman didn't kill her sister with an iron."

"Looks can be deceiving." He fingers the paper in his hand. "Did you notice her expression when I questioned if she had wanted to meet with Deena? Fake, if you ask me. I'll have someone make us an appointment for interviews at the Onslow residence in Halifax for Friday. Do I smell chicken?" He pretends to sniff the air. "Let's leave. Meet you at the park tonight."

On the drive home, Stella's mind drifts away from the case. She hasn't seen this enthusiastic and boyish side of Aiden since they were teenagers. He's been morose and depressed most of their time together over the past two years. Who will arrive with him tonight?

****

Nick remains distant—a disappointment. Stella lets his mood ride. Aiden will soon be here with his new flame, and she'll see what happens. After she changes, she finds him in the kitchen basting the chicken. "Smells wonderful," she says, touching his back while he's turned toward the oven.

"Don't worry. I'll make sure they're fed well with garlic smashed potatoes and roasted veggies to go along with the bird. There's pecan pie from the hotel."

She provides a thumbs up.

"I ran into town after Duke went home. Didn't take long. Kiki enjoyed the ride."

Stella brushes her lips against his neck. "I expect we'll enjoy a fabulous evening, my love."

"In deep investigation discussions?" The edge still hasn't left his voice.

"Nope. Aiden bought a new house. Details to follow."

"I hear gravel crunching. Run and welcome them. I'll check the vegetables again. Tell them dinner in thirty minutes."

She watches through the screen. The vehicle is Cavelle Painter's electric blue sedan. Aiden emerges from the driver's side as Cavelle pushes open the passenger door and extends a long leg to plant a platform heel on the crushed stone.

Stella's breath catches in her throat. Cavelle? Aiden and Cavelle? Her mind struggles to interpret what she sees. She watches her friends. Cavelle, in tune with Trixie's style most of the time, is subdued in beige linen pants, a white shell and a beige leather jacket. One long gold necklace and her signature bracelet watch comprise her jewellery, except for the hoops in her ears. She carries a small black clutch and not the satchel which most often accompanies her when she's away from the office.

Aiden waves. "Hi. I brought Nick's favourite beer." He hoists a six-pack in the air.

"Hi," she squeaks, as Cavelle ascends the veranda stairs. She opens the door and the bear hug from her surprise guest is immediate. The frothy smell of gardenia settles in her nostrils— Charlie by Revlon. You can't miss the sandalwood, either.

"Are you shocked? Aiden wanted me to shock you," she murmurs.

Nick will be the one who's gob-smacked, Stella thinks, but replies, "Yes. In a good way. Come in, you two. Nick's still hovering over a hot stove." She picks Kiki off the floor, and they muddle through to the kitchen, since they decided earlier a formal dinner by the fireplace wasn't necessary. Although, under normal circumstances, she lets her guests go first, Stella leads. She doesn't want to miss the expression on Nick's face. "They're here, Nick. Aiden's date is Cavelle."

Flushed from the oven, Nick stands, turns, and his wide eyes reveal that their most recent Aiden-conversation is replaying in his brain.

"You said a half hour, right? We'll settle with drinks and sit in the living room until supper's ready," Stella recites.

Aiden places the beer on the counter.

"They brought your favourite." She has filled in as much air space as she can while Nick stands in stun-mode. "Say hi, Nick," she mumbles, from behind his shoulder while she reaches for glasses.

"Hi, Aiden, Cavelle. Welcome."

"Wine, Cavelle? There's white in the fridge. I assume Aiden wants a beer." She directs her remark toward Nick with another nudge.

Once everyone receives a drink, they move out of the kitchen. "Now, tell me. I'm curious. Why did you not drive your car, Aiden?"

"Simple answer." He's settled on a sofa. His leg touches Cavelle's. "If she parks at the office, people assume she's at work. They call, leave messages, even bang on the door. The easier choice is if I park further along the street, and we use Cavelle's ride instead."

"Why don't you tell Aiden and Cavelle what's on the menu, Nick? You've worked hard." She produces her most supportive expression, although there will be no avoiding her teases once they're alone.

Nick rattles off the details, leans over and retrieves Kiki, places her on his lap, and says he'll take the dog out for a minute or two before he serves supper.

After he's gone, Cavelle whispers, "We've shocked poor Nick, eh, Stella?"

"I bet he's more relieved," Aiden quips.

She's surprised at Aiden's comprehension of their circumstances but doesn't bite.

Over dinner, Aiden describes the house he's acquired—Ruby Wilson's previous home, which faces the flats. Years ago, people from Ontario purchased the derelict New England colonial, gutted the inside, and added a two-story, windowed addition on the back. Ruby Wilson, the bank manager at the Shale Harbour Savings and Loan, invested in the property. After her conviction for Lorraine Young's murder, the asset hit the market once again. A young local couple bought the showpiece via Cavelle and Grey Cottage Realty. They tried their best, but the payments were a challenge even though they were aware of the interest rates from the outset. "The contract includes pieces of furniture. You remember those L-shaped cognac leather sofas and the coffee table ottoman."

Stella nods.

"Those are part of the purchase agreement, along with the Lucite dining room suite. The set isn't my style. Neither are the pink stone countertops, but Cavelle says," he pats her hand for emphasis, "I can replace the countertops and sell the furniture, which is worth a pretty penny."

"When do you move?" Nick asks after they retire to the living room.

"A month. I need more furniture and appreciate Cavelle's help. We're off to Halifax." He touches her hand again. "Most of the stuff from Port Ephron will stay in case Rosemary ever returns. If not, I'll rent the place, or sell."

As she leaves to sort the dirty dishes, Cavelle tags along. Once alone, Stella remarks, "You and Aiden sound serious."

"I agreed to shop for furniture with him because I can make sure what he buys suits my tastes. I have the distinct impression what he chooses might be mine soon." She savours the moment with a deep breath.

"He's married, Cavelle, not to overstate the obvious. And Rosemary has mega problems, jealousy being the least of them. Listen. You need to understand the woman threatened me."

"Aiden explained what happened, but honestly, he suspects she fixates on you because she's focused on history. I'm not worried. You live with Nick, Trixie has Val, Jacob confessed he's dating an old chum of Lucy's, and for God's sake, Hester has Angus, from what I can gather." Her eyes glow. "The time has come for me to enjoy more than the odd real estate convention."

Stella leans into her friend as they finish the dishes. "I often wondered how you occupied yourself at those events." Her eyes twinkle.

CHAPTER 18

I Wouldn't Know Her

She closes the inside door after watching Aiden and Cavelle pull out of their parking lot. With her back still turned, she asks, "Are you worried because I'm in a car with Aiden driving to Halifax on Friday?" She can't keep the tease out of her tone.

"Okay. You were right, which makes me wrong. I won't worry anymore." She attempts sternness when she looks at him.

"The good detective has finally gotten over you." He smirks as he grabs her hand. "Let's make tea."

As usual, when they discuss events, they sit together on the sofa. Tonight, the aroma of cranberry wafts while they share opinions.

"Isn't Cavelle concerned, Stella? Rosemary's reaction will be wild when Aiden leaves the marriage. I can't imagine anything less."

"I asked her point blank. I told her Rosemary threatened me and there's a possibility she might be in danger now, too. She replied that Aiden shared the story, but he thinks his wife will continue to focus on me because of our history. Rosemary lives in the past most of the time, so the present isn't a priority."

"Seems thin. I see the woman as jealous and vindictive. Her behaviour becomes exaggerated because of her illness. I don't trust her."

"Agreed. I suspect Aiden is mistaken. I hope he doesn't put Cavelle in a risky position."

"The one at risk when the woman's discharged from hospital will be you." Fury edges into Nick's voice. "She'll spend the summer on our veranda."

"You're probably right, but she can't come out here unless someone drives her."

"And his plans for the trailer? Aiden won't encourage her, even with Toni or Mary Jo in tow. Surely not," he huffs.

"Any options are possible, but I'm certain if she visits the park, her sisters will supervise. I didn't ask. I'll bring up the topic when we're on the way into the city Friday." She snuggles closer. "Tomorrow, I'll help you with any outside work you might want finished, but, thanks to my *dear* friend Cavelle," she blushes, "I'm interested in focusing on other areas tonight. I've missed you."

****

He fetches her from the park, and they leave in his car. "Here's the information we've gathered on the Onslow family." Aiden hands her four manila folders while she settles. She notes each file contains one sheet of paper except Rupert's. His has an offence summary sheet and a dozen documents which itemize his assaults against civil society since he turned eighteen.

"Thanks. I'll read while we drive."

"Sure. Dinner and your support were both great on Wednesday. Cavelle and I enjoyed a wonderful evening." He pulls the Caprice into traffic on the highway, and they begin the two-hour trek to the city. "Were you surprised?" He turns for a quick glance at her face. "Nick was shocked. He's figured I set my eyes on you from the time I moved back into the area."

She measures her words, so there's no room for error. She won't betray Nick's trust. "We are both happy for you if your goal is a separation, Aiden. Your arrangement leaves Cavelle vulnerable, though. Can we discuss Rosemary?"

"We can discuss whatever you want."

"Cavelle says her threats toward me are based on her fixation with the past and not the present. She said she needn't worry because there's no concern Rosemary might focus on her."

"True, Stella. I'm more worried about her release when she sets her sights on you. Her hatred won't transfer to Cavelle."

"But, since she's a real estate agent, Cavelle's in the public eye and accessible at Grey Cottage Realty. The two of you should rethink your approach and not make assumptions." She lifts her hand, palm flat. "My opinion."

He nods. "Point taken. And the second topic?"

"Shall I expect Rosemary at Shale Cliffs over the summer?"

"No. I've rented the trailer for the entire season, to a family from Ontario with twin boys. She won't be on site. Me either, except if they call me. I planned to tell you, but they don't arrive until after school closes. I'll give their number to you."

Relieved, she tells him the contact information she'll need and opens Finn Onslow's file. He's their first interview.

****

The Onslow home sits on a quiet residential street in downtown Halifax, near the children's hospital. The house is one of those salt-box narrow affairs like those which survived the explosion of December 1917. Renovated into two flats years ago, they enter the small front foyer and press the bell for the left-hand door. A voice yells, "Come on upstairs." Finn expects them.

A thirty-year-old man, chubby and unkempt, greets them at the top of the steep and straight stairway. "You must be the cops." He doesn't make the remark in an accusatory fashion, more a statement of fact.

"Yes. I'm Detective Aiden North and," he points to Stella, "my colleague, Stella Kirk. We're here as part of our investigation into the death of your mother."

"Come inside and sit. Can I offer you coffee or tea?"

"No, thank you," Aiden replies. He doesn't check with Stella but makes a successful assumption.

"Rupert Onslow, your father, lives here in the upper flat with you. Correct?" Stella establishes basic information, as a precursor to their discussion.

"Yeah, when the old man isn't in the slammer. I take care of my grandparents downstairs. They raised me 'cause Dad wasn't around, and my mother disappeared when I was five."

"You've kept in touch with your Aunt Odette." Stella moves him along with a fact.

"She's been good to me. If I didn't do chores for Gramma and Gramps, I'd ask her if I could live with her. I would find a job; help her. Odette's great." He fidgets in his chair, clasps his hands between his legs, and twists each finger without mercy.

"We're sorry for your loss, in the death of your mother, Finn. You never met her again after she left?" Aiden studies Finn's response.

His shoulders heave and he focuses on the pine floor. "Aunt Odette gave me a picture I keep in my wallet." He digs in the back pocket of his trousers and retrieves a battered billfold. "See?" He offers the crinkled photograph to Stella first.

Indeed, the faded image shows Deena and Odette. Although taken at the time of their parents' sudden death, if one judges by the clothes they're wearing in the photo, neither woman has aged much over the years.

"I wouldn't know her. Did either of you ever meet her? Aunt Odette said she looked the same as when they were teenagers."

"We met your mother," Aiden contributes, as he takes the picture from Stella. "The photograph shows an excellent likeness."

How was Odette aware Deena hadn't aged appreciably, Stella wonders, as Aiden checks Finn's whereabouts on the day of Deena's death? He has no alibi because he says he remained alone after he helped his grandparents earlier.

"Do you want me to call the old man? He's below. Gramma's oven is on the fritz, and he claims he can fix appliances." Finn chortles. "Musta learned in jail."

"Thanks. If you could send your father upstairs, we'll have a private conversation with him. Please stay downstairs for the extent of the interview."

After the thunder of his shoes, as they bang each of the worn treads, has faded, Stella turns toward Aiden. "He's a nice enough young man, if you take into consideration what Odette has reported, but how could Odette tell him Deena's looks haven't changed in twenty-five years?"

****

She assesses the apartment while Aiden completes his notes. Sparse, used, tattered, even dirty are words which come to mind. Splatters of grease, and a crimson stain, like someone threw a drink, cover the wall behind the stove. She's curious to see downstairs. Aiden and Stella wait ten minutes before Finn's father appears.

"I assume you two expect to pin Deena's murder on me, right?" Rupert's rounded midriff shakes as he stomps into the living room. His guffaw fills the space. "Incarceration. Don't ya' love the word? Best alibi for a guy with my record." He approaches them both, seated on the battered sofa, and stares down. Body odour wafts around them. He needs a shave. His jeans appear new, but they don't fit—a size too small, at least.

"Did the kid find you somethin' to drink?" Rupert's bluster continues.

"No, thank you, Mr. Onslow. I'm Detective Aiden North and Stella Kirk, here, is my community consultant. We appreciate your time so we can ask you questions related to your ex-wife, Deena Finch."

"We called her Deena Onslow after she married me, and we never divorced." He slumps into the armchair. "The murdered woman, as reported by her sister, was my wife. No denying the obvious." The muscles in his cheeks sag. He struggles for control.

"She left you because of abuse, Mr. Onslow." Stella lets her remark hang in the air while she observes his reaction.

He offers an engaging and open facial expression in response. "Aren't you a smart cookie? Done your homework. I respect attention to detail." He leans toward Stella. His elbows are on his knees while he maintains his contrived, in Stella's estimation, guise. "I wasn't prepared for marriage any more than her. Finn suffered the most because she left the kid. Happened twenty-five years ago. I'm sixty now, for God's sake. Water under the bridge. I forgave her for leavin'."

"Did Finn?" Stella finds Rupert Onslow off-putting for countless reasons.

"Well, you 'investigators' shoulda asked Finn that question." He sits back, relaxes, and crosses his legs. "Finn ain't bright. He ain't tough, either. My dad tries his best when I'm not in the picture, but the kid's a mess."

"When were you released from jail, Rupert?" She has the answer to her query in the file but wants to create a conversation which will direct him to reference his contacts.

"You should have my dates, Missy, but Deena died on the fifteenth of last month and they didn't spring me until the twenty-ninth. As I said, a rock-solid alibi."

"Any friends from prison?" Aiden follows her lead.

"Nope. No associations."

Stella sees his muscles tense.

"I didn't pay a cell mate to kill the wife I haven't seen in a lifetime. You're nuts."

She watches his body language. He inhales and calms. She can see the struggle in his eyes. Rupert has a temper he dares not show, and less control than he expects when faced with a challenge.

"Okay, Mr. Onslow. We'd appreciate an opportunity to meet with your parents, now. If you don't mind, please lead us to their apartment."

Aiden has refocused Rupert with a modicum of success. They follow him into the lower unit and along a narrow hallway toward the kitchen. Finn sits at a battered and cigarette burn-scarred maple table with his grandparents. Herman Onslow, a heavy man with crooked fingers and a pronounced stoop, obviously in his eighties, lifts himself away from the furniture to greet them.

****

"Go on back upstairs, boy. No need for you sittin' around here. The detectives want to talk with me." He waves his arm toward the stairs. "You, too, Rup. Scram." Once Finn stands, he points at two chairs for them. "Isla, fetch our company coffee."

"No thanks, Mr. Onslow. Let me introduce ourselves. I'm Detective Aiden North of the Port Ephron and Shale Harbour RCMP, and my colleague, Stella Kirk. We appreciate your time and want to ask questions focused on your late daughter-in-law." They both accept a seat.

Isla, who stood when instructed by her husband, sits once again. She hasn't opened her mouth.

"Mr. Onslow, the purpose of our discussion today is to collect background information on the victim, who called herself Deena Finch. We understand she left the common domicile twenty-five years ago. Did you ever contact her?"

"Call me Hermie. Deena was a first-class bitch if you get my drift." He winks. "Rup couldn't control her. She was no mother, either. Too young. Once we found out Rup knocked her up, we shoulda paid her off instead of lettin' the kid marry her."

"You and your husband raised Finn, correct?" Stella wants Mrs. Onslow included in their conversation.

"Yeah, we gave the boy a proper home. No need to ask her." His hand flutters in his wife's general direction. "We've been married for over sixty years. I can tell you what she's thinkin'. Isla, you was told to fetch the police their coffee. Now, as I was sayin', Finn ain't smart, but he minds pretty good. He drives my car, does our errands, takes us to our appointments. He eats here and has a place to live. I give him pocket money. He likes takin' the bus and explorin' the city." The old man shrugs. "Finn's okay."

"What happened when his mother left?" Aiden refocuses the discussion.

"They tussled, her and Rup. She said he broke her arm, or wrist, or somethin'. Isla drove her to the hospital while I was at work. The bitch laid charges."

Stella watches as Isla opens her mouth, but Hermie continues.

"The police blew in and dragged Rup outta here, in front of Finn. Deena came back until I posted bail. Then she left for good. Somebody lost their patience and killed her. Easy to lose patience with Deena, as I recall. Odette, her sister," he taps his index finger on the table for emphasis, "now she's a flake, if I ever met one. Maybe Odette's your culprit. She called and said Deena had died—murder suspected. I couldn't care less. You talked to her, right?" He harrumphs. "She musta told you where we live. She blamed us because Deena disappeared."

Isla opens her mouth again, but clamps her lips shut when her husband continues.

"I guess Odette blames our family for Deena's death, too. Rup sat in jail, and we was here. You're barkin' up the wrong tree."

"Could we talk together in the front room, Isla?" Stella nods toward Aiden before the two of them make their way into a parlour which mirrors the one upstairs, except with newer furniture, as if they furnished the top flat with hand-me-downs from the lower unit.

Dull and expressionless eyes stare at Stella. "I can't offer you any more information, Ms. Kirk. My husband most often talks for both of us."

"Understood, Isla, and please call me Stella. Will you describe Deena's departure in your own words? Hermie said you took her to the hospital the day Rupert broke her wrist. This incident became a life-changing event for her, I assume." Her intent is to communicate that she understands. "Tell me what happened."

Finn's grandmother settles into her chair. The muscles of her face relax, although she glances at the door before she begins. Her voice is hushed, and she leans toward Stella before she speaks. "The doctor called a hospital social worker who came for an interview. She said we should pack our bags, take Finn, and drive to a shelter right away. I couldn't leave Hermie. He's tried over the years. Hermie worked, took care of me, bought our house when the place was a wreck, renovated from top to bottom, and wanted us to be happy. He's rough, perhaps even ignorant," she explains, "but he's my husband."

"Did Deena take the social worker's advice, but without Finn?"

She sits straighter. "Soon after. Hermie always rode the bus to work to save money, and I used the car for errands. I promised Deena to give Finn a proper home, which I did, and still do," she adds, "and I drove her to the shelter once Hermie made Rup's bail." She leans across the space between them. Her lips are near Stella's face and her breath smells of stale coffee. "I've never told Herman or Rupert. I let on that she took off, and I didn't know what happened."

Stella preserves her blank expression. "Did you maintain contact with her?"

While she stares at her lap, she whispers, "Twice. Both times she waited across the street until Herman and Rupert were gone to work and she met me and Finn. He didn't recognize her because she dyed her hair and wore sunglasses and an enormous hat. Finn thought she was a spy from the movies. The first time, she told me she wanted to move away and wouldn't be in touch anymore."

"Your grandson didn't think the woman was his mother?"

"No. I said she was a girl I used to work with years ago. She came back once more. I gave her money I'd saved from the groceries. They," she nods toward the door, "paid no attention to a small boy's ramblings."

"Thank you for your honesty, Isla. Did you see Deena after she returned to the province and moved to Shale Harbour?"

"I gave up drivin', so have no opportunity to sneak away. With my husband retired and at home, he keeps a close eye on my movements. You understand?" She peers at Stella. "I'm okay. No need to alert a social worker. My marriage is under control. I let him feel he's the one who calls the shots. My secret to success. Don't worry," she insists.

On the return trip to Shale Cliffs, Stella provides Aiden with a clearer picture of Isla Onslow. Aiden's private interview proved less productive. Herman showed Aiden his workshop in the back and Aiden spent his time hearing detailed descriptions of the specific advantages of five different models of saws.

When he drops her off at home, cobalt darkness has settled over the park. She stares at the veranda lights, imagining a warm supper and a glass of wine. Could she ever live Isla's life, acting a part for the sake of survival? She closes her eyes before she opens the car door. "A useful day, Aiden. We learned more than we expected. There's a possibility Herman and Rupert Onslow conspired to kill Deena, but motive escapes me. Odette may well be our most logical suspect."

"Or someone at the G-plex," he mumbles. "Must run. Cavelle and I are meeting at the hotel for supper."

As she trudges up the steps, bone tired, her thoughts wander back to Aiden, and the pretenses he maintained while in a marriage bound for failure.

Chapter 19

She Wanted to Hide

"I'm ready for you." Earlene leads them into her apartment and shows them to chairs at her dining room table. Her face does not betray the emotional tremble in her voice.

Stella and Aiden exchange looks. "We're here today to review your formal statement and decide whether you want to add information." Aiden produces his notebook from an inside pocket in his overcoat.

Earlene, dressed in a shiny polyester suit with a tight skirt and box-style jacket, perches on the third chair, back straight and knees squeezed together. "I assumed you scheduled a visit with me because you are of the opinion that I killed my husband for the insurance money. His business teetered on the edge of bankruptcy at the time."

"Do you have more details related to the death of Richard Marigold?"

"No, but Deena acted both unkind and suspicious whenever she spoke of poor Richard's sudden passing. She asked me questions most rational people consider inappropriate. Her manner threatened me." She frowns. "I assumed you'd heard the rumours throughout your investigation, and now want to address them with me."

Setting the woman's obvious paranoia aside, Stella begins. "Describe Deena's behaviour, Earlene." The owner of the G-plex may be on the precipitous of revealing a motive for her tenant's murder. She watches as Earlene clasps and un-clasps her hands.

"I didn't kill Deena." She stares into space. "I can't deny I often wished I could evict her, but there are rules, as I'm certain you're aware. She tormented me and suggested I murdered Richard." Earlene pauses while she meets Stella's gaze. "How he died is obvious to me, and the circumstances may well lead you, as officers of the court, to hypothesize I participated in orchestrating his demise, but there is no way I intentionally hurt poor Richard."

Stella finds her formality unnerving.

"Your husband died of a coronary."

"Correct, Detective North, but he enjoyed easy access to my foxglove seeds and there's the possibility he poisoned himself. The results mirror a natural heart attack."

"You studied poisonous plants with Opal Painter." After her discussion with Hester, Stella is well-aware of the adverse effects of foxglove.

"Yes, and her unusual sister. I went through a phase where I became fascinated with local deadly flora—the useless occupations of a woman of leisure." She sighs. "Opal—no surprise once you two unveiled her behaviour—was happy to teach me her tricks of the trade. I adored foxglove and created personal varieties. I kept jars of seeds in the basement of our home." She tilts her head and produces a sad smile. "As much as they were my favourite flower, I've planted only ornamental shrubs around the fourplex." Her eyes drift toward the front window.

"Did Richard want to commit suicide?" Aiden squints while he focuses on the woman before him.

"One might generously describe poor Richard as mentally unwell. His business struggled on a troublesome downhill trajectory. The alarmingly high interest rates over the last few years meant people pulled their investment portfolios and purchased GICs at the bank. He said he lost money every day. The house was at risk."

Aiden leans back in his chair. "Your opinion is that your husband used seeds from a poisonous plant, where the toxin mirrors a heart attack, to mask the poison and guarantee you could collect his insurance."

"Possibly, in the same way a simple, although massive, coronary is possible. I expected you to arrest me for fraud, Detective." She touches her handbag on the table in front of her. "I am prepared."

To Stella's surprise, Aiden refocuses the conversation back to Deena. "Did our murder victim ever mention insurance fraud, or the potential of insurance fraud, Mrs. Marigold?"

With closed eyes, Earlene whispers, "No, not directly. She accused me of forcing Richard to eat poison, and she suggested the result was a fake coronary. I repeatedly told her the coroner reported the cause of death, not me."

Stella's tone encourages her. "How did she threaten you, Earlene?"

"Deena suggested cheaper rent for not telling the others who would report me and instigate an investigation. She scared me, entered my apartment illegally, waited for me until I came home, and took personal possessions when I wasn't here. We called the police several times, as you know."

If Earlene sensed any potential threats, and if she was compromised in her husband's death, why risk a call to authorities about Deena's behaviour? Stella sits mystified.

Earlene answers the unasked. "Deena hid issues of her own. She suggested Velvet and Tess could do the deed. She said that if she told them, either one would report concerns. I became curious. Why did she want to avoid personal involvement in humiliating me? She struck me as the type who would seek out all the credit. Once we discovered she lived under an assumed name, I understood. She was hiding. I expect she collected disability cheques under false pretenses, too."

"Thank you for your help and your candour today, Mrs. Marigold. We'll call when your statement is ready for a signature."

"And the insurance, Detective North? Will you arrest me for collecting on my husband's sudden death?"

"The coroner said your husband died of a heart attack. I am aware of no evidence that Mr. Marigold went near your foxglove seeds." Aiden reaches for his coat and turns toward the outside door. "We'll make our way round to Ms. Boone's. Thank you again."

Stella bustles behind him after a quick and vague nod in Earlene's direction. Once out of earshot, she asks the obvious. "You don't expect to charge her?"

"Not for insurance fraud."

"Good, because she didn't kill Deena, either."

****

Seated in Tess' minuscule apartment, Aiden begins with the same introduction as provided to Earlene. "We're here to collect any added details you might want included in your statement." His voice has the familiar formal quality Stella finds both repellent and reliable.

"I told you how she broke into my unit. Once, I found her at my table with a drink in her hand—a drink she took from my refrigerator. She remarked on my cheap taste in wine."

Stella blocks a gasp with a gulp. Deena was bold, she ponders in silence. The woman possessed no moral compass or filter. She said whatever crossed her mind.

"There are other issues I didn't mention." Tess bites her lip and stares at her lap. Her shoulders heave as if burdened by the worries of the world. "The last time she broke in, she read pages from my current manuscript. They were on the table since I planned on completing a round of edits after I returned from Harbour Manor."

"What happened?" Aiden sounds curious.

"Deena talked like one of those book critics you might hear on the radio. She said my writing didn't inspire the reader. She insisted I had copied another equally talentless author's work, word for word."

Stella attempts neutrality. "She accused you of plagiarism."

"Yes." Tess's voice vibrates and her eyes fill with tears.

"Did you?" Aiden asks the obvious.

"Yes," she repeats. She sits straighter in her chair. "Not word for word, as she said, mind you, but I mirrored an idea from my favourite book. Deena threatened she'd tell Earlene and Velvet."

"You feared a humiliating exposure." Stella understands the woman's pain.

Tess' eyes widen and she brushes a tear off her cheek. "Few people have seen my books except Theo and me, but there's always the off chance a publisher in the future may appreciate my work. God forbid Frances…." She sniffs and touches her nose. "I didn't kill Deena. On the occasion in question, she told me the real reason she came into my apartment was because someone followed her home. She used her key, entered the lounge via the patio door, secured the slider, and crept in here instead of her place. She wanted to hide from whomever. Since we are now aware of how Deena managed access," she squints in recollection, "I guess I might do the same, given the circumstances. The prospect of being pursued by an unknown person unnerved her."

Aiden squirms in his chair and refocuses the interview. "If I understand, Ms. Boone, Deena Finch threatened exposure of you as a plagiarist, at least to your bridge partners. Any reason she didn't complete the threat?"

"Because she died. I expected she'd make a grand announcement at bridge the next afternoon, but we found her dead instead."

"Did she give you any hint who she thought followed her or why?" Stella frowns. *Did Deena suspect Odette?*

"Not a clue. Deena presented a good front, but I could tell she was worried."

They leave Tess and trudge around the building. Movers are busy with Mary Jo's possessions when they walk past her door toward Velvet's apartment.

"Before I forget, will you conduct second interviews with Tess' sister at the manor, Mary Jo, and Cavelle? Wise if I'm not involved in those conversations, specifically Cavelle and Mary Jo. Take Moyer along as your partner. I'll be busy at the hospital, focused on Rosemary's discharge tomorrow."

She meets his gaze. "Her homecoming is faster than expected, I gather." She doesn't wait for a response. "Okay. I'll contact each of them and you make sure Moyer rides shotgun if your bosses don't mind. You can't be certain I won't get an idea in my head and run with it." She guards her insecurities with teasing.

"Thanks." He presses Velvet's doorbell and elbows her arm.

****

They discover Velvet seated at her worn kitchen table. She didn't rise, but hollered "enter," while she remained slumped in her chair.

"Take a seat." Her eyes are downcast. She has her hair in an asymmetrical braid over her left shoulder—a nautical pattern one might see used for a fishing boat tethered at the dock in a harbour. Dry, unruly sprigs of black and grey poke out from the twists.

Aiden begins. "Ms. Carmichael, Stella and I are here to review your statement and offer an opportunity for you to add any details, perhaps missed, in your initial remarks."

Velvet, unkempt in a green wool jumper with food stains on the front, scowls. "I guess I should tell you the whole truth and nothing but the truth."

Stella's breath catches. "You haven't been honest with us?"

She touches the end of her braid, which hangs wet and sticky. Stella suspects her of a serious episode of chewing before they arrived on the scene. Velvet's eyes flash a momentary defensiveness. "I didn't lie."

"We need more clarification." Aiden clicks his pen.

"Odette said she wrote a note and hoped Deena collected her message from the Groceteria." She sits straighter. "I never told Deena that Odette and

I were friends—not at first. But Deena appeared here one night and said someone was watching her movements. She told me about the note. She read it aloud and then suggested Odette waited at the grocery store and followed her so she might find out where she lived."

"What did you say in response?" Stella suspects Velvet caved, which added to Deena's unease.

"I pointed out that her sister would never scare her in such a way and emphasized Odette left the note to give her an opportunity to contact her family." She grabs her braid. "After years of therapy, the technique of refocusing a conversation comes easily to me. Dr. Visser has been an excellent teacher. I changed the subject and showed an interest in her son. I can manipulate people when necessary." She curls her lip in a defiant smirk. "I really tried to settle her."

"And Deena's response?" Velvet's demeanour reminds Stella of Rosemary. She wonders if Aiden has noticed.

"Deena acted afraid, and I mean afraid with a capital A. I suggested she pack her bags, if she felt unsafe here, and was determined to avoid contact with her sister. I wanted the woman gone and hoped Mary Jo might move in, even though I never said as much." Her eyes widen as she continues. "I didn't kill her so my friend could live here." She chuckles. "Yeah, the crazy lady always has a motive, right?"

"No one has suggested you murdered Deena Finch because you wanted to gain Mary Jo as your neighbour, Ms. Carmichael, but the victim may have threatened you if you accidentally let slip that you were friends with Odette."

Her cheeks flush. "Odette might have followed Deena because she wanted contact with her. She was convinced Deena needed to develop a relationship with her son. I can't remember his name. Reminds me of fish."

"His name is Finn, Velvet, and Odette could knock on the door whenever the time suited her because Deena lived in the same building as you, and you gave Odette that information earlier."

"I told Deena I knew her sister," Velvet stutters in a hushed and hesitant afterthought. "You should be aware, I told her." She gasps and clamps her hand over her mouth.

"And?" Aiden sits straighter in his chair.

"She blew a gasket. Her face turned purple, and I worried, for a minute, about my safety. After ranting and spitting accusations about trust and stupid, crazy people, she said her world was full of mentally unstable kooks who wanted to hurt her. She left, thank goodness."

"When did your confrontation happen, Velvet?"

"Two days before she died."

****

They park in front of Cocoa and Café because they planned on tea after their interviews. Both sit focused on the deck of the restaurant, silent and thoughtful. Stella begins their conversation. "Each has motive and opportunity, but none of them killed Deena Finch."

"Come on, Stella. Earlene Marigold said that Deena threatened to tell Velvet and Tess that she, Earlene, had a hand in the death of her husband, or at the very least, committed insurance fraud."

"Understood. She didn't murder Deena, though." Stella stares straight ahead.

"Tess Boone suggested Deena accused her of plagiarism—enough motive."

"Correct, but no."

"Velvet Carmichael has a history of mental illness, was constantly intimidated and tormented by Deena, and confessed she was friendly with Deena's sister. She told Odette where Deena lived."

"Which, in my mind, makes Odette more of a suspect than the hair-chewing Velvet."

"Why Odette?"

"Anyone who committed this murder was emotional and used a weapon at hand. It wasn't planned. Odette was abandoned by her sister. They finally meet and confrontation ensues."

"Okay. Okay. They each have motive and opportunity."

"Understood, but none of the residents of the G-plex hit poor, paranoid Deena Finch with an iron. Although the logical choice, I am troubled with the idea of Odette as the killer, too. Let's talk with her again, Aiden."

"We can, but I want you to re-interview Cavelle, Mary Jo, and Tess' sister first, before we drop any of the three bridge partners as suspects. I'll handle Duke, because he dated Deena and might shed more light on her as a person, but interviewing Cavelle and Mary Jo is inappropriate for me." He peers at her from behind the wheel. "Because you're convinced Earlene, Velvet, and

Tess aren't guilty, verify your instincts with those best able to vouch for the G-plex residents. I expect Mary Jo has finished with the movers. Ask her to take a break from unpacking and give you her full attention."

"What's the story with Rosemary?"

"She's discharged tomorrow and moving into Toni's for the next week to ten days while I settle in Shale Harbour. Toni wants to help her adjust to living in our old house alone. She and Mary Jo promise to stay with Rosemary on alternate nights, once she's back, until she gets into a routine, and they think she can live unsupervised."

Stella senses a hesitation. "Will the plan work?"

"Not a chance. Mary Jo is reluctant. I gave them both strict instructions not to reveal my new address, but Rosemary will access the detachment in Port Ephron. I intend to avoid the office there at all costs for the time being." He pouts. "Trouble is unavoidable, I expect. Sounds callous." He shrugs. "But if she confronts me and behaves badly, I'll file committal papers again. Either she acts like a normal person, or back she goes. No coddling." He turns to her, and his voice develops a monotone. "She'll live in a pleasant house, receive a comfortable income, and enjoy the company of two sisters who love her. Enough for anyone."

Doubtful. "Okay." Stella feels his plan will never work but says nothing more. "As for tomorrow, I can meet with Cavelle, Mary Jo, and Connie. Your goal for my interviews besides 'dig deeper'?"

"We've determined none of them consider their friend or family member capable of killing someone, even our victim. Their views are obvious but look for more. Find out whether they discussed details. Maybe you'll discover an angle we haven't seen yet." He glances at his watch and taps his hand on the wheel. "Too late for tea, Stella. Sorry."

Once inside her Jeep, she plots the next day. Staff would prefer her to visit Connie in the afternoon. Mornings are busy at the nursing home. Cavelle arrives at her office by nine. She'll leave a message at Grey Cottage Realty for Cavelle to collect tomorrow, since chances are she'll be with Aiden tonight. Mary Jo's phone won't be connected yet, so a stop on her way back to the park to suggest coffee after ten might be wise.

When she drives into the parking lot at the fourplex, the movers are gone. Mary Jo and Toni's cars sit side by side. She trots around to the backyard, past Tess' side entry, and despite the chill April air, finds Mary Jo's door ajar. "Knock, knock," she shouts.

Toni appears. "Stella, what a delightful surprise. I'm helping Mary Jo unpack her kitchen." She then adds with a stage whisper, "I just became aware the woman cooks. I expected that ten minutes and we'd have her organized, but I've been here for over an hour unpacking her dishes. Come in and visit."

"No, thanks. On my way home but need a word with Mary Jo first."

"You want me? What can I do?"

"Why is your front door wide open? The weather isn't overly warm."

"Smells kinda sickly sweet in here. I expect the odour to be dried blood under the Lino. Earlene said they replaced the floor, but I suspect they didn't bleach underneath." She frowns and mumbles her displeasure.

"I suggested they tear everything out again, and expose the cement to a disinfectant wash, but Mary Jo doesn't want to ask Earlene." She glances over her shoulder at her sister.

"That smell is hard to handle, Mary Jo." Stella wrinkles her nose. "The reason I'm here—can you take time for coffee tomorrow and review your witness statement? Aiden has asked me to revisit the details with each of our collateral contacts, of which you are one."

"No problem. Toni has her meeting with Aiden at the hospital, and I'll be plugging away knee deep in my mess." She glances around at the piles of boxes. "Unpacking will take forever. I forgot what I stuffed into storage." She throws her hands in the air. "Come at ten, okay? I'll find the pot and make you coffee."

"Perfect. Gotta run. Nick expects me. Bye, Toni. See you in the morning, Mary Jo."

$$\mathbf{W}$$

Chapter 20

Uncontrollable Variables Are the Enemy

Sergeant Moyer stands at the back entrance of the detachment, his legs apart and his hands clasped across his belt, while Stella pulls her Jeep into the parking lot on Tuesday morning. His familiar jumbo size and kind face make the prospect of three interviews without Aiden more bearable. He performs a mock salute and approaches her driver's window.

"Let's take the cruiser."

Reluctant to ride around in a marked police vehicle, she hesitates. "You could hop in with me." She points to the passenger seat with her thumb.

"No thanks, Stella. I can't be much help when you talk with people, but I'll be your driver." His grin is toothy and stained.

She complies and exits her Jeep.

"Where are we off to first?" He settles his hefty frame behind the wheel.

"Grey Cottage Realty. I left a message for Cavelle Painter last night and told her I hoped she could meet with us near nine o'clock. She knows Earlene Marigold because she managed the sales of both the Marigold home and the property where Earlene built her fourplex. Her sisters, Opal and Hester Painter, taught Earlene about poisonous plants."

Moyer's head twists toward her as he navigates the sharp turn off the RCMP lot. "Did Mrs. Marigold kill her old man? Lots of chatter when he died but never came to charges."

"He wanted to die, according to Earlene. I'm doubtful she killed him." Even if Richard Marigold used her foxglove seeds as a poison, Stella's convinced Earlene isn't their murderer. "We'll cross the Ts." She grimaces. "My job today."

Once they arrive and park on Birch Street, near the office, Stella leads the way. Moyer assumes a post by the entrance, which confirms he doesn't want direct involvement in the actual interview. Cavelle exudes perfection in a deep plum pantsuit draped with a coordinated shawl. She greets her in a rush. "I heard your message. Farley will cover the front, and we can use his space." She glances at the empty desk in the corner. "We've organized interviews for another agent and an administrator." She leans toward Stella's ear. "I hope Farley lets me move into Meredith's office once we settle on new staff."

Stella masks her shock. A year has passed since Meredith Tompkins' conviction for her part in the murder of her husband's lover and Stella's friend, Paulina McAdams. Farley assumed the brokerage role at Grey Cottage Realty but still avoids meeting with clients. Poor Cavelle works as a one-woman show most of the time. "You deserve your own spot with privacy, Cavelle. I bet he couldn't run the operation without you."

"I'd shutter the place, Stella." Farley emerges from behind a closed door, and the awkward silence, that comes after someone overhears a disparaging remark, passes. "You can talk in here." He points an index finger over his shoulder. "And Cavelle, let's clean out Meredith's office for you. I've found us an administrative assistant." He answers her quizzical expression first with a nod. "We'll talk later."

"I'm glad you visited today, Stella. You forced my boss into a commitment." She winks. "There's a young woman over at Stephens and Stephens who asked about a real estate job. I hope he's hired her." She rests her elbows on the battered desk. "Now, what can I do for you?"

"We're reviewing statements with collateral witnesses and trolling for added information."

"Aiden said he couldn't talk with me about my relationship with the Marigolds." She glances toward the ceiling. "The idea could be considered inappropriate by his superiors, under the circumstances." Her eyes widen. "I am smitten, Stella. Haven't felt cherished in a long time."

"I wish you my best, Cavelle." She pauses before she makes her concerns known to her friend. "You are aware of this, but Rosemary can be dangerous. Be careful." She lifts a finger to her lips. "Enough attention on the Norths. Tell me your observations related to Deena Finch and the Marigolds."

"Okay. And thanks for your concern. Someone else who has my back." She folds her hands on top of one another and focuses on Stella. "I wasn't acquainted with Deena Finch, but many people spoke of her caustic attitude when she worked at the Groceteria. As for Earlene, I enjoyed a professional relationship with her and Richard. Earlene, on her own, too. I sold them property. They were fair-minded, kind, and responsible business owners. Interactions were pleasant and easy. I ran into her on two or three occasions out at the farm while she studied botany with Opal and Hester. Hester only 'consulted', as she often describes her input." Cavelle offers a bemused giggle. "You know Hester."

"Did Earlene kill Richard, or help him die, so she could collect the insurance?"

Cavelle frowns. "Not Earlene. And for the record, Stella, she didn't kill Deena, either, although I suspect Deena threatened to tell people she poisoned Richard or committed fraud." The phone has rung with steady persistence since they closed the door of Farley's office. He answered two calls, but the answering machine clicked in for the others. "Rumour suggests Deena faked her injuries. I doubt if Earlene felt threatened by her. The tables could turn in a flash." She stands. "I'd better return to the front. Farley gets overwhelmed in no time."

Stella follows her lead. "You've helped solidify my first instincts, Cavelle. I appreciate your candour." She wants to caution Cavelle again, but inwardly rejects the idea, despite being convinced Cavelle's romantic involvement with Aiden will not end well.

Back in the car, Moyer asks, "Why should Ms. Painter's opinion be important, Stella? She wasn't involved with the murder at the fourplex."

"Individual impressions, Moyer. People create alliances at different levels. Cavelle knows Earlene Marigold through real estate, and because she studied poisonous plants with Opal. Hester and I discussed the same topics. I approach an issue through the perspectives of others."

"I guess there's lots to learn. I assumed you'd only want to interview the person you suspect of murder. Who killed Deena Finch?"

"Not sure. I could tell you who didn't kill her, but not yet."

****

When confronted with Mary Jo's closed door, Stella hopes the smell of dried blood has dissipated, but no such luck. She and Moyer enter the living room and dining area where the sweet and sickish scent wraps around them in the warm air. "Sorry. Still stinks," Mary Jo grumbles while she leads them into the wider, open kitchen space. "Who's your sidekick, Stella?"

Stella introduces Moyer, who has taken his post by the exit, feet spread, and hands clasped in his familiar stance. "Aiden assigned Sergeant Moyer as my partner today, since he's busy and his superiors could frown on his involvement with particular witnesses."

Moyer nods in Mary Jo's direction.

Her clear Pyrex coffee pot—the type of percolator Stella recalls from childhood—rests on the back of the stove. Tobacco-coloured stains blur the parts inside—a glass tube and stand, the metal basket with the built-in spring, and the metal cover. The lid sits on the counter nearby. Mary Jo fills the pot with water, heaps tablespoons of grounds into the basket, and sets the antique on the burner to perk.

"I've reviewed my various observations and contacts with Deena. What a witch." She attempts to smooth sprigs of unruly hair behind her ears. Her receding hairline enhances her masculine appearance.

"A witch." Stella repeats, noncommittal.

"Yes. Not only did she treat Tess and Velvet terribly, but Deena also made threats toward them and entered their apartments, for God's sake. I most often subbed for Earlene—no first-hand knowledge of how she talked with her landlady, but I expect not much better." She heaves her ample rump off the chair. "I'll pour your coffee. Sergeant Moyer?"

"If it's no trouble, Ma'am."

"Nope."

The initial sip gives the impression of motor oil laced with molasses. Strong doesn't come close to describing the concoction. Stella adds milk, feels her stomach lurch at the insult, and hopes for the best. She squints at Moyer, who sips with enthusiasm.

"You were forthright with her." Again, Stella makes a statement and waits for Mary Jo to fill in the empty spaces.

"I fight for folks, especially women who can't defend themselves, and Tess and Velvet are two of those. I forced Deena to admit, once when she and I were alone in the lounge, how she fled an abusive marriage and stayed under the radar. Someone followed her home more than once, and that made her scared most of the time. She said her ex-husband's family members are lunatics. She never admitted the fact, but I suspected she birthed at least one kid, after her hissy fit, when I criticized the way people rear their children. I was right in the end."

"Yes." She can't drink any more of the coffee.

"Deena Finch was a hard woman to read. I guess we understand why now."

"Will you tell me your opinion of the other three women and whether you suspect one of them committed murder?"

"Not in a million years," Mary Jo puffs while she pours more brew into her cup and refreshes Moyer's mug. "None of them has a violent personality, not even Velvet." She squints at Stella. "Velvet's mental health challenges mirror Rosemary but without the mean streak." She pauses before she continues. "Now, if I had lived here, you might investigate me." She guffaws at her self-deprecating joke.

As much as Stella wants to discuss Aiden and Rosemary, she's uncomfortable with Moyer alert and positioned at the door. As Toni and Aiden work out the final details of Rosemary's discharge, Mary Jo has distanced herself from the process. She approaches the sink, tips her full cup near the drain, and runs the water. Mary Jo need not be told how horrible her brew tastes.

"How did you drink that coffee, Moyer?" They are back in the car. He will return to the detachment while she drives to the park for lunch. Nick promised cinnamon buns, although the elastic waistband of her pants may not appreciate his efforts. She and Moyer plan to meet at Harbour Manor at one o'clock.

"Her brew was tasty. Could sit and drink with her anytime." He meets Stella's gaze. His eyes are soft.

Stella squeezes her lips together, so words don't spill out between them and spoil his image. She hovers over a compromise. "Mary Jo isn't your type, Sergeant."

****

Olive Urback, the nursing supervisor, reported that although in bed, Connie insisted she meet with Stella. They walk along the wide corridor. Moyer straggles. He said he's uncomfortable in hospitals and wanted to wait in the car. She convinced him to stand at the entrance to Connie's room.

"Good afternoon, my friend." Stella strolls through the door after a quick tap and takes her place at the foot of the bed where Connie can easily see her.

Her head lolls on the pillow as her eyes search for Stella. Her attempted smile imitates a grimace, but Stella knows the action shows Connie's pleasure with the visit. They enjoy each other's company. "Talkin's hard, now," she rasps. "Won't help much." Her mouth seems full of potato chips. "Nobody but Jasper understands me."

"I understand you fine." Stella drags a chair, the office stackable variety, to the foot of the bed and sits. "Can you see me?"

She bobs her reply. "Who's your friend?"

"Aiden wanted second interviews with collateral witnesses today, but he couldn't attend. Meet Sergeant Moyer." She turns toward the door and motions with her hand. "Come over near me and say hi to Connie Gee, Sergeant. She's Tess Boone's sister."

Moyer shuffles over. "Pleasure." His eyes stay downcast.

"You too, Sergeant." Connie's expression tells the tale. Neither insist he make eye contact, because of his obvious lack of experience with the sick and infirm.

"Can't tell you much." She coughs.

Stella jumps and wipes the spittle from her chin.

"Thanks. No more smokin' for me." She pushes air as she whispers. "Quit. Tobacco will kill ya." Her eyes dance and her lips quiver.

Her time with Connie will be limited today. She gets straight to the point. "Did Tess ever discuss Deena, or say she felt threatened?"

"Yup. Deena tormented Tess and called her a pretend writer." She pauses and forces a swallow. "Theo Gorman printed her books because no publisher took her on. Tess lost what little confidence she had." Connie gasps.

Their conversation won't last much longer, and Stella wonders if Connie's aware of her sister's admitted plagiarism. "Does Tess ever express her inspirations, Connie? Where does she find her ideas?"

Connie's chest heaves as she fights for more air. "She told you how she copies notions?"

Stella nods.

"I've suggested to her often," she gulps, "she should write her own experiences—our story—or describe her assault to the world." She gasps. "Call the work fiction but use her personal knowledge and pain." She shakes in frustration. "Instead, she takes other people's ideas. Time's run out for me now. I can't help her anymore."

"Who else knows about her plagiarism, Connie?"

She bends closer as Connie puffs, "Frances, but she's never told Tess."

"Could Tess, in a fit of anger, hurt Deena to keep her secret hidden?"

"Oh, no." She flails back and forth into the pillow. "Tess never loses her temper. Tess slinks away and enjoys a pity party." She coughs, this time with frightful ferocity. "I'm okay. I hope the cough knocks me out for good sooner rather than later."

Her chin requires another wipe. Connie's appreciation flickers in her eyes. "Sorry, I can't be more help."

"You're a great resource, Connie." She strokes the woman's arm. "Should I call anyone before we leave?"

"No need. Switch on the TV. I'll be fine."

Back in the police cruiser, Moyer turns the key in the ignition but doesn't put the unit in drive. "She's not long for our world. Poor woman."

"Connie Gee doesn't want your sympathy, Moyer. She has faced a debilitating and horrible disease with dignity and grace."

"I learned from watchin' you today. You ask simple questions. You let people talk."

"Correct. First off, Tess hasn't hidden her plagiarism from her sister, but doesn't know her author-friend, Frances Ellis, is aware. And Connie's considered opinion, although biased, suggests Tess doesn't possess the personality to precipitate the lack of control required to commit such a violent murder."

****

She arrives home for the second time today, near three o'clock, to an empty house. Duke's VW bug sits unoccupied in the lot. Nick and Duke, plus Kiki, must be out on the property or in the workshop. She fills the kettle before she enters her office to compile her notes in anticipation of a later conversation with Aiden. The blink of the answering machine light catches her attention, and six message slips sit on her desk. She thumbs through the stack. Each holds a request for reservations. Nick has told them Stella will call back. Her shoulders heave. Too much work and too few hours in the day.

Tea in hand, she jots her notes and remains convinced Tess, Velvet, and / or Earlene did not murder Deena Finch. She retrieves her calendar and map from the reception desk and returns the phone calls. Everyone has a spot. She even manages room for three trailers side by side in the middle of July. If the weather holds, and the septic system works as advertised, she expects an exceptional year. Uncontrollable variables are the enemy, she reminds herself.

"Lasagna's built and ready for the oven, Stella. I invited Duke. Cloris ran off to a meeting tonight—Duke's assessment. He wasn't happy." Nick stands in her office doorway and fills the space in that way he does, where her heart flips and heat travels across her chest and along her neck.

"You are the boss, my friend. Where has Duke gone?"

"He and Kiki took a walk and assigned me to make tea." He winks. "I see you have yours." He nods toward her, now cold and half-empty, cup. "Refill?"

"Yes, thanks. I contacted the people who left messages, including the ones still on the machine. Busy day. Give me instructions and I'll finish supper. Do we need a salad? A loaf of bread from the freezer?" She wraps an arm around his waist, and they make their way into the kitchen.

Later, and after their meal where Duke regaled them with Cloris and Duke couple stories, and said he had a great "consultation" with Aiden, she returns to her office. As for Duke, he's trying hard to preserve his current liaison. Perhaps the fourth time will be the charm. Neither wants marriage again. Avoidance of any formality may be the secret to success.

Aiden answers on the first ring. "Hello."

"Hi. I decided to call your old house, but if you weren't there, I'd wait until you contacted me."

"Shale Harbour tomorrow." His words are cryptic. He sounds impatient. "They will install my phone by Friday, and I'll give you the number as soon as the telephone guys provide one."

"Arrangements turned out well today?" She doesn't ask direct questions. No matter what their history, she won't pry.

"Rosemary's discharge into Toni's care happens at the end of the week. I'm removed from any non-financial involvement for at least sixty days— allowing her time to become comfortable with life on her own."

"Did you see her?"

"Oh, yes. She acted pleased to be rid of me—cordial and cooperative."

"The medication?"

He grunts. "Not sure. Don't care. Will unpack a box or two after work each day. We need to do more follow-up interviews, so I can't take a vacation." He sounds preoccupied. "How did your visits go?"

190

"No revelations, Aiden. I've jotted notes for your files. Deena threatened Earlene, according to Cavelle. Deena understood Earlene could suggest to Patricia Brooks the possibility she faked her injuries, which left them in a stalemate. Deena told Mary Jo that Rupert abused her." She omits the part where Mary Jo said, unlike Rosemary, Velvet wasn't violent, but reported none of the women believed any of the fourplex residents could have committed murder, regardless of the victim's behaviour. "We need to re-interview the Onslow family for sure. Connie is aware of Tess' plagiarism. Frances Ellis knows but hasn't confronted Tess about her ethics. Connie says her sister never defends herself, so murder is a stretch. No real breakthrough information, although I agree with all three. None of the G-plex residents killed their neighbour. Another interview with Odette is important now, too."

"Okay. Let's go to Halifax tomorrow and talk with the victim's in-laws, ex-husband, and son. We'll see Odette on the way home. No appointments. Let's arrive and catch each of them off guard." He pauses. "Duke was no help, although he thought he was. Speaking of help, how was Moyer?"

"Supportive. Happy he came with me. He didn't take part, but he stood sentry and listened, except for Cavelle. He remained outside Farley's office when I spoke with her. We debriefed after each interview."

"Excellent experience for him. I'll use him in the field on major cases more often."

CHAPTER 21

An Undefined Nervousness

"Good morning. Stella Kirk for Detective North."

"He hasn't come in yet. Can I take a message?"

"No, thanks." She checks her watch and decides she'll leave right away and arrive at his new house before eight-thirty. With a two-hour drive to Halifax and five interviews to conduct, starting their trip as soon as possible is the wise option. Last night, he didn't suggest she should meet him at home, though.

As she parks the Jeep in what once was Ruby Wilson's driveway, recollections of the bank manager who murdered Lorraine Young litter her thoughts. The case propelled her toward her status as a consultant with the RCMP. Aiden returned to Port Ephron with Rosemary in early 1980 because he assumed he would see an improvement in her condition if she lived near her sisters, Toni and Mary Jo. He's tried, but hard enough? Rosemary remains unwell and unmanaged. She promises herself she'll continue to hide her opinion on the matter until he asks. As in most situations, Stella feels people should avoid direct queries as to her personal assessments and opinions— unless they want direct answers.

She stops for a moment as she ascends the stairs toward the garden doors and deck. The location of the renovated century home, with the two-story addition on the rear, always impresses. Behind the main drag in Shale Harbour, the house faces the tidal flats. The view changes by the hour.

Aiden drags open one of the glass doors before she presses the bell. "Never made the drive to work. Too busy on a search and rescue mission for my coffee pot." White hair slides across his forehead and into his eye. "No luck."

His disorganization may be temporary, but his lack of focus worries Stella. She takes over. "We can grab coffee from Tiffany on the way out of town. I see your RCMP issue in the yard. I gather you'll drive." Although the investigation is her primary concern, she notes the Lucite dining room suite and the cognac leather sofas. Before Trixie educated her to current style demands, such detail was unimportant. Trixie informed her of the finer points of high-end furniture when they performed their recognizance mission at Ruby's back in the summer of 1980.

Once on the road, coffee in hand, Aiden sputters his frustrations. "We'd better not be chasing shadows, Stella. Whoever killed Deena Finch, the person was neither Hermie nor Isla Onslow."

"Agreed." She paces her response. *Keep him focused.* His current move and Rosemary's status mean he has more on his mind than work. "Hermie and Isla's observations and opinions might help us narrow the field." She further explains. "If we assume the murder wasn't random, and the other residents of the fourplex aren't guilty, Hermie or Isla may shed light on whether Rupert, Finn, or Odette were involved. One of them killed Deena." She taps her knee for emphasis. "I'm certain we're on the right track now."

The awkward silence, broken by a brief call on the radio from Moyer, suggests to her that Aiden might not agree. She had hoped their drive to Halifax would allow time for uninterrupted speculation and theory presentation. Instead, he fumes, and she worries.

****

Crammed into the narrow front porch for the second time, they ring the bell for the lower unit of the Onslows' dilapidated house. Hermie's gravelled voice hollers, "Come on through. Not standin'."

As they push the original oak-panelled door inward, wood scrapes across the century-old and warped threshold, reminding Stella of a cat with a caught tail. She cringes. Isla rushes forward while she slides both hands along the front of her apron. She twists her face away from them. "The cops are here again, Hermie. Did you know they were comin'?"

She turns her attention toward her guests as her husband replies, "What the hell?"

"Good morning, Isla. Detective North and I were in the neighbourhood and hoped to ask you a few more questions—tie up loose ends. You understand." She meets the woman's eyes and counts on their previous encounter for cooperation.

"Come in. Come in." She mutters with confusion. She takes a quick glance toward the ceiling. "Happy to help, but I don't know what we can tell you."

They follow her into the kitchen and sit at the table covered in breakfast remains—crumbs, an open bottle of gluey strawberry jam, plates, and stained coffee cups. Hermie concentrates on his task of filling syringes. "Gittin' my needles filled ahead. The home care nurse says I should manage with no help. What do you two want today?"

Without an invitation, Aiden and Stella sit at the table. Isla leans against the stove. She doesn't remove the dirty dishes or offer them coffee. Stella isn't interested, anyway. She senses a reluctance from Isla, an undefined nervousness.

Aiden clears his throat. "We're hunting for more background. You raised both Rupert and Finn. With Deena's disappearance and Rupert in and out of jail, you took on the responsibility of your grandson. You carried a big load."

"We sure as hell did," Hermie croaks, as he packages his filled needles in a plastic container and hands them to Isla. She tucks the box into the fridge, while he reaches for his smouldering cigarette. "We were stricter with Finn." He breaks into a fit of hacking. "Doc says my lungs ain't no good," he gasps. "Told me to quit." He waves the smoke away with yellowed fingers. "Can't tell me what to do."

Stella looks at Isla, who closes her eyes.

"I knocked sense into the boy. Not gonna lie," he continues, when his coughing subsides. "We was too easy on Rupert. Finn's not smart. I beat the livin' daylights outta him a few times afore he learnt who was boss."

Isla studies her nails while she leans against the counter. "Once, when I took him to the doctor, they asked if I dropped him on his noggin'." Her grim expression says volumes. "The kid does what I tell him now."

The old man coughs again, louder and longer this time.

"He's thirty years old. Can he not make his own decisions?" Stella struggles to assess Finn's status. They treat him as if he's still an incorrigible teenager who must do as they bid.

Hermie lights another cigarette. "From the time Isla caught the cancer, I put my foot down. Do as I say with no arguments. His job is to take care of us."

"Will you discuss your illness?" Aiden has placed his notebook on the table and focuses his attention on Isla.

"Not much to tell. The doctor found a spot on my lung, and they lobbed a lobe, as the surgeon said. I'm fine." She shrugs. "Finn was twenty and kinda crazy, but he took stuff more serious after I was sick."

"Because I threatened to pitch him into the street if he didn't help. Funny, Isla caught the cancer and not me." He sucks another drag and sputters. "I hope youse don't want to talk to Finn today. He left before seven on one a his explorin' trips. Uses his bus pass and wanders everywhere."

"Yes, we did, Hermie. And Rupert?"

"He must still be in bed." Isla squints at the ceiling. "He'll come downstairs for coffee or bang on his floor if he wants a cup brought upstairs. Haven't seen him." She settles her gaze on Hermie. "When did Finn leave? I never noticed."

She sounds stilted, rehearsed, as if the words are what they planned to say if anyone asked. Stella watches Isla wipe her hands on her apron again. She pushes both palms across her front. They aren't wet. "I'll go fetch Rupert, if you want." Her face lights. "And call you when Finn comes home."

"Thanks, Isla. We'll check on Rupert ourselves. You've been helpful. Sorry for the unannounced visit." Aiden sets a business card on the table, rises with a nod, and Stella follows.

After they buzz the upstairs apartment, Rupert bellows, "Open the door." They find him at the top of the stairs, in blue jeans, his chest bare.

"May we ask a few more questions, Rupert?"

"Can't stop the cops." He turns toward the kitchen as they make their way to the second level. "Pardon the mess. Late night, and Finn took off early."

Stella sits on the edge of a dirty wooden chair and holds her handbag in her lap. Aiden stands—all business. "Just a few loose ends. How did your parents treat your son when he was their responsibility?"

"They were hard on the kid. He's kinda slow. Let's face facts. At thirty, he still lives here and takes care of them." He flaps his hands in obvious frustration. "No future, no job, no prospects. He rides around on city buses and wanders, for somethin' to do if Dad and Mom don't need him. Sad."

"And how do you fill your days, Rupert?" Aiden maintains his position of authority in the space. He gazes at Rupert, who doesn't act bothered.

"Oh, one gig or another. Stayin' outta jail." He pauses. When Aiden remains silent, he continues. "I help at the gym and the bar down the road. They still need a bouncer every weekend. Five more years before I'm a pensioner. Can't wait to get me some Old Age Pension." He roars at his own humour.

Stella voices her assumption aloud to gauge his reaction. "Your father abused you and your son."

"We was both knocked around, if that's what you mean. Finn more, I expect. Dad figured the boy needed to be kept in line." He shrugs. "Finn don't have brains enough to stray too far in the first place, if you ask me."

"Please tell Finn to contact us the minute he returns, Rupert. We want to talk with him again, and soon."

"Sure. He'll be home for supper. Never fails." He takes the card Aiden offers.

In the car, on their way to lunch, Stella ruminates aloud. "Deena made the best choice when she left the Onslows, although horrible for her to leave without her son." She shudders. "Hard to imagine the family violence, despite Hermie's colourful descriptions, that would precipitate such a decision. Those two should be in a care home."

"I agree, but who supports Finn then? Rupert? Doubtful."

He navigates the sedan into the downtown core and creeps along a one-way backstreet until he comes near a less-than-savoury establishment. Not the type of business Stella envisaged.

"Aiden? I expected we'd eat a quick bite at a bistro and drive to Port Ephron for the interview with Odette afterward."

"Surprise. I'll park here and we can go inside."

"A bar?" She's mystified.

****

Aiden holds the brown metal riveted door and ushers her through. "The restaurant is upstairs."

The seedy looking drinking establishment occupies the lower floor. Open stairs, where she watches the patrons below nurse their drinks, rise to a second level peppered with over-stuffed furniture and coffee tables. Each vignette possesses an element of privacy provided by the high backs on the deep grey chairs and the circular position of the pieces.

"Come. Come. Sit over here." He touches the small of her back as he hustles her into a corner with a tiny, reserved sign, hand-written in calligraphy, on the centre table.

Dread washes over Stella. Aiden has brought her to a romantic hideaway. The lights are low. The servers whisper. Although noon, candles grace the tables, reflecting the amorous ambience. She swallows, unbuttons her coat, and sits as directed. Her appetite has disappeared as her stomach churns. She scans the room for directions to the Ladies. Aiden may no longer make his life with Rosemary, but his plans cannot include her. *What about Cavelle?*

She points at the sign and trots along a narrow hall. In a small bathroom, she splashes water on her flushed face. *Focus on the case. Ask a question. Keep him occupied.*

Once she returns, she states with undue emphasis, "We need to locate Finn, Aiden."

He waves his hand between them and bats her inquiry into unimportance. "If Isla calls tomorrow, I'll instruct Halifax police to bring Finn into Port Ephron. If not, we can call. Now—what's your opinion of The Lost Loft?" Before she compiles an answer, he continues to prattle. "A guy at the detachment suggested the place and I tried it out last time I was in town. I love the atmosphere—private, intimate, if you understand."

His eyes are clear and confident when he looks at her. Her body shrinks into her core before she responds, then opts for the obvious. "Let's discuss Deena, okay?"

"Order first. Wish we could enjoy a drink, but no such luck. They serve a fine turkey salad and cranberry open face sandwich. The side-salad has nuts and berries. Great. I've tried to concoct the citrus dressing at home, but the mix didn't taste the same."

Right now, she's sure even the best lunch will resemble cardboard. "Okay. Whatever you suggest. I'm not hungry."

Aiden ignores her remark, swivels in his chair, and motions toward the wait staff, huddled in the back corner. A young man, wrapped in a black apron tied in the front, glides between the furniture vignettes, and arrives at their side. "Settled? May I offer you a drink?"

"No alcohol, thanks. We're in the middle of a workday. Stella?"

"Tea, please. Chamomile, if available. And a glass of water."

"Coffee. Thanks." He raises a finger. "We'll order when you come back."

The diamond in his left pierced ear twinkles when he nods and then floats away. Stella assesses the space. She notices two other couples in the room. Each person clutches a glass of red wine. One pair has lunch—salads in enormous white asymmetrical china bowls. The outer surface mirrors a wavy sea if the sea were white. Candlelight bounces off the ridges.

"What's our approach with Odette Greer later today? I expect she'll tell the same old story. Any ideas?"

"Okay, we can discuss the case, although our investigation isn't the reason you're here." Aiden winks.

She withers. He's brought her to a hideaway where lovers meet for a meal. Above a bar and almost dark, muffled voices and quiet contemporary listening music are the only sounds. She senses an uncomfortable confluence of events on her immediate horizon.

"About the case. Let's imagine Finn thinks Odette killed his mother. Maybe he's at her apartment."

"Why would he consider Odette murdered his mother, Aiden?"

"He understood that she felt abandoned as he did. Makes sense for him to figure she went to see his mother and lost control."

Their drinks arrive, and they order the turkey sandwiches and salad. Stella doesn't care. She remarks, "I assumed you saw Rupert as the candidate."

"No. Rupert was incarcerated, remember? He didn't hire anyone, and his parents wouldn't help him, I'm certain. Odette's our murderer and Finn has figured the scenario out before us."

"We'd better gobble lunch and return to Port Ephron." She glances toward the wait station, but no sign of their meals.

"The Onslow car was in the driveway. There's the bus which leaves at two. We'll arrive before him if I'm right." Aiden sips his coffee and studies her expression. "Are you nervous, Stella?"

"Hitchhiked?"

A cloud crosses Aiden's face. "Perhaps." He squirms in his seat. "Once lunch arrives, I need your opinion—not about the case, but important."

Stella avoids eye contact and refocuses on Deena Finch's murderer. "Let's hurry. If your assumption is correct, Finn could be in danger."

"Here comes our food." They thank the server. "Dig in. Here's my question."

She mentally braces for a conversation about their decades-old liaison which, to her, no longer exists. With Rosemary partially out of the way, Aiden may have a different mind-set. *Sound nonchalant.* "What, Aiden? Now I'm curious."

He places both elbows on the table and peers into her face. "Honest answer, Stella. Do you think The Lost Loft could serve as a good back drop for me to ask Cavelle if she'll move in with me?"

Her hot cheeks and a wave of dizziness overwhelm her. The excess mayonnaise in the sandwich makes her queasy. She averts her eyes and stares at her lap. *Is humiliation possible even if no one else knows?* She swallows hard before she lifts her chin. "I'm sure you don't need a trip to Halifax, Aiden." *Did she croak? He hasn't noticed.*

"Oh, you've misunderstood, Stella. I've planned every detail for this weekend with Cavelle, so we can run away for a romantic couple of days. You, of all people, should understand." His eyes twinkle. "I booked Sunday brunch here before we return to Shale Harbour, and I want to ask her. What do you think?"

Is my mouth open?

"Well?"

"They use too much mayo, but the atmosphere hits the mark." *Don't be churlish.* "Cavelle will love the place."

With half her sandwich untouched and her salad rearranged on the plate, they leave Halifax and make the trip back to Port Ephron in record time. For a moment, Stella thinks he'll turn the emergency lights on. She sits, arms crossed with her elbows clutched in her hands, while she holds her mortification crushed into her taut chest. To move away from her internal self-recrimination, she returns to the safety of the case. Ironically, she finds solace in their murder investigation. "Finn could be visiting Odette because he enjoys spending the day with her. We may knock on the door and he's inside. No harm, no foul."

Aiden, bent over the wheel, grimaces at the windshield. "I expect Odette has disappeared because Finn has been hunting for her, if he believes the woman killed his mother."

As she ponders Aiden's theory, Stella re-examines their witness statements in silence. Did Odette give Finn accidental access? Did Finn find Deena and tell his grandfather? "We'll arrive in ten minutes at this pace, Aiden. I think today is the day we discover who killed Deena."

CHAPTER 22

Significant Miscalculation

They arrive at the Pharmasave where Odette works. Since the drugstore chain is a recent addition to the business district, Stella expected a renovated and modern store. Instead, they're greeted by the familiar rundown facade, previously Fuller's Pharmacy. The new owners covered the old sign with paint, and a contemporary backlit one now hangs twelve inches above.

Aiden and Stella enter via a plate glass door, which creaks when pulled open, and make their way past a 1950s soda fountain toward the dispensary in the rear. A harried and emaciated gentleman of indeterminate age gives them a brisk nod before he resumes a methodical count. "Give me a sec. Be right with you." His sparse auburn moustache twitches as his voice scratches. He needs a lozenge.

"Detective Aiden North. We want to speak with Odette Greer, please."

The pharmacist's eyes narrow. "She called in sick. Said she'd be out for the rest of the week." He pauses, makes eye contact, and coughs. "I can't ever call in sick."

"Thank you. Sorry for the trouble. I see you're busy." Aiden turns on his heel and marches toward the exit. Stella remains silent.

They park in front of the bungalow where Odette lives in the basement apartment. Her entrance is on the side. The property appears well-kept, but Stella suppresses a thankful moan for having never found herself in circumstances which forced her into a below-ground living space. They tread, single file, down the cement stairs toward Odette's unit. She doesn't answer repeated knocks, but Aiden persists. He's convinced she's at home. After five minutes of annoyance, the door cracks open an inch and Odette asks them what they want.

"We are concerned for you and Finn. We need to find him for an interview. May we come in?"

She glances behind her.

The sliver of an opening reveals dark quarters in complete disarray. A pile of clothes covers the couch. Kitchen cabinet doors are ajar. Heaps of mismatched dishes sit in the sink. The area has a distinct odour of garbage. A suitcase rests on a hassock. Two closed doors frame the primary space. Stella assumes they are a bathroom and a bedroom.

"Taking a trip, Odette? You must stay nearby until we complete our investigation." Aiden's abruptness lets Stella know he's lost his patience. "I made myself clear."

Odette fiddles with pieces of clothing after she reluctantly permits them entry. She packs blue jeans in her suitcase, examines a blouse, and tosses the flimsy garment toward the sofa.

"Sit, Ms. Greer."

She complies. Her hands tremble once inactive.

Stella makes a direct statement. She hopes to rattle the woman. "We suspect Finn is here at your house. May we check?"

"He's not here and no, you may not." She frowns at Aiden. "Don't you need a warrant to wander through my place? They do on TV." She emphasizes her response when she shoves her nose in the air.

"I asked the purpose of your packing. You are a pivotal person in our investigation into your sister's murder, and you are required to remain available."

"Do you see any point in me staying? Deena didn't want to meet me or Finn." Her shoulders slump. "A few days away won't hurt," she pleads.

"Running off to avoid the funeral?"

Her response is a shrug.

"No, Odette. Stay here in Port Ephron." He glances in Stella's direction.

"Where's Finn?" Her tone sounds sharper than she intended.

Odette's eyes dart around the room.

Stella muffles her suspicions. "Finn left Halifax earlier today. If he didn't come here, where did he go? You two are close," she continues.

Aiden's voice elevates. "You are not to leave Port Ephron, Ms. Greer. Do you understand? Whether you tell your boss you're sick, or you take vacation days, matters not. Please stay available to my staff."

She stares at her lap and nods.

Back in the car, before they return to Shale Harbour, Aiden radios the Port Ephron detachment. "I need a unit to watch Odette Greer's residence. We suspect Finn Onslow is inside her apartment. Apprehend him if he ventures outside. The windows require surveillance as well. He may try an end run. I'm on my way to Shale Harbour."

"He's with her, Aiden. She kept us from examining her other rooms. He's there."

"I know. They'll catch him." He holds the car keys in his hand. "We'll sit nearby until the units arrive."

"One of the two killed Deena." Stella closes her eyes and imagines first Odette, then Finn, smashing an iron into the skull of their victim. "Deena's murder was violent and merciless, Aiden. Do you suppose everyone possesses a vicious streak where, under the right conditions, they could kill a sister, mother, or lover?" His gaze weighs hot on her cheek. "Trixie and I have our issues, but really?"

"In my experience, anyone can commit murder if the motive and opportunity present themselves. Assess the cases we've solved. Love or money. Motive, with few exceptions, is love or money." He watches the house. "Lorraine Young's death involved money. Lucy Painter's reflected love of the unhinged variety. Paulina McAdams died because of love, again, twisted and warped by jealousy, but present. As for the boarding homes, money motivations preceded proper care and deaths were the inevitable consequence. Love or money, Stella."

"If I follow your logic, Odette or Finn murdered Deena because she abandoned and refused to love them. Odette never married and has no children." She shrugs. "She was jealous that Deena could reconcile with Finn and afraid he would no longer be interested in a relationship with her? Stranger things…."

"One of them killed Deena, and we'll know within the next day or two. Here come our reinforcements."

****

Stella arrives home in time for supper. Nick expected to be busy. He planned to clean new sites which need extra attention after the winter. The rich aroma of chili and fresh bread wafts toward her while she removes her shoes at the door. Nick turns the corner from the kitchen as he wipes his hands on a tea towel. Kiki trots behind him. She scurries forward when she spies her second human. Stella has little chance to appreciate the soft expression borne by her lover as the dog approaches.

"I'm glad you're back. We worried."

"Long day." She lifts her face and kisses him on the lips, while Kiki wriggles between them. Unease mars her enjoyment of the moment. If she misjudged Aiden's motives, she might misjudge Nick's as well. She could easily convince herself their connection is not as deep as she has accepted, albeit with reluctance, over the last years. There's the possibility Nick has boosted her confidence to such a degree she presupposes she can be desirable in the eyes of other men. Her disquiet sloshes inside and she bites her lip.

Nick expresses his curiosity with a frown but as is the norm when she and Aiden work a case, he doesn't ask direct questions but remains a sounding board when she needs one. He must expect her reactions to be because of the investigation. She gathers her emotions, lifts her shoulders, and asks, "Do I smell chili? Did you make bread? How could I survive without you?" She leans into him as his muscular plaid arm wraps around her shoulder.

"Home to a cold, dark house and an empty fridge, for starters." Nick keeps her close while she carries Kiki, and they toddle into the warm kitchen. He pours them each a beer, with no confirmation necessary. He assumes what she wants and proves correct more often the longer they're together.

"We can't locate Finn Onslow. Tried to find him in Halifax, but he wasn't at the house. We interviewed Odette Greer again in Port Ephron. She'd called in sick, and we found her home at her rental. I'm certain Finn hid at her place, but she refused to cooperate." She dips a spoon into the chili and tastes. "Oh, Nick. Best chili yet." Her face flushes from the heat.

"Where did you go for lunch?"

"Does The Lost Loft sound familiar?"

"Yeah. Isn't that a bar?" His brows furrow.

"With a cozy bistro hideaway upstairs."

He stops with his beer near his lips and peers at her over the top. "Aiden took you into a bar with a 'hideaway' upstairs? Are you serious? Is he done with Cavelle already? Should I be concerned?"

She struggles with her response and decides a partial truth will be the best tactic. "Not in the least. He wanted my opinion on whether the place provided a suitable backdrop for he and Cavelle while on their weekend away—he wants to ask her to move with him into his new house in Shale Harbour."

"What did you tell him?"

"The cook used too much mayonnaise on my sandwich."

Nick bellows. His beer rolls in the glass. Kiki jumps out of her bed and runs around the table to see if he's okay. "Stella, my love. Did you make an unnecessary assumption, too? Do I sense significant miscalculation by each of us?" He chortles again. "Serves you right for enjoying my shock on the night he brought her to the park for supper."

Although he has seen through the plight, she doesn't bite. "He's moving too fast for Cavelle, I'm sure. Rosemary's still in the picture." She gulps her beer and swallows the urge to share more. "As you may expect, he wasn't interested in my assessment."

They are lingering at the table with tea and store-bought cookies when the phone bleats. Stella reaches behind her and answers the wall-mounted unit. "Shale Cliffs RV...."

"Hi. Have you and Nick made plans for Easter dinner?"

"Hi, Trixie. How are you?" She catches Nick's eye and lifts her brows as he clears away the rest of their dishes. "No, we've got nothing planned." Her tone adopts a facetious quality. "Nick, did we make plans for Easter?"

With his back to her, he shakes his head.

"We were waiting for you to call. Which day?"

"Easter brunch on Sunday at the hotel. Can I count on you?"

"Okay, Sunday is the best choice for me, too. I expect our investigation will ignore Good Friday. I'm disappointed we're not invited to your house." Trixie loves to entertain now that she has a stunning home for the first time in her life. "Why the hotel?"

"Val and I are painting the downstairs. I've covered the furniture and the cabinets in drop-cloths. Too much work to straighten the place mid-stream. I am aware you and Aiden are in the middle of a case. As for Brigitte, she's open more often now, and the poor hotel needs business. We'll be us, you two, Brigitte, Carter, and Mia and I'll ask Cavelle and Aiden, but I expect Cavelle will want to stay at home with her siblings—family togetherness like us, eh, Stella?"

"Right," she responds to the tease, and continues, "Don't bother asking Cavelle. She's invited on a weekend getaway with Aiden over Easter. He told me today he has every detail planned, which includes their Sunday brunch. I expect we'll interview suspects both tomorrow and Good Friday, but they'll leave for the city on Saturday."

"Okay. No problem and I'm not surprised. Cavelle and Aiden spend as much time together as possible."

"Where does Rosemary fit? She could cause Cavelle no end of grief. Cavelle doesn't realize how dangerous a person Rosemary can be."

"I don't agree, Stella. What Rosemary doesn't know won't hurt her, and how could she follow Aiden's movements here in Shale Harbour?"

Watching Nick from behind as he scrubs dishes, she can't explain, right now, why the gentle rhythm of his hips while the sponge circles the plates proves oddly erotic. "Mary Jo lives in Shale Harbour. I'm sure Toni and Rosemary will visit their sister occasionally."

"Point taken, but they'll be fine. Cavelle deserves a measure of love in her life."

Later, much later, with her soapy sponge and swaying hip issue resolved, she stares at the ceiling and ponders the concept of silent humiliation. Nick sounded jealous for a moment, too, until he learned the details. She now assesses how she felt as within the boundaries of anyone's reaction when in similar circumstances. Her biggest problem is being too hard on herself. She snuggles closer. Tomorrow, they'll find Finn.

****

As she digs sheets out of the dryer, Aiden calls. "Good morning. I've got news."

"Did they catch Finn when he left Odette's?"

"No. Odette called earlier and told us Finn is with her. The Port Ephron team is picking them up and I'm on my way over with Moyer. We'll deliver them back here for interviews. Are you interested?"

"Need you ask, Aiden?"

"We will hold both overnight, but let's talk with Odette as soon as possible and Finn tomorrow. I assume you can come into the detachment on Good Friday, unless you and your family made plans." He pauses and when she doesn't reply, he continues. "I've contacted Rupert and asked if they want to hire a lawyer, but no interest. I'll call Carter Stephens and see if he and his cousin, Brent, will handle legal aid work. They represented Hector Greene and Maura Martin, which wasn't easy, but I imagine the pay from those two was significant despite the outcome."

"When should I arrive at the detachment?" No need for her thoughts to drift toward JanlonNS, the murderous boarding home company owned by those two.

"Around two. Odette killed her sister, and Finn knows. She'll throw Finn under the bus and then we'll untangle the details and get at the truth."

She avoids any discussion of her opinions for the moment. "See you later."

The first order of business will be caffeine, before she folds the sheets. Aiden has decided Odette is their murderer, but she finds the matter unclear. She fills the pot with water and reaches for the cannister of hazelnut coffee. When she lifts the lid, she stops for a moment and inhales the nutty, sweet aroma. Okay, Odette knew where Deena lived because of Velvet. She contacted her sister via the Groceteria. She sat outside the fourplex, probably often. Stella frowns. There's the possibility Finn followed his aunt. Maybe he lost his temper. We don't know if the killer was male or female.

With the sheets folded and tucked into the linen closet, she reaches for Kiki's leash and her thermos. The fluff ball hurls her body off the couch and rushes toward the back door. With Nick in Port Ephron buying parts for the loader, she is stuck in the yard until he returns. They share the Jeep because the old truck is fit for local trips and park work alone. He'll be home for lunch.

The property suffers from a certain bleakness in the early spring. The grass struggles to transition from brown to green. Perennials ponder the production of sprouts. The garden beds need attention. She gazes out over the cliffs and listens while the waves break below her. Everyday comfort, despite this often-dreary shoulder-time of year.

Shale Cliffs RV Park reflects its name, perched atop steep cliffs which overlook the bay and the ocean horizon. Her family home faces the water, and she never tires of the sound of breakers against the sand. She and Kiki walk along the main road, which dissects the park and ends one hundred feet from the cliff. Years ago, the pavement ended one hundred and fifty feet from the cliff, but erosion and Mother Nature steal a measure of her property each year. The park has three crossroads, when she counts the road which parallels the sea. Kiki trots beside her. Nick often lets her run ahead, untethered, but Stella couldn't gather the courage today.

Mildred's trailer rocks gently in the stiff breeze, as do Aiden's and the Black's. Buddy McGarvey and Bell's unit reflects the mid-morning sunshine. Ted Metcalfe's place sits safe and sound, further back from the cliffs. She must give him a buzz today and let him know. He frets all winter that his property will sustain damage, but never entertains the idea of paying for undercover storage in one of the local agricultural barns used for RVs during the off-season.

Standing for a moment, near the wooden stairs, available for access to the beach at low tide, she squints across the bay at the Painter farm. Once they resolve the Deena Finch case, a call to Hester will be in order. She'll invite her friend, plus her new beau Angus Raspberry, over for dinner. And Cavelle? She cringes at the idea of Cavelle moving in with Aiden. Rosemary is a real and present issue. No one else has expressed concern. Stella's the only person Rosemary has threatened directly, but any risk to Cavelle remains the root of her fear. Perhaps, if Trixie intervenes, she can dissuade Rosemary from possible destructive behaviour. Rosemary likes Trixie and enjoys her company, while Cavelle is Trixie's dear friend. A topic of conversation at brunch on Sunday if the opportunity presents.

With her back against the wind, and turned toward the house, her mind revisits lunch at The Lost Loft with Aiden. When she described her experience to Nick, he felt jealous and upset until she told him about the actual motivation for Aiden's choice of venue. She was relieved by his amusement. The weight of her concern vaporized as their mutual and unspoken understanding emerged. Aiden is no longer an issue, real or imagined, to their partnership. They're a team. She lifts her collar as the Jeep turns into their parking lot. A warm meal is in order, and she picks up her pace.

"Out for a walk with my little one?" Nick shouts above the wind. Stella has let Kiki run toward Nick, and the leash drags on the ground. He scoops her into his arms and coos. She never imagined him as the type of man to coo until they adopted the dog.

"Decided I needed exercise and a ponder."

He frowns.

"Don't worry. Aiden asked me to drive into town after lunch for an interview with Odette, then Finn tomorrow. He said Odette called and told them Finn appeared at her house and remained overnight. He and I don't agree on which of the two of them murdered Deena. I took my walk-time to analyze what information I'm privy to at this point. Soup?"

"Sounds great. I'll take the Jeep to the machine shop and unload my purchases. You don't want them rattling around when you go into town." He hands her the dog. "And I stopped at the café for croissants." He reaches into the front of the vehicle and places a butter-stained paper bag in her free hand. "They'll be scrumptious with soup." He kisses her forehead before he climbs into the vehicle. "Back in ten minutes. Promise."

She sets the dog on the ground. Kiki leads the way up the veranda stairs and into the living room. The buttery smell of warm croissants makes her stomach growl. "Come on, little one. Let's see what kinds of soup are in the pantry. I'm hungry now." She realizes domestic contentment has temporarily trumped any speculation about murder. Such appreciation for her relationship has been rare and often smothered by inadequacy.

CHAPTER 23

Complications Happen

Obviously, Odette doesn't expect to remain overnight. She's dressed as if on her way to a cocktail party. She can't cross her legs in her too-short skirt. The sweater she chose is a size too small, and her high heels seem inappropriate for an interview at the police station. As a suspect in her sister's murder, they can hold her in custody for twenty-four hours. She has no idea.

Their conversation begins at two o'clock. Carter Stephens represents Odette. Stella expects Brent to accompany Finn tomorrow. Stella sits in her preferred spot at the curve of the conference table, angled toward the interviewee and Carter. Aiden is in a position across from Odette and starts the conversation. "Ms. Greer, you called us earlier today and informed me you were harbouring Finn Onslow and he was in your home yesterday when we questioned you."

"Correct, Sir." She fiddles with the strap of her shoulder bag and avoids eye contact.

"Please explain your actions."

"Finn killed his mother and I want this mess to be over. As much as I've tried to remedy the fact my sister abandoned him and ran off when he was five, I could never do enough. He finally cracked." She lifts her face and widens her eyes. "I was afraid, to be honest."

"For your life, Odette?" Her manner presents as contrived. She's tossing Finn under the bus, Stella ruminates. Aiden may well be correct, and Odette is their murderer.

Odette furrows her brow and squints at them. "I never felt like he would hurt me, but lots of issues don't make sense."

"Examples, please?" Aiden wants to catch her in a lie. He'll elicit as much information as possible. Stella hangs back.

"You consider me a suspect, but you're wrong. If I didn't kill my sister, and her bridge friends didn't, then Finn or an intruder murdered her." A tear trickles along her rouged cheek. "There are questions I can't answer."

"What questions, Odette?"

"Did he follow me when I drove to the fourplex? I called Isla, and she said he borrowed the car on the day Deena died. He might have driven there if he figured out where she lived." She rummages inside her purse for a tissue and blows her nose with extraordinary force. "I can't remember if I told him she worked at the grocery store at one time. Let's say he waited for her. I handed over a picture. Everybody shops for groceries." She tilts her head and her eyes mist. "I gave him the tools he needed, and when he found her, he lost control."

"Why is Finn a man unable to control his emotions, Ms. Greer?" Aiden pushes.

"He's not learning disabled, Detective, but he's not bright." She glances toward the ceiling. "And healthy role models were at a premium. With a brute for a grandfather, a jailbird for a father, and the epitome of milk-toast for a grandmother—no backbone—he never stood a chance." Finished, she clutches her handbag in her lap while her shoulders sag, as if done with the entire ordeal.

"Let's take a break, Ms. Greer. An officer will fetch you and your lawyer cups of tea." He makes a call. When the constable arrives, tea in hand, Stella follows Aiden into his office.

Aiden falls into his chair and points to the one opposite his desk for her.

"Did she kill Deena?" Stella remains unconvinced.

He scrapes a strand of white hair off his brow. "First, her contacting us, followed by her sudden enlightenment, sound contrived." He reaches for the phone. "Let's check that alibi."

"Good morning, Mrs. Onslow. Detective North here."

"Correct. We are talking with Odette and your grandson. Quick question, if you don't mind."

"On the day of your daughter-in-law's murder, Finn suggested to us that he remained alone after he did a few errands for you. Did you and your husband leave the house for an appointment?"

"Yes, memories can fade. We wondered if you would confirm you were with Finn on the day in question."

Aiden leads her along and Stella squirms in discomfort.

"Oh, I see. Finn was alone because he left in the car." Aiden closes his eyes for a moment. "When you said he was alone, you didn't mean at home."

"To be clear, on the day Deena Finch died, Finn helped you and your husband do errands, after which he took the car for a drive. Correct?"

"Thank you, Mrs. Onslow, for your cooperation." He places the handset back on the base in a manner one could describe as a slam.

"Odette told the truth, Aiden. Finn had obvious motive, means—the car and the iron—and opportunity if Deena let him in. She surely recognized him."

"From my perspective, she rehearsed her answers. Why check Finn's alibi herself?"

"She was right, though. Finn took the car, and the Onslows lied or omitted the complete truth."

"Let's go back and finish. I want her in custody until we speak with Finn. I'm still not convinced."

Unimpressed with Aiden's instruction that she is to remain in cells until after Finn's interview the next day, she cries and whines as she explains she's made plans with girlfriends for supper and drinks. They'll be upset when she doesn't appear, and she has a hard time making friends in the first place. She asks if she'll need a lawyer again and Carter assures her that he'll be available. She uses the telephone and calls one of her friends.

"By the way, Detective," she shares, before she's escorted to a holding cell, "Finn has been upset for months, and after Deena died, he mellowed. I wonder if her death removed the bottled-up anger he's carried around for so long."

****

On the morning of Good Friday, April 9, the streets of Shale Harbour are quiet. Stella notices the yellow bunches of daffodils waving in the bright sun. The days are warmer and people with bulbs planted near their home now reap the benefits. No spring flowers and not much activity today in the RCMP detachment parking lot.

She nods at a familiar constable on the front desk and makes her way along the corridor toward Aiden's office. He's on the phone. She stands in the hall before he motions her inside.

"Okay. I understand. I'll reschedule our trip for this Sunday evening in Halifax. We can go into the city after brunch and come back home on Monday afternoon."

"Sure. One night away will be my consolation prize. We deserve the break. See you later."

Hesitant when she hears him on the phone and expecting the person at the end of the line to be Cavelle, she doesn't sit until he's finished.

His shoulders sag when he leans into his chair. "Good morning. I guess there's been a change. Cavelle and I, along with Jacob and his new girlfriend, and Hester and Angus, will join you and your family for brunch at the hotel on Sunday."

Trixie shouldn't have asked Cavelle after she heard Aiden's plans. Stella fumes.

He shrugs. "Can't argue with family. Speaking of which, I must call Mary Jo and make sure she doesn't take Toni and Rosemary to brunch at the same time."

Stella lifts her brows.

"Complications happen," he justifies.

"Rosemary will learn about Cavelle eventually, Aiden." She points her finger toward him. "Face the music, my friend, since you want Cavelle to move in."

Aiden glances at his watch. "You're right. You're right. I'll call for Finn to be escorted upstairs. I imagine Brent Stephens is here by now."

"You have successfully avoided one issue, but regarding our current matter, Odette didn't kill her sister."

"Really? What is Finn's precipitating factor if your theory is he killed Deena Finch? He hadn't seen his mother for twenty-five years. He was impatient to meet her, not murder her. Makes no sense."

When they reach the interview room, they observe Finn perched on a chair while a constable keeps watch.

They both acknowledge Brent with nods before turning toward Finn. "Good morning, Mr. Onslow. I hope you spent a pleasant night here at our little resort."

Stella expects a slur for a response, but her breath catches when he says he has stayed in worse places and liked the food. Brent Stephens reports they met earlier and prepared.

With a quick nod from Aiden, Stella begins. "We understand your life hasn't been easy, Finn. Detective North and I want you to describe the struggles and successes you've experienced."

His eyes widen. "I expected you to ask what I did the day my mother died."

"In good time. Let's start with you."

He squirms in his seat before he leans forward. "Deena. She left me. I was five. Dad has been in and out of jail since I was born. My grandparents raised me, by force, I guess." His voice develops a hard edge. "I wasn't smart at school but made grade nine before I quit. They didn't care, because the house was too much for them and the old man was never around. Gramps taught me how to help and fix stuff." He squares his shoulders. "They depend on me now. Once I learned to drive, they started lettin' me use the car. I moved upstairs, and we were mostly okay unless my useless father arrived home."

"Your grandfather was hard on you." Stella omits details they gleaned from both Odette and Isla.

"Gramps can throw a punch. He often locked me in a closet or out on the back porch." Finn's face lacks expression, as if the story belongs to someone else.

Stella prompts him, and he continues.

"Sometimes they didn't feed me." His eyes glaze. "Once I got taller than my grandfather, he laid off." He pauses. "Dad's another version of Gramps, only meaner. Funny, but I'm happier when he's in jail. Man, he uses his fists first and asks questions later." He unbuttons his shirt and reveals bruises on both arms and across his chest. "Can't say much around him. He punches hard."

"I've told Finn we can discuss assault charges," Brent contributes.

"Not interested," Finn mumbles.

"Do you ever hit back when you're assaulted?" Aiden's eyes are black with rage.

"Nope. Keep my feelins' to myself. Learned a long time ago how fightin' makes matters worse."

"You must blame someone for the abuse you've suffered." Stella waits for his response.

"My mother. I had no chance for a decent life when she left me behind. She sacrificed me to save herself. My grandparents made that clear from the time I was little." He scratches his chin and day-old stubble. "Gram tried, but most of the time, she stood back and watched. Scared, I guess."

"You're close with your Aunt Odette."

"Yeah. She's a good person. She didn't kill my mother." He tugs at his collar and a sheen develops on his brow. He swallows twice before he adds, "One of the other women in the building killed her." Finn fidgets in his chair.

He's lied. "Tell me why you decided Odette didn't murder your mother."

Silence weighs heavily in the interview room. Aiden and Stella exchange glances before she closes her eyes for a moment. She hopes Aiden will stay quiet until Finn shares more. He must describe to them exactly what happened. Brent opens his mouth and Finn twitches.

"You needn't answer their questions, Finn. I told you earlier that I can speak on your behalf."

Ignoring his lawyer, he sputters, "Aunt Odette didn't kill my mom. Aunt Odette couldn't hurt a flea. She slipped one day and gave me a clue and I found my mother."

"What did she say, Finn?"

"She said Deena hadn't changed from the picture. I figured Mom lived in the area. I followed Aunt Odette as often as I could use the car." He clasps his hands in his lap. "I wanted to talk to Mom; to meet her and tell her how much I missed her—and how she ruined my life." His shoulders shake.

Aiden rests his elbows on the table. "What happened, Finn? Take your time." His voice is flat; resigned.

"I expected I'd knock on the door, she would answer, put her arms around me, and be happy to see me." Tears well. "I found the front door unlocked, and I stepped inside. She turned the corner and treated me as if I was some random intruder; like I broke into her place and wanted to steal from her."

"Your mother didn't recognize you." Stella visualizes the rest of the story.

"No. She made me mad. She had no clue who I was. I slapped her."

"Go on, Finn."

In between blubbers, he describes the moment he grabbed the iron and hurled the appliance at her head. "The whole day is a blur. She ruined my life. I never even existed for her."

"There must have been a good deal of blood, Finn." Aiden pushes, making sure he hasn't conjured a story to cover for Odette.

Before Brent intervenes, Finn answers. "Gram and Gramps didn't know where I took the car. I put my clothes in the washing machine and climbed into the shower. You can check because Gram wondered why I did a wash on Monday. She does the laundry every Wednesday. I told her I slipped in the mud."

Confident in Aiden's staff to verify the details, she can't help but sympathize. In Finn's mind, his mother was the root cause of his violent upbringing.

Back in his office, Aiden says their decision to go to brunch and postpone their weekend trip is good, because paperwork will gobble up tomorrow. "You were right, Stella."

"Deena wronged everyone—the residents at the fourplex, her employer, her sister, and her in-laws—but no one as much as Finn. We're aware Finn's family was brutal. Even though he claims he never fought back at home, his rage has bubbled for twenty-five years."

****

Easter Sunday, and Trixie's wearing her bunny fur jacket. Stella muffles a smart remark while fluffy Trixie wobbles on platform heels toward the private dining room entrance. "Thanks, Pepper." Stella acknowledges the hotel employee who has escorted them into their family gathering. "I guess we're in the right place."

"Stella, Nick. Aren't the decorations perfect?" She sweeps her arm around the room and doesn't wait for an answer. "Come say hi."

Scattered at or near four antique tables, flanked by mismatched pressed back chairs, Stella sees Carter, Brigitte, and Mia. They dressed the child in the red velvet frock Stella gave her for Christmas. Her heart swells. Carter stands and shakes their hands while Brigitte manoeuvres past the table, holding Mia's fist, to deliver hugs.

"We expect the Painter entourage any minute," Brigitte whispers in her ear. "I hear Jacob has a new flame and Hester invited her neighbour, Angus Raspberry."

While her face remains near Brigitte's, Stella informs her niece how Angus may be more than a neighbour and friend. "And Jacob's date?"

"No idea. Another surprise."

"I see the hotel doesn't subscribe to the concept that less is more in the decoration department." Over-sized Easter basket centre pieces grace the tables. Stuffed bunnies cover the sideboard.

"Mia insisted the stuffies were for her when we came over to plan details for today with Pepper. I bought one to contribute to the display. Now she can take a bunny home. Pepper told me she could choose. My purchase will replace whatever she wants. Cute, eh?"

"Clever parenting." She stares across the space. "Val looks out of his depth." Trixie's boyfriend sits in the corner, focused on the opposite wall. "Trouble in paradise?"

"Oh, no." Brigitte waves her hand in dismissal. "He hates groups, but Mom insists. She'll never change."

"I'll go talk with him." She touches Mia's soft curls before she makes her way past an empty table and perches beside Val. "Another one of Trixie's shindigs, eh Val?"

"Couldn't convince her otherwise. Now the Painter family will be here, too." He nods in the vague direction of the door. "Too much chit-chat, Stella. Hard to understand people."

"Have you met Jacob?"

"Yeah," he grumbles.

"And Nick."

"Nick's good people."

"You'll be fine. Trixie's in her element." She leans closer and whispers in his ear. "Act happy, and she'll be none the wiser. I've practiced the art for years." She smirks. "Here comes Nick." Her love brushes her hand as they pass each other.

She smiles at Carter, in a raucous game of patty cake with Mia, and makes her way toward the commotion at the door. Trixie and Cavelle squeal their delight. Aiden touches Cavelle's shoulder and then sidles into the room. Could Jacob's date be Maeve Cavannah? They're standing next in line. She cranes her neck and sees Hester with her hand tucked into the crook of the arm of a bulky and tall man unfamiliar to Stella. His bright red hair, which requires a cut, coupled with untidy whiskers, conjure images of people who have been long missing in the wild. They both appear lost at this moment—or ready to run for the hills.

"Move over, girls. Hi, Jacob. Nice to see you, Maeve. Still in the home care business?" She continues her banal banter routine while she elbows her way toward Hester. "Hello, my friend. What a pleasant surprise."

"Thank you, Stella. We will eat brunch with you because your sister invited my sister. We are the extras, I gather."

Stella suppresses a giggle. "We are here because of our fabulous company." She winks, although Hester doesn't react.

"Please meet Angus Raspberry. He has a farm around the cove from us."

"Pleasure, Angus. I'll introduce you to my partner Nick as soon as we can find our way through the high heels." Trixie and Cavelle remain near the entry.

Hester, in an uncharacteristic gesture of affection, places her hand on Stella's arm. "Remember our conversation? We aren't only friends."

Stella attempts to respond, but Hester pulls away. "I'm happy for you, Hester. We'll talk. You and Angus come for supper before the season starts. Shall we make a date?"

She briefly glances up at Angus, and then returns her attention to Stella. "We will both be delighted to enjoy a meal at Shale Cliffs. I will bring you jam."

Within a few minutes, everyone makes their way into the dining room, and Trixie completes the introductions. Pepper materializes to tell them her staff has replenished the buffet. They can fill their plates in the room next door. Stella lags and Nick leans closer.

"What are your thoughts on Angus Raspberry? I've invited them to supper." She's curious and wants his opinion.

"He behaves much as Hester did when we first met her. Did you notice?"

"Yes, although her social skills cross the line into bluntness territory when she points out the obvious, he's reluctant to engage with anyone besides her. He makes her look like the interactive one." They reach the doorway, which leads into the room with the food. Watching Angus and Hester discuss ham or turkey, she remarks, "They're a cute couple. Remind you of us?" She snuggles into his shoulder.

Later, after they choose their desserts, and the ever-present Pepper serves tea, Stella finds a moment to visit with Trixie. "We finished the case."

"Aiden and Cavelle told me earlier. They'll take off to the city once we're done here."

"Right. Trixie, any chance you can discuss Rosemary with her, or even speak with Rosemary once she's aware of Aiden's involvement with Cavelle? I'm worried about Cavelle's safety."

"The woman is dating a cop." Trixie pats Stella's arm. "Cavelle's a big girl.

She knows Aiden's still married. Their affair is their business—her right, by the way. No one has mentioned divorce, marriage, or whatever. Don't fret."

"Okay, Trixie, but if the opportunity comes along, will you check Rosemary's state of mind? She likes you. Determine if Cavelle's in any danger?"

"I won't interfere, Stella. You're the busybody in the family, not me. Now, I must pay attention to poor Val. He'll be hunting for a new girlfriend if I force him into too many more of my little functions."

Stella watches her trot across the room with her arms extended. Val stands and wraps her in a hug. Angus and Hester hold hands under the table. Jacob and Maeve listen with enthusiasm to a story Nick is telling them. She makes eye contact with Aiden and finds a chair beside him and Cavelle. "Ready to take off for Halifax?" She glances at Cavelle's shocked expression. "He doesn't report every detail," she teases.

Aiden blushes. "Yes." He checks his watch. "Shall we do end-of-case interviews at the fourplex on Wednesday? I'll call them on Tuesday and make the arrangements. You speak to Mary Jo first because I shouldn't take part."

"Let's go early in the morning because they play bridge in the afternoon. We can't block their card game."

CHAPTER 24

We Held the Higher Cards

As Stella pulls her Jeep into the lot at the front of Earlene Marigold's fourplex, she struggles to come to terms with the fact that only a month has passed since Aiden called and advised of a sudden death on this property. Now she will visit with the new tenant in Deena Finch's former apartment. She doesn't expect Aiden. He won't interfere with Mary Jo's post-event debrief, even with Finn Onslow's solid confession, which has resulted in a closed case.

She knocks on Mary Jo's door and hears a gruff voice holler, "Come in."

The angle of the kitchen entry enables her observation of Mary Jo as she lifts a pan of what her nose suspects are pumpkin cookies out of the oven. "Hi, Stella. Hold on."

"No problem." The smell wafting through the apartment is heavenly and appears to have successfully masked any residual odour of blood. "I assume you're on dessert duty for your bridge game, but you don't bake."

"This recipe represents the full spectrum of my abilities, although I can find my way around a chicken or a pork roast with no trouble. Pumpkin is a fall flavour, but the girls must endure." She turns and grins at her guest. The act exposes large teeth and generous gums. "I added chocolate chips to this batch. Velvet will be happy." She grabs her spatula and moves the cooling cookies from the sheet onto a rack. "Care for a sample?" She pushes one toward Stella. "People say you can't enjoy a cookie before noon. We've almost met the bar." She snorts her satisfaction and nods encouragement as Stella takes her first bite.

Warm and soft, with the chocolate still at the melting stage, refusal was never an option. In between morsels, Stella explains her visit. "I gather the detachment called and told you I'd be over for a debriefing on the case."

Mary Jo reaches for the biggest cookie and drags a kitchen chair out from the table. "The constable said Aiden wanted to speak with me, but he's cutting a wide swath around any in-laws right now."

"Understandable." Stella frowns.

"I bit my tongue and didn't say exactly what was on my mind, when he called me last week and suggested I not take Toni and Rosemary for Easter brunch at the hotel."

"He provided a reason?" Stella nods so Mary Jo will elaborate, curious whether Aiden has been honest with his sister-in-law.

"Oh, yeah." She reaches for another cookie and raises her eyebrows at Stella, who declines the wordless offer. "I'd heard he and Cavelle Painter are an item. You don't live in a building with three other women and not become privy to every snippet of local gossip floating around. I told him he has no worries from me."

"Why?"

"I've cut most ties with my sisters for now. I explained to Toni that I prefer to carve out a place here in Shale Harbour. Complications from Rosemary might create obstacles for me. I don't want her influencing Velvet." Mary Jo makes eye contact with Stella and holds her gaze. "And she will, if given the opportunity."

"Did Toni understand?"

Mary Jo examines chocolate on her fingers before she pops the rest of her cookie into her mouth. "No. Not at all. Rosemary hasn't moved back into her own house, yet. While she's under Toni's roof, Toni will monitor her medications. Toni says I've abandoned her, and that's right." She stands and reaches across the space between them for a napkin. "I bet the girls will love my contribution." She shares a playful and chocolate-trimmed grin.

Stella focuses away from the food, taking the conversation back to Cavelle. "Might Cavelle be in danger because of her association with Aiden?"

"From Aiden, for sure, Stella. He'll drop her the minute Rosemary behaves as if she's a normal person again. I've watched them for years, even when Aiden worked out west. The second she acts wifely, he's home. Cavelle becomes the loser."

Regret may follow her next remark, but she voices her concern. "Cavelle is moving in."

The expression on Mary Jo's face doesn't change. Stella sees no momentary shock, horror, or puzzlement. "Happened before. Happening again. Aiden won't permit threats to Cavelle, but the affair will end. On the surface, he'll suggest the break-up is for her sake, but he'll race back into my sister's delusional and mentally unstable arms."

After she swallows her disbelief, Stella mutters, "No need for me to stress anymore, I guess."

"You're not familiar with Aiden, the philanderer, Stella. Toni and I worried for you, in case he tossed a monkey wrench into your partnership, but you and Nick are solid. We both admire how you kept Aiden at arm's length. Half of Rosemary's problem results from her husband's behaviour." She settles her elbows on the table and studies Stella. "You hadn't figured him out. I'm surprised."

Her cheeks flush as she recalls the lunch at The Lost Loft. "No, I hadn't. I appreciate your candour." She refocuses. "Let's change the subject. I'm here to tell you that Finn Onslow murdered Deena Finch, nee Greer, and Onslow." Stella rattles off the information Aiden asked her to share. "Deena abandoned him when he was five years old, leaving home so she could avoid further domestic abuse. Deena's sister, Odette Greer, discovered Deena's location by accident when she and Velvet Carmichael became friends."

"Yes. Velvet feels guilty because she blabbed to Odette."

"We'll address her concerns when we gather in a few minutes. You may attend, by the way."

"No. I'll stay here and give you folks discussion time. Not too excited to meet face to face with Aiden," she explains.

"Okay. To continue, Finn figured out his Aunt Odette had an idea where his mother lived and followed her until he confirmed the location."

"How did he gain access to the apartment?" Mary Jo turns toward the area where the other residents found Deena's lifeless body. One can't ignore the death of a woman in the unit, despite the new floors.

"She left her main door unlocked, and he walked in. He said she didn't realize who he was and acted as if he was an intruder. He lost control."

Mary Jo rests her face in her hands. "And the kid's age now?"

"Not a kid. Thirty."

"As hateful as she behaved most of the time, one can't expect a mother to recognize their child after twenty-five years, I'm sure. She never stood a chance."

Stella glances at the clock on Mary Jo's wall and avoids comments. "Almost time. I must go."

"Okay. I'll let you into the lounge so you can meet with the others. Bang on the door when you finish your talk if I haven't made an entrance yet. Poor, hateful Deena."

****

"Deena Finch's son, Finn Onslow, has confessed to her murder."

As Stella slips into the lounge at the fourplex, she sees Aiden seated at the bridge table, deep in conversation with Earlene Marigold, Velvet Carmichael, and Tess Boone, each sitting wide-eyed and hanging on his every word.

"What else can you tell us, Detective?"

Velvet interrupts. "Her death is my fault. I told Deena's sister, Odette, where we lived."

"You told us you discussed your neighbours with a stranger, Velvet." Tess taps the table with the pencil which Mary Jo placed beside her tally card when she prepared the room.

"I didn't know they were sisters. I described our place to Odette." She hesitates but doesn't jam a piece of hair into her mouth. "I talked about each of you. I was nice, complimentary, even." She shivers. "I'm worried I was complicit in Deena's death."

Stella, thankful Velvet avoided her compulsion, moves closer and retrieves a fifth chair from the side of the room. Aware of how the current circumstances could push Velvet into an episode, Stella tries her best to remedy the situation. "Don't blame yourself, Velvet."

"Go on, Detective." Earlene leans forward and motions for Tess to drop the pencil.

"Finn Onslow is thirty years old now. Deena abandoned her abusive marriage, and her son, when he was five. I won't detail the trauma he suffered, but once he discovered the location of his mother, he became obsessed with meeting her. On March fifteenth, a month ago tomorrow, while you three and Deena prepared for your bridge game, he entered via her unlocked front door. He lost control."

Velvet's eyes fill with tears. "I wonder if he tried to talk with her and she presented her normal nasty personality."

"Deena acted mean with everyone," Tess inserts. "I suppose the logical conclusion for you people was that one of us killed her. I imagined murdering her many times myself." She gazes around at the faces focused directly on her. "Not in reality, you understand, but I admit I hated her. She lied and stole."

"We explore every possibility, Ms. Boone. That's our job. Stella and I questioned several suspects. Our perpetrator expected the police to accuse one of you three. He assumed he wasn't under suspicion because his mother lived in a building with other people and felt accusing a resident was the obvious option."

"Fate deals the cards in the end."

Aiden's puzzled expression encourages Velvet, who carries on in an explanation, despite the cautionary glances from the others.

"When we play bridge, if the person on my left leads a low card and I expect they held back their King or Ace, or if my partner has the King or Ace and doesn't play either, I can try to make my Queen take the trick. I fail when the person on my right slaps a higher card on before I play my Queen. I can only hope I have a smaller card to forfeit, but will no doubt lose my Queen in the end. Deena jumped at any chance to point out someone's failure. Ironic." She sits straighter in her chair and frowns. "Deena's son attempted to finesse his behaviour in the hopes our alibis and circumstances were unreliable." Her shoulders heave with satisfaction. "In the end, we held the higher cards."

Earlene dismisses Velvet's analogy with an impatient wave of her hand. "Detective. Stella. May I pour you each a cup of tea before our game? Mary Jo isn't here yet." She glances in the direction of Mary Jo's entrance, a frown threatening her perfect makeup.

"She should be here anytime." Stella nods at Aiden. "I visited with her earlier. She baked pumpkin cookies—a treat for you today. And I, for one, always appreciate a cup of tea."

They each turn toward the click, as Mary Jo props her inside door with her hip and balances a crystal plate piled high with cookies. Velvet runs over to help. "Thanks, old girl. I'm not late, am I?"

"No, Mary Jo. Stella and Detective North are joining us for tea before we begin. Those smell yummy." She points at Mary Jo's offering.

Mary Jo gives Stella a withering look but continues into the room.

****

Later, while they stand beside their cars, Aiden expresses his appreciation to Stella for her collaboration with the notifications. "Will you drop off a brief report within the next few days? Final interviews with involved players aren't a big priority, but the case is done and dusted once they're recorded. Did your talk with Mary Jo go okay?"

"She claims she's keeping as much distance as possible from her sisters for now." Stella recalls Mary Jo's assessment of her brother-in-law. If she takes into consideration what Mary Jo revealed, she expects the one heart soon to be broken is Cavelle's. The woman may or may not be in danger, but she sees little she can do, and any intervention on her part is inappropriate at this stage. "You needn't worry. Your wife and sisters-in-law won't be standing unannounced on your doorstep."

Aiden's eyes widen. "You've changed your tune. You were concerned for Cavelle's safety."

"Trixie reminded me you're a cop. My fears are unfounded." She opens the car door. "Now, besides the paperwork you requested, I expect to spend my time, in the foreseeable future, with Nick. Over the next month, we're involved in serious preparation for what we hope will be a stellar season. I'll be training a new assistant and welcoming my seasonals." *Does she sound too formal?* "Are you coming out on Victoria Day weekend to open your trailer?"

"That's the plan, although I have time before my renters arrive."

She jumps into her vehicle. "I'll leave my report at the front desk of the detachment. With any luck, I won't see you until the twenty-first, at the earliest." After the words leap from her face, she forces a more conciliatory tone. "I meant what I said in the nicest way."

No, she didn't.

****

Saturday AM, May 8.
Thirteen Days Until Shale Cliffs RV Park Opens

"Eve. Hi. Are you ready for your start date next Friday?"

"Stella, I want to be at the park right now, but I need to write one more exam. Are the plant beds a mess?"

Her heart warms as she hears Eve Trembly's enthusiasm. "The gardens and a spring clean of the bathrooms will be your agenda items for the week before we open. You're happy with the same detail as last year?"

"Oh, yes," she bubbles. "I expect I'll miss Alice, but Merrilee sounds excited to start her new job. She said she'd drive Paul, too."

"Right. I must call the others. See you on the fourteenth."

****

"Good morning. Merrilee Wild speaking."

"Hi, Merrilee. Are you still beginning work here next Friday? This is Stella Kirk, by the way," she hastens to add.

"Bells are on, Ms. Kirk. Stella. One last paper to complete for my accountancy course, and afterward, my total attention for the summer will be focused on you and your business." She pauses. "I'm sure my next remark is inappropriate, but I look forward to our work together."

"Not inappropriate. Your enthusiasm is great. We'll meet here on the fourteenth, Merrilee."

****

"Good morning, Cloris. Might Duke be around? Just confirming our start dates."

"Oh, he plans on spending days at the park as of Monday. He told me Nick needs his help and I should move my trailer over to my site at the same time. Okay?"

"No problem. I'll tell Nick. He'll check and make sure your spot is prepared and we can hook in your services. You two will be the first seasonals with septic attachments, Cloris. We'll celebrate with coffee and muffins." She rattles her plan as thoughts of a busy season dance through her mind. She's surprised how the idea of an open park and people around again, without murder as the theme of the day, could uplift her to such a degree. Back in the groove. "See you both on Monday, Cloris."

****

One more call. She dials the Morgans with no need to check the number. She misses Alice, even now, before the season starts. "Good morning, Mrs. Morgan. Stella here. I'm calling to confirm Paul's start date here at the park. Is he nearby?"

"Lovely to hear from you, Stella. Alice says she's homesick for you folks already. And you've found her replacement?"

"Yes. I understand my new hire will replace Alice as Paul's driver, too."

"Here he comes."

"Thanks."

"Hey, Stella. Ready when you are. How's Nick?"

"He's well, Paul." She smiles into the phone. "You're prepared to start work next Friday with Merrilee Wild as your chauffeur?"

"Right. Eve introduced us. I asked Eve if I could ride with her on her scooter, but she said a better idea was for me to carpool with Merrilee."

"Sounds like a plan. See you Friday."

****

With her confirmation calls behind her, Stella makes her way into the kitchen. Kiki and Nick greet her with hot coffee and fresh banana muffins. "You've made yourself useful," she remarks as she eyes the cooling racks.

"We need a stash in the freezer since the staff will hang out here next weekend. We can make a different batch every day until Friday."

She sips her brew and reaches for a warm muffin. "Smart you started today. Cloris told me Duke wants to begin work on Monday, and she'll be with him to move her rig. She and Duke have the honour of being our first sewer set-ups." She winks while she munches. "Isn't life fine?"

****

Engrossed in discussions of the various staff personalities, Stella and Nick both jump when the telephone on the kitchen wall bleats. Nick reaches for the receiver.

"Hester. Hi. Yeah. She's right here. Hold on." He extends the phone toward Stella.

"Hi, Hester. You're using the phone. You never call. What's wrong?"

"I need your help—urgently. Can you come to the farm and drive me to town?"

Has she heard a modicum of emotion in Hester's voice?

"Yes, I'll fetch you right away. Tell me the problem. Are you hurt? Alone?"

"I'm too upset to wait until you arrive, so I'll explain now." She takes a shallow, broken breath. "Angus came for supper last night. We had roast pork. When he arrived home, he saw a truck parked by his old barn. When he investigated, he found a man Sergeant Moyer believes is the guy who stores gear on the Raspberry property, dead on the floor, the body still warm. He called the police right away." Her words punch through the phone line. Stella has never heard her friend so agitated. "They closed off access to the farm and arrested him," she continues. "I was unaware of this until Sergeant Moyer telephoned me. He did Angus and me a favour by calling and I'm not sure he obtained authorization, so please don't tell Detective North. Can you come?"

"Aiden hasn't contacted me in relation to the case, Hester. I will help you and Angus, however possible. I'll be at your house in thirty minutes, and we'll go to the detachment together."

"I'm sorry, Stella. Jewel or Jacob would probably take me, but I want you to be there with me."

"Understood, my friend. On my way."

When she replaces the receiver, she's met with raised eyebrows and a puzzled expression. "Hester says the police arrested Angus Raspberry. He found a dead guy on his barn floor when he arrived home last night."

"Aiden hasn't called." Nick's voice exudes calmness while he states the obvious.

"No, he hasn't." *I don't care if he calls.* Moyer wanted her to know, which is why he broke protocol and contacted Hester. After her discussion with Mary Jo three weeks ago, her contact with Aiden has been non-existent. She wrote her report and dropped the paperwork at the Shale Harbour detachment on a day when, unknown to her, he was in Port Ephron. She has avoided inviting the couple for a meal and they haven't entertained her and Nick. Cavelle moved in with him late last month. In their most recent conversation, Trixie described Aiden and Cavelle as entrenched in domestic bliss. Stella decided not to reveal the information she heard from Mary Jo. Cavelle and Trixie are close friends.

As she gathers her handbag and jacket before she rushes out the door, she realizes she promised Trixie she'd help with Brigitte's wedding, set for June 26. She shrugs. Hester will be her priority for the moment. The police can't consider Angus Raspberry their perpetrator. He spent the evening at the Painter farm with Hester. He has witnesses. *Did Hester mention a warm body? And a truck parked at Angus' barn when he arrived home?*

About the Author

L. P. Suzanne Atkinson was born in New Brunswick, Canada and lived in Alberta, Quebec, and Nova Scotia before settling on Prince Edward Island in 2022. She has degrees from Mount Allison, Acadia, and McGill universities. Suzanne spent her professional career in the fields of mental health and home care. She also owned and operated, with her husband, both an antique business and a construction business for more than twenty-five years.

Suzanne writes about the unavoidable consequences of relationships. She uses her life and work experiences to weave stories that cross many boundaries.

She and her husband, David Weintraub, make the fabulous Summerside, Prince Edward Island, Canada their home.

Email – lpsa.books@eastlink.ca
Website – http://lpsabooks.wix.com/lpsabooks#
Face Book – L. P. Suzanne Atkinson – Author
Face Book – lpsabooks Private Stash

Titles:
Emily's Will Be Done (2012)
Ties That Bind (2014)
Station Secrets: Regarding Hayworth Book I (2015)
Hexagon Dilemma: Regarding Hayworth Book II (2016)
Segue House Connection: Regarding Hayworth Book III (2017)
Diner Revelations: Regarding Hayworth Book IV (2018)
No Visible Means: A Stella Kirk Mystery #1 (2019)
Didn't Stand a Chance: A Stella Kirk Mystery #2 (2020)
Sand In My Suitcase: A Stella Kirk Mystery #3 (2021)
Fictional Truth: A Stella Kirk Mystery #4 (2022)
Mallory Gorman Won't Be Buried Today: A Stella Kirk Mystery # 5 (2023)
Fate Deals The Cards: A Stella Kirk Mystery # 6 (2024)

Watch for:
My Inescapable Vow: A Stella Kirk Mystery #7
The seventh in a series of cozy mysteries, set in Shale Cliffs RV Park
Coming in the spring / summer of 2025